I0555974

# ALL IN

## SHERRYL D. HANCOCK

# VULPINE
## PRESS

Copyright © Sherryl D. Hancock 2019

All rights reserved. No part of this publication may be reproduced, stored in or introduced into a retrieval system or transmitted in any form or by any means, electronic, mechanical, photocopying, recording or otherwise without prior written permission from the publisher.

This is a work of fiction. Names, characters, places and incidents are either the product of the author's imagination or are used fictitiously, and any resemblance to any person or persons, living or dead, events or locales is entirely coincidental.

Published by Vulpine Press in the United Kingdom in 2019

ISBN 978-1-83919-305-7

Cover by Claire Wood

www.vulpine-press.com

Also in the *MidKnight Blue* series:

Building Empires

Empires Fall

Where Loyalties Lie

Treachery Rising

Betrayals Stand

For all Intents and Purposes

Blood in the Water

Means to an End

Past in the Present

Just for Now

Here and Now

Rules to the Game

Roll of the Dice

# CHAPTER 1

Christian, Stevie, Joe, and Jordan arrived in Monaco the day after Christian and Stevie's Christmas Eve wedding in Las Vegas. The four made an extremely attractive group as they entered the lobby of the Hotel Metropole, with its beautifully appointed seating area and skylight above. Stevie was stunned by the hotel, which was over a hundred years old. It was so elegant and opulent that she felt both awed and incredibly out of place at the same time. She was waiting for someone to kick her out. The rooms they were shown to were no less incredible in their appointments, with rich-looking antiques and a marble tub big enough to swim in. She and Christian had a suite all to themselves. On their private balcony, she stared out at the incredible ocean view and could not believe she was there.

"This is like a fairy tale!" she exclaimed, her eyes sparkling in the fading sun.

"Gotta say, I'm feeling a bit starstruck." Christian nodded toward the ocean, his arms encircling his wife's waist.

"You and me both, handsome!"

The first two days in Monaco were spent at the beach and in the casinos. At one point, while Christian and Stevie were taking some alone time in their room, Joe was sitting at the high-stakes black jack table, with Jordan watching him play.

"Joseph Sinclair, what a surprise to find you here!" exclaimed a highly sophisticated English-accented voice.

1

Joe turned to see Geneva Glasstone standing to his right. His eyes narrowed for a moment, then he glanced around to locate his cousin. Geneva and Christian had reportedly been a couple for about six months before Christian had been forced to come to America. Christian hadn't bothered to keep in touch, much to Geneva's dismay. Joe was fairly sure that was why Geneva was greeting him like a long-lost friend.

They had indeed been friends of some sort at one point, having grown up in the same society circle in London. Geneva had always been a wild girl who was willing to do or try anything. That type of girl had always appealed to Joe's tastes, so he'd spent time with her and her friends. Eventually their lives had gone in totally different directions, but it was obvious that Geneva didn't note the long distance between them. She never did notice things she didn't choose to.

"Geneva," Joe said, inclining his head politely. He turned his head to Jordan. "Jordan, this is Geneva Glasstone. Geneva, this is Jordan Tate."

Geneva's eyes widened as she recognized the famous rock star. "Joseph, I see your circle of friends has improved," she said, her tone reflecting her surprise.

Joe's eyes grew much cooler, a look Geneva remembered well as displeasure. "No, Geneva. I still hang out with those lower life forms known as the working class."

"Oh, Joseph, you know I'm only kidding," Geneva said, trying hastily to cover her mistake.

"What is it you want?" Joe cut in, his tone as icy as his light blue eyes.

"I…" Geneva hesitated. She knew she was now on the defense. "I was merely surprised at seeing you. Pleasantly so, of course."

2

"Of course," Joe replied evenly. "And I'm sure it had nothing to do with my cousin, right?"

Geneva tensed at the mention of Christian. She sincerely hoped Christian hadn't told Joe the nature of their relationship. Geneva had in fact paid Christian Collins to be her "escort" to parties. She liked having a handsome man take her to parties so her friends wouldn't fix her up with any of their stodgy friends. Christian Collins had been the epitome of the devastatingly handsome companion. He'd also been incredible in bed. She'd yet to find better.

"How is Blue?" Geneva asked, managing, she thought, to sound casual.

Joe looked back at her for a long moment. Then his lips curled in a derisive grin. "Oh, he's doing great. He and his wife are here somewhere." He almost viciously emphasized the word "wife" for her benefit.

"Wife?" Geneva almost choked.

Christian Collins had gotten married? She couldn't believe it. Christian Collins was not the marrying kind. Even if he'd gotten some girl in trouble, he'd be the type to tell her to "deal with it," not to be gallant and marry her. The idea that Christian might have married for love never occurred to her. She remembered quite well his attitude about that. Geneva had made the mistake of uttering the words "I love you" to him once. His reaction had been quite literally violent. Geneva figured his new wife must have money. So he could be bought into marriage? Perhaps he needed a better offer.

"Well, that is just lovely," Geneva said sweetly.

"Uh-huh," Joe said, nodding, his eyes narrowing again.

He had the distinct impression that Geneva Glasstone had just changed plans. Good God. What had he done?

3

He shook his head as Geneva walked away, after uttering an appropriately polite departing comment.

"What?" Jordan asked, having watched the exchange with interest.

"I think I just caused Christian more trouble than he needed," Joe said, getting up from his stool and gesturing to the dealer to hold his place.

"Where are you going?" Jordan asked as she followed him away.

Joe took her hand. "Gonna find a phone. I can't get a damned signal in the casino," he said over his shoulder. "I need to at least warn him."

"Warn him?"

"Yeah, Geneva is a predator in the worst way, and Christian's the one that got away from her. I think she's liable to try anything to get him back."

"Yeah, but…" Jordan trailed off as he stopped at a phone and made a call.

"Trust me," Joe said, then winked at her perplexed look.

The phone in their room rang. Christian groaned loudly, even as he reached for it.

"What?" he said, sounding worn out.

"Hey, man, it's me," Joe said. "You're never gonna guess who I just ran into."

"Who?" Christian asked, sounding unconcerned.

Stevie turned over and snuggled against him, peering up at him with one emerald green eye open.

"Geneva Glasstone."

4

"What!" Christian exclaimed before he could contain himself, moving to half sit up. "Where the hell was she?"

"Down here in the casino."

"Lovely," Christian said, grimacing.

"I told her you were here with your wife," Joe said, grinning.

"Great, and she wished me well, I'm sure," Christian said, regaining his sense of humor.

"Oh I'm sure," Joe agreed. "Just thought I'd warn ya, man."

"All the more reason to stay in bed with my wife."

"Indeed," Joe said, laughing.

They hung up a few moments later, and Christian lay back down.

"Who was that?" Stevie asked as he put his arm around her, pulling her closer.

"Joe."

"And?" she said, raising a dark auburn eyebrow at him.

He shrugged. "And he was just telling me that he ran into someone I know downstairs."

"Uh-huh…" she said, narrowing her eyes. "Who?"

"Someone I knew back in London," he said simply.

"Knew?" she queried, ever the investigator.

"Yes," he replied, moving to kiss her to stave off the rest of her questions.

She responded to his kiss, her hands sliding up his chest, moving through his hair. Pushing him to his back, she leaned down over him, kissing his lips. As she kissed his neck, his eyes closed, and then he gasped when she bit him.

5

Christian opened his eyes to find his wife staring down at him, her emerald green eyes sparkling with barely leashed malice. "You fucked her, right?"

He pursed his lips, his light blue eyes staring back into hers. "I fucked her, yes."

Stevie nodded. She kissed his neck where she'd bitten, then moved her lips to his ear. Her teeth grazed his earlobe.

"Next time just tell me that," she said, sliding her tongue over his ear, making him groan deeply as she slid her body down onto his.

They made love, with more fire and heat. Christian knew she was taking her jealousy out on his body. He found that he enjoyed that she was still jealous, even though they were now married. Theirs was not going to be a common relationship.

Afterward, they lay together catching their breath, and Christian explained who Geneva Glasstone was.

"So she paid you to take her to parties?" Stevie said.

"Yeah."

"And you fucked her."

"And I fucked her," he replied, his grin impossible to hide at his wife's way of cutting things down to size.

"Did you love her?" Stevie asked, her eyes narrowing slightly.

"I didn't believe in love then."

"Not until Susan."

"Not until Susan."

Stevie nodded, obviously satisfied with his responses. She was not the common woman, his wife, Christian realized, not that this was news to him. He levered himself up, moving to lean over her and kiss her lips softly.

6

"I love you," he whispered, staring into her eyes. "More than I've ever loved anyone in my life."

Stevie's eyes softened at his words. She stared up at him for a long moment, then narrowed her eyes slightly. "Good," she said, grinning. "Keep it that way."

"I fully intend to."

He lay back down half on his side, his body partially covering hers, his arm around her shoulders, one leg thrown possessively over hers. His lips touched her cheek, her temple, then trailed to her neck, kissing her skin and nuzzling her. For a man that never wanted to be near a woman after having sex with her, it was an extreme difference.

It was not a difference lost on Geneva Glasstone, even as she shoved the thought away as she stared down at them three hours later. It had taken that long to bribe, cajole, and out and out threaten the hotel staff to not only tell her what room Christian Collins was in, but to let her into the room to "surprise" him.

My God, he looked incredible still. Even more so, if that was even possible. His hair was longer than it had been before, falling a couple of inches past his shoulders now. His back was still well muscled and tanned. His profile was slightly scruffy from not shaving, his jet black brows still slightly arching and stark against his skin. His arm, thrown over that woman, was well muscled too, so attractively strong-looking. Geneva remembered well the strength he had, the way his body had felt, how he'd made her feel. She trembled just thinking of it again.

She'd somehow managed to forget what a vicious bastard he'd been to her at their last meeting. How he'd practically raped her because he'd been drunk and she'd called him her property. Even that had excited her and also terrified her, but she didn't care. She wanted to possess this man like no other man she'd ever met, and she intended to. If this woman had managed to offer him enough money to marry her, Geneva knew she could offer more. It was that simple. She'd never thought to approach that with Christian Collins, afraid of his anger and cruel words. But perhaps he'd softened some over the years; maybe he would remember her fondly.

Stevie woke to the feeling that she was being watched. Her eyes met the blue eyes of Geneva Glasstone.

"What the—" was the first thing that came out of Stevie's mouth.

Christian stirred as Stevie moved to sit up, her eyes taking in Geneva's extremely groomed appearance. *I thought this broad was older,* was what Stevie was thinking. Geneva didn't look old at all. She looked young and fit, and far too attractive, as far as Stevie was concerned.

"What?" Christian said as he opened his eyes, glancing up at Stevie and then at who she was staring up at. "Oh, Jesus," he said, his irritation already starting as he sat up, one arm snaking around Stevie's waist, pulling her back against him.

Stevie didn't even bother to cover her nakedness. Let the bitch see that she wasn't exactly a slouch in the figure department. She leaned back against Christian comfortably, exuding arrogance and confidence in her place.

"So, this would have to be Geneva," Stevie said calmly.

"This would be Geneva," Christian confirmed.

Stevie nodded, giving Geneva an assessing look, then shrugged. "She's resourceful, I'll give her that," she said evenly.

Christian chuckled, leaning down to nuzzle her neck, his light blue eyes on Geneva.

8

Raising his head, he said, "So what is it you want, Eve?"

Geneva was taken aback. This was not the Christian Collins she remembered. He was different, but still the same somehow. And this woman he was married to was not at all what she'd thought she'd be. Geneva was wary suddenly. Perhaps this hadn't been an altogether good idea. As usual, however, Geneva Glasstone's way of handling mistakes was to bluff her way out.

"It's good to see you, Blue," she said, her tone lowering an octave. "You're looking well, as usual."

Christian nodded, not saying anything, still waiting for her to answer his question.

There was a long silence. Stevie dropped her head back on Christian's shoulder in a dramatic show of weariness.

"Bored now," she sing-songed, her lips curling in derision as she looked at Geneva. "Did you come here to bore us? Or was there something else you wanted?"

"Leave it to an American to be so crass," Geneva said derisively.

"Leave it to an English snob to be so senseless," Stevie countered calmly.

"Senseless?" Geneva echoed. "What have I been senseless about, little girl?" she asked condescendingly.

"About the fact that you're way out of your league here," Stevie replied, still composed.

"Out of my league?" Geneva repeated, exuding a superior air. "Little one, you have no idea what league I play in. You can't even begin to imagine." She gave Stevie an assessing look, then canted her head to the side. "Certainly you don't imagine that Blue is in love with you?" she asked contemptuously. When Stevie didn't reply she

9

went on, pressing home her advantage. "Trust me, little girl, there is nothing you have that I can't match or better. There is nothing money can't buy, especially the man you're currently married to."

Stevie's looked was complacent, even as a wintery smile curled her lips. "I don't have any money," she said simply. "But then, that's the thing, isn't it?"

"The thing?" Geneva asked, shocked by Stevie's admission that she wasn't rich.

Stevie's hand slid over Christian's arm around her waist, moving to touch the wedding band on his left ring finger. Then she looked back at Geneva with guileless emerald green eyes.

"The difference between you and me," Stevie said softly.

Christian hadn't said a word. In fact, he was staring back at Geneva with the oddest light of amusement in his eyes. She didn't like it.

"And what would that difference be?" Geneva snapped, not liking the way things were going.

Stevie's grin was sardonic. "I don't have to pay him to fuck me," she said, so simply Geneva couldn't believe what she'd heard for a moment.

Christian's chuckle was the only sound in the room. Geneva's eyes connected with his, even as he shook his head to show her she'd just been made a fool of. Without a word she turned and left the room.

"Dayum…" Christian said, leaning down to kiss Stevie's temple. He grinned. "Remind me to let you take out the trash from now on."

"Uh-huh." Stevie moved to sit up and away from him, turning around. "I thought she was some old broad," she said accusingly.

Christian's lips curled as he grinned, lowering his head then looking back up at her through the veil of black hair that fell forward on his face. "I never said she was that old, babe."

"You never told me she was a fucking gorgeous woman either," Stevie shot back.

"You think I'd sleep with an old hag?"

Stevie looked thoughtful for a moment. "Okay, good point. You never sleep with anyone that isn't top shelf."

"Damned right," he said, and pulled her closer.

"Don't think you're off the hook here, Collins," Stevie said, trying to keep the grin off her face.

"I'm off the hook," he said knowingly. "'Cause I married the sexiest woman I've ever met."

"Oh, now he's kissing ass…"

"I don't kiss ass, love."

"You just bite them."

"Indeed," he said, kissing her deeply.

They made love again after that, and Geneva Glasstone was forgotten.


Three days after getting to Monaco, Joe left Jordan playing at the craps table and went up to their room. Jordan found him sleeping four hours later, lying on the bed on his stomach, his arms wrapped around the pillow under his head. He'd only taken the time to kick off his shoes. Jordan didn't disturb him, going back into the other part of the suite. She watched TV for a while, then read a book she'd bought downstairs in one of the shops. It was seven o'clock at night when there was a light knock on the door between her and Joe's room and Christian and Stevie's.

"Come on in," Jordan called softly, not wanting to wake Joe.

Christian opened the door, glancing around for his cousin.

"We're getting ready to go have dinner," Christian said. "We wanted to know if you and Joe would like to join us."

Jordan nodded toward the bedroom. "He's asleep."

"He is?" Christian asked, sounding surprised.

"Yes, he's been asleep all afternoon," Jordan said. "Why?" she added, noting the change in Christian's expression to one of concern.

Christian shrugged. "He could just be tired," he said, noncommittal.

"Or?" Jordan asked, sensing that Christian was worried.

Christian leaned against the doorjamb, crossing his arms in front of his chest. "Joe has a history of getting pneumonia," he said. "And I've noticed he's been coughing the last couple of days."

Jordan bit her lip. "A history of getting pneumonia?"

"Yeah," Christian said. "It starts off with a cough, then a fever and him sleeping a lot." He shrugged. "Randy's always said it's his body's way of making him slow down when he's overdoing it."

Jordan's head came up slightly at the mention of Randy. She felt a stab of unreasonable jealousy. It bothered her that Randy knew Joe so well, and apparently always would.

"So what should we do?" she asked.

"Not much we can do," Christian replied, his eyes narrowing slightly, having noted the look of jealousy in her eyes. "He knows what he needs to do if it gets bad."

Jordan nodded. "Have fun at dinner," she said, sounding dejected suddenly.

"Can we bring you two anything?" Christian asked.

"No, that's okay. I'll order us something from room service when he wakes up."

"Alright," Christian said, straightening. "Let me know if you need me, okay?"

"I will. Thanks."


Joe never did get up that evening. He slept on into the night. Christian came back and checked on them when he and Stevie got back. He shook his head wearily when Jordan told him that Joe still hadn't gotten up.

"He's getting sick," Christian confirmed. "He never sleeps this much if he's not."

Jordan nodded uneasily.

Later that night, when Jordan crawled into bed next to Joe, she noticed that he'd shed his clothes at some point. They lay in a pile next to the bed. That was unusual for him; normally he was fairly neat about his clothing. She knew that was probably another good indicator that he was sick. Getting into bed, she could feel the heat emanating from his body. She knew he had a fever before a touch to his forehead confirmed it.

"Joe?" she whispered, loath to disturb him but wondering if he should take something to break the fever.

He didn't stir.

"Joe?" she repeated, louder this time, feeling the beginnings of alarm when again he didn't rouse in the slightest.

He was always so alert, even when he was sleeping. Whenever she'd crawl into bed after he was asleep, he'd wake instantly.

"Joe!" she repeated, much louder this time, shaking him a bit.

Finally, he stirred, groaning softly and reaching out to touch her waist, pulling her to him.

"Joe, you've got a fever, babe. You need to take something," she said softly, reaching up to touch his face.

He nuzzled his face against her hair, then was asleep again. She lay worrying about him for the next hour. Finally, she got up and fetched a wash rag to try and cool him down. He slept on obliviously. By morning she was worried sick. His fever only seemed to be getting worse, not better, and he had begun coughing. It had a rattling, hollow sound to it that made her feel that he was direly sick.

At 8:30 a.m. there was a light knock on the bedroom door.

"Come in," Jordan called softly.

Christian appeared in the doorway, his eyes going to Joe's sleeping form immediately.

"He looks bad," Christian observed.

"He's had a fever all night," Jordan said. "I tried to cool him down, but nothing seems to be working. I'm scared to death here, Christian. What can I do?"

Christian's look was assessing. She could see that he was worried too, but felt unsure about their options.

"What?" Jordan asked.

Christian shook his head. "I was just thinking this set in damned fast this time. I'm wonderin' if his cancer scare last year weakened his lungs again."

"Cancer scare?" Jordan asked, paling significantly.

"Yeah, he got an infection that made a spot on one of his lungs, making the doctor think it might be cancer. Scared the shit out of

14

him and the rest of us. That's why he quit smoking finally."

Jordan nodded, looking down at Joe and realizing that this man she was in love with had really been through a lot in his life. It was amazing he was in as good a state of mind as he was.

"So what do we do?" she asked again.

Christian blew his breath out, shaking his head in frustration. "Nothing at this point. There'll be no convincing a French doctor that Joe's getting pneumonia, not until he shows real signs of it. But looking at him, that won't take too long." His lips tightened in anger. "I just fucking hate to let him get that sick."

"Is it bad?" Jordan asked, not sure she could handle seeing Joe so sick.

He'd always seemed so strong to her. In the time she'd known him he'd been this pillar of strength, taking everything in his stride. She knew that she would have to handle whatever came, because she loved him, but it worried her. She didn't know for sure how strong she was herself.

"It can be," Christian confirmed. "Try to get him to take something to get the fever down—it's not good for him to be that hot for that long. I'll go down and see if I can get ahold of some Albuterol, or at least something for his cough."

Jordan nodded, feeling a little less nervous, since Christian obviously knew how to handle this situation. She wondered what she would have done if Joe had gotten sick when his cousin wasn't around. She knew she would have called a doctor, but according to Christian the doctor wouldn't have known it was becoming pneumonia. Would she have figured it out, or would Joe have just gotten more sick? It bothered her that she knew so little about him, really. She knew she was just being ridiculous, but she thought a lot about

15

that anyway.

Getting up from the bed, she went to her purse. She had Tylenol she always carried for the frequent headaches she got. That was as good as anything to break the fever. She got a glass of water and then walked back over to the bed. Putting the glass and the pills down on the nightstand, she reached over, nudging him firmly but whispering gently to him, "Joe?"

Again, he didn't react right away. After a few minutes of shaking him gently and calling his name, he seemed to come out of whatever fog he was in, waking slowly.

"Joe, I need you to sit up, babe. I need you to take these," she said, holding the pills out.

Joe sat up groggily, reaching up and rubbing his eyes. He reminded her of a young boy then, looking so sweet and sick at the same time. He looked up at her, and it was obvious just from his eyes that he was very sick. His usually bright light blue eyes were almost gray.

"Oh, honey…" she whispered, reaching out to touch his cheek, biting her lip as tears sprang to her eyes.

"I'm okay, babe," he said, his voice gravelly from the coughing.

"You're not okay, Joe," Jordan said. "But Christian seems to know what to do to make you at least comfortable."

Joe nodded, looking like he was ready to sleep again.

Jordan handed him the pills, then the glass. She watched as he swallowed the pills and drank the water. It was then that her eyes fixed on the wedding band he still wore. It dragged at her. Did he realize he was still wearing it? Was that saying things that he wasn't? Was he still in love with Randy? She squashed all the questions that came instantly to her head. Now was not the time to bother him with

16

this. It was important that she know, but right now his health was more important.

"Try to drink some more, Joe," she said. "Your body needs it."

He nodded, draining the glass. He started coughing then, over and over, his body racked with convulsions. Jordan saw that he was gasping for breath, and tried her best not to panic. She sat down next to him, smoothing her hand over his back.

"Joe, calm down, slow down. You've got to breathe easier, babe. Just try, okay? Try."

Joe nodded, feeling his lungs constricting painfully as he tried to draw breath in.

"I need Albuterol," he gasped painfully.

"Christian went to try and find some," she said softly. "Just try to calm down." Then she had a thought. "Wait, come here," she said, pulling at him, getting him to stand.

She put his bathrobe on him and tugged him into the bathroom, sitting him down on the counter and closing the door. Reaching into the shower, she turned it on full blast on hot. Steam rolled out of the shower head as the hot water jetted out. Moving back to Joe, she smoothed her hand over his back, talking to him in as calming a voice as she could muster.

"Okay, babe, this should help. This should loosen things up. Just breathe in the steam, slow and easy, babe, slow and easy."

Joe coughed a few times, but then it became obvious he was breathing easier. Jordan climbed up on the counter next to him, pulling him to her so he could lean against her. Finally, she turned to put her back to the wall next to the door, and coaxed him to lie against her. He was breathing easier at that point, and it was obvious he was relieved. She stroked his hair, kissed his temple.

17

"It's okay, babe. I'll take care of you, I promise," Jordan said, making Joe smile weakly in spite of how horrible he felt.

"I love you," he said softly.

"I love you too, Joe," she said. "I just want you to feel better."

"I will."

Christian found them still in the bathroom a half hour later. A cloud of steam rolled out as he opened the door. He raised an eyebrow at Joe and Jordan.

"Isn't this a little bit too kinky for you, old man?" Christian asked, grinning.

"Fuck you, kid," Joe said, his voice very hoarse but a grin at his lips.

Christian held up a small bag. "Got you some Albuterol."

Joe nodded, coughing again, moving to get off the counter and glancing at Jordan. Her hair was damp from the steam and she wore no makeup, but she still looked incredibly beautiful. She smiled at him weakly, and he held his hand out to her.

The three of them walked back into the bedroom. Jordan helped Joe lie back down, making sure he was warm, not wanting him to catch a chill from the temperature change. The movement had Joe coughing again, violently. Christian got the Albuterol out and handed it to Joe. He sat up, and between coughing fits managed to take a couple of puffs of the medicine. His cough calmed considerably then, and within minutes he fell back into an exhausted sleep.

Christian and Jordan looked at each other.

"Shower was a good idea," Christian said.

"I remembered it from the last time I had a nasty cough during a tour. My tour manager made me sit in the bathroom with the shower on for almost an hour. I hated his guts till I realized my cough was gone," she said, grinning impishly.

"Well, we owe your tour manager one, then," Christian said, grinning back at her.

"Where is your wife?" Jordan asked, realizing she hadn't seen Stevie that morning.

"She went in search of a doctor," Christian said. "We asked the hotel, but their staff doctor is still on vacation."

"Think she'll have any luck?"

"Well, she can't speak a word of French, but she's beautiful as all get out, so she might," Christian replied, a mischievous grin on his lips.

"Never send a man when a beautiful woman can get so much farther," Jordan said, laughing.

"Too right," Christian agreed wholeheartedly.


That afternoon, Stevie returned, telling them that a doctor would be there in about an hour.

"And how did that go?" Christian asked, narrowing his eyes.

Stevie looked at him. "Well, I fucked him, of course," she said, her tone serious.

Jordan's mouth fell open, but then Christian started to laugh.

"You realize I'll have to kill him then, right?" he said.

"Of course, that was the plan all along," Stevie replied, batting her eyes. "Saves on expensive doctor's bills, right?"

Jordan shook her head. She wasn't sure if she'd ever get used to the way these two dealt with each other.

The doctor arrived as expected, and unfortunately announced

19

that Joe had a cold, as expected.

"Doctor…" Christian said, shaking his head. "He's getting pneumonia. He gets it every time he gets like this."

"*Non*," the doctor said, then continued in heavily accented English, "It is a mere cold—it will pass."

Christian narrowed his light blue eyes dangerously. "I'm telling you, it isn't a bloody cold. He's sick. He needs antibiotics or he's going to get worse."

"I am sorry, monsieur, but the antibiotics will not cure a cold."

Christian took a menacing step toward the smaller man. Stevie's hand on his arm stopped him. "Listen, you stupid little fuck," Christian growled. "If my cousin gets a lot worse because of your lack of concern, I swear I'll beat the living shit out of you."

The little man drew himself up to his full height of five feet six. "It will not do to insult or threaten me. I am a physician. I cannot prescribe medication that is not warranted. I go."

With that the little man hurried from the room. It took both Stevie and Jordan to keep Christian from going after him and carrying out his threat.

"Let's not end up in prison here, babe," Stevie said soothingly.

"We won't if we hide the body really well," Christian growled.

Stevie nodded, holding back a grin. Christian caught her look and narrowed his eyes. Before long he was grinning too.

"Okay, so killing the little twit won't help," he acquiesced. "What do we do now?"

"I need to go home," Joe said from the bed, his voice almost a croak.

"Joe, the flight'll only make it worse," Christian said.

"Staying here without meds'll kill me, man," Joe said seriously.

Christian drew in a sharp breath, then nodded. "Okay, I'll make some arrangements."

Joe nodded.

Christian and Stevie left then, going back to their room to make calls.

Jordan lay down next to Joe, pulling him to her and letting him rest his head against her shoulder as she stroked his hair.

"I'm sorry," he said simply.

"For what?" Jordan asked, surprised.

"For messing up your vacation."

"Joe, I'm just sorry you're so sick. Don't worry about the vacation. I just want you to be better," she assured him.

A little while later, Jordan's cell phone rang. She picked it up, feeling annoyed, because she was sure she already knew who it was. She wasn't wrong.

"Jordan, it's Mark," he said smoothly.

"What?" she asked, without any attempt to sound polite.

"Nice," he said sarcastically. "What's your problem?"

"What is it, Mark? I'm busy," Jordan said, feeling her irritation rise.

"Poor girl, can't get fucked often enough by the white knight?"

"Either get to your point or I'm hanging up," Jordan replied, her voice barely controlled.

"Fine," Mark said shortly, surprised that she hadn't risen to the bait. "We've got some cancellations."

"Why?" Jordan asked, surprised. "And how many?"

21

"About six shows," Mark replied, all business now. "And because there have been some severe storms here. Places are flooded. Don't you get out of bed long enough to watch the news?"

Jordan ignored his last comment. "So when do I need to be back?"

Mark was silent for a minute. "I think you need to get back here and do some rehearsal time—"

"Bullshit. When is my next show?"

"January fifteenth. But I think—"

"I don't care what you think," Jordan said, cutting him off again. "I'll be back on January fourteenth. Where should I meet up with the band?"

"Look, I don't know what or who is up your ass—" Mark began nastily.

"Don't fuck with me, Mark. I'm so not in the mood right now. Tell me where to meet the band, or I'll call Tommy and get the information."

"Rome," Mark answered tightly.

He didn't like the way things were going all of a sudden. Jordan had always been easy to handle before. What the fuck was this Sinclair doing to her? He couldn't be that good of a lay!

"Fine, tell them I'll be in Rome on January fourteenth," she said.

"Where will you be if I need to get ahold of you?" Mark asked, thinking he'd at least get an idea of what was going on this way.

"At the other end of this cell phone," Jordan replied, and hung up.

Mark stared at the receiver in his hand. She'd hung up on him? Was she really so caught up in Sinclair that she'd forgotten what he had over her? Did she really think Sinclair would want her if he knew what they'd done? Sinclair would probably take his blue blood and run like hell. And maybe that's what needed to happen... Mark grinned, thinking about what he would do.

Jordan tossed the phone down on the floor, wanting to get away from Mark and his nasty insinuations.

"He's being an asshole again?" Joe asked, his voice gravelly.

"Yeah," Jordan said. "Nothing I can't handle, though."

"Jordan..."

"Joe, don't worry. Let's just worry about getting you better, okay?" Jordan said, not wanting to get into this with him again.

They'd had numerous discussions about why Joe didn't want her around Mark. Not the least of those reasons was that he knew Mark had hurt her a few times. Joe was afraid that Mark would hurt her again when she went back to the tour. He had a plan in mind to keep that from happening. Being sick wasn't going to help that much, however.

Joe was asleep two hours later when Christian came back to the room.

"We can't get out of here until tomorrow," he said, sounding harried. "Every fucking thing is booked solid."

Jordan nodded. "You and Stevie are leaving too?" she asked, surprised.

"You're gonna need help with him," Christian said, indicating Joe. "He's gonna be worse by tomorrow, and I seriously doubt you can support his weight."

Jordan bit her lip. The prediction that Joe would be so much worse he would need help to walk was scaring her again.

23

"Hey," Christian said, reaching out to touch her hands, which were clenched in her lap. "He'll be okay, Jordan. He just needs to get on antibiotics quick. This really is the best way."

Jordan nodded, still worried, and aware that he was just trying to allay that fear.


Christian had been right—the next morning, Joe was much worse. He coughed constantly, his fever was way up, and he went between sweating and getting chills so bad that his teeth chattered.

By that afternoon, Jordan knew there would have been no way to get Joe to the airport without Christian's assistance. In the end, Joe leaned heavily on Christian the entire walk through the terminal. Stevie watched her husband carefully, seeing him wince at the soreness in his bad shoulder, which he used to support Joe's weight at one point simply because the other shoulder was so tired. By the time they made it to the gate, Stevie had a Vicodin out, and she handed it to Christian as he sat down. He took it gratefully, and washed it down with a bottle of water. He leaned back in the seat, moving his sore shoulder around gingerly, gritting his teeth.

"Is he okay?" Jordan asked Stevie, glancing at Christian and seeing him wince in pain again.

"Yeah," Stevie said. "He has a bad shoulder from saving my life a while back. The Vicodin should help pretty soon."

"From saving your life?" Jordan asked, surprised at the simple way Stevie had said it, as if it were an everyday occurrence.

Stevie nodded. "He took an AK47 round trying to protect me."

"Wow..."

"What she neglects to mention," Christian put in, "is that she'd already taken three AK47 rounds herself."

"And the fourth would have more than likely killed me," Stevie said.

"I should have stopped the first three too."

"Bullshit," Stevie said. "Then you'd be dead."

"Better me than—"

"I'm not dead, Collins. Damn it, stop that," Stevie snapped.

Jordan watched, seeing the way they argued so passionately. It was clearly the nature of their relationship, all fire and passion. She could also see why Christian had been devastated at losing Stevie to Joe. He was very obviously deeply in love with her. And Jordan was fairly sure a man like Christian Collins didn't love lightly. From what she'd seen of him, he more than likely loved with a great deal of strength; he probably scared Stevie to death with the intensity sometimes. Jordan wondered if that was the reason they'd had problems, if Stevie had been afraid of the depth of feeling such a handsome man bestowed on her.

Glancing down at Joe, whose head lay on her lap, his body stretched out on the one couch they'd cajoled, harassed, and basically threatened other travelers off of. Joe was a different sort of man; his love was more of a sweet, romantic type. But then there were so many times when his passion was overwhelming in its intensity too. Jordan knew that she was terrified to give herself totally to loving him, in fear that he'd turn back to the life he'd had before he met her. He'd been married for thirteen years to the same woman; he still wore her ring on his finger. How could Jordan commit totally to him, wondering constantly if he was just replacing Randy? Again, she forced the thoughts back out of her mind. Now was not the time to overanalyze her relationship with Joe. He needed her to be there, not to be off

25

worried about things that she couldn't change.

She stroked his hair, noting how heavily he was breathing. The coughing fit he'd had when they'd made it to the gate had eased now that he'd taken the Albuterol again. Jordan was beginning to worry they'd run out of the medicine before they made it back to the States. It was a long plane trip.

In the end, the Albuterol was of no use. Joe's cough wouldn't be abated by anything. By the time they were two hours out of San Diego, he was coughing uncontrollably. He'd lain across the seats in first class. The seats did not fully contain his six foot, two inch frame. Jordan insisted on sitting on the floor next to his head, trying to soothe him. When he began coughing again, he took the cloth napkin she handed him.

Jordan, Christian, and Stevie had already assured their fellow travelers that Joe was not contagious. That he had pneumonia, and not to worry about the cough. Christian had been loath to explain anything to anyone, but Stevie and Jordan had understood the horrified looks they'd received from other passengers at the alarming sound of Joe's cough.

As Jordan was smoothing Joe's hair back, she glanced down at the napkin he held and saw blood. She gasped loudly, terrified. Christian was beside her in an instant.

"What is it?" he asked.

Jordan pointed to the napkin. Christian saw the blood and nodded, reaching down to pull out his cell phone. He dialed and held the phone to his ear, looking his cousin over then glancing back at Jordan.

"Hey, San, it's Christian. Midnight in?" he asked smoothly.

"Great, thanks." He reached out and touched Jordan on the shoulder, giving it a reassuring squeeze. Midnight came on the line a moment later.

"Blue!" she exclaimed. "Why are you calling me from Monaco?"

"I'm not, I'm on a plane," Christian said. "About two hours out of San Diego, as a matter of fact."

"What? Why?" Midnight asked, a note of alarm creeping into her voice.

Joe began coughing again right at that moment.

"Shit. He's sick, isn't he?" Midnight said, recognizing the sound.

"Yeah," Christian said. "He's bad."

"You guys have only been gone five days."

"I know. It hit him hard and fast this time."

"Shit," Midnight said, her mind racing. "Okay, what do you need from me?" she asked, knowing Christian wouldn't have called just to tell her.

"He needs to get to a hospital as soon as we land," Christian said. "He's coughing up blood now."

"Oh my God," Midnight said, closing her eyes. The thought of her best friend coughing up blood made her feel sick. She pulled it back together immediately. "Okay, I'll have an ambulance there when you land. Leave everything to me."

"I knew I could count on you," Christian said.

"Always."

"We're getting in at two thirty-five, Air France."

"Concorde?" Midnight asked, knowing it was Joe's preferred way to get to Europe.

"No, couldn't get anything booked on short notice," Christian

27

said with a grimace.

"Yikes, he's been on a regular flight, up that long?" Midnight asked, then grimaced, knowing that made it sound like an accusation that Christian had screwed up. "Look, you did what you had to."

"I know," Christian said, sounding unconvinced.

"I'll see you guys in about two hours," Midnight said, not wanting to belabor the point, realizing Christian would only beat himself up more.

Christian hung up then.

"Okay, Midnight'll get us to the hospital as soon as we touch down," he assured Jordan.

"We'll have to go through customs and all that..." Jordan began, knowing even her stardom never got her out of that.

"Not in Midnight's city," Christian assured her.

Jordan was skeptical, but was convinced when, two hours later, they touched down. Joe was nearly unconscious by that time. They managed to get him down the gangway. Two harbor police officers were waiting at the end of it. They assisted Christian and took Joe, putting his arms over their brawny shoulders. They ushered the group out to the curb, where an ambulance waited. Jordan walked along with a sense of unreality. No one stopped them; in fact, doors were opened for them by other officers, each of them looking either concerned or deeply respectful. It was like one of their brothers was fallen, and they were respecting that. Jordan saw that sentiment more as the day went on. The ambulance was escorted by San Diego PD motor officers. At the hospital people were waiting to take Joe into ICU. Within two hours of touching down, Joe was resting comfortably in a hospital room with Jordan sitting by his side.

Midnight walked in, noting Jordan's vigilant expression and

taking it to heart. Christian had already assured Midnight that Jordan had been "incredible" about taking care of Joe when he was sick. That had earned Jordan more respect from Midnight Chevalier-Debenshire than could ever be expressed. Seeing the world-famous star sitting next to Joe's bed, wearing no makeup, her hair up in a loose bun, her clothes rumpled from sitting on the plane floor for most of the flight, was a testament to her love for Joe. That sincerity of emotion translated itself in Jordan's actions, and the depth was not lost on Midnight.

"Hey," Midnight said softly.

Jordan looked up. "Midnight, hi," she said, smiling.

"How's my second?" Midnight asked, reverting to the name she'd always called Joe from back when they ran FORS together.

"Second?" Jordan questioned, not understanding the term.

"Second in Command," Midnight explained, smiling, realizing that Jordan didn't know all the lingo they used. "When he and I started working together, he was my second in command. I still call him that sometimes."

"Oh," Jordan said, smiling warmly at yet another piece of information about Joe. "He's better. They're getting ready to administer some antibiotics intravenously so he can start combating the pneumonia."

"Good, that's what he needs," Midnight said, nodding. "The Gang's outside."

"The Gang?" Jordan asked, then nodded, remembering. "Oh, all you guys' friends."

"Family," Midnight corrected.

Jordan nodded, remembering Joe had called them that too.

"So how are you doing?" Midnight asked, seeing that Jordan looked extremely tired.

Jordan smiled wearily. "I'm okay. Relieved that he's in good hands now."

Midnight looked at the younger woman for a long moment, then nodded. "He was in good hands before that too."

"I don't know about that," Jordan said skeptically.

"I do," Midnight said with confidence. "You're a good addition to the family."

Jordan looked back at Midnight with surprise, then began to shake her head sadly. "I don't know that I'm permanent in his life…"

Midnight canted her head to the side. "Why?" she asked. "You not planning on sticking around?"

"Me?" Jordan replied. "No, I mean… I just, I don't think he's ready for any more permanent additions."

"What makes you say that?" Midnight asked, narrowing her eyes, her investigative skills starting to come out.

Jordan shrugged, looking down at where her hand held Joe's, her fingers brushing back and forth over his wedding band. Midnight's eyes caught the movement, and narrowed more.

"The ring?" she asked.

Jordan looked up, and saw that Midnight was staring at her. "Yeah…"

Midnight shook her head. "That's just jewelry to him, Jordan. That's not what his marriage was about."

"But he's still wearing it—don't you think that means something?"

Midnight shook her head. "I think it means he just hasn't

30

thought to take it off yet. It's been there for thirteen years. It's like his watch—half the time he forgets to take that off too."

Jordan bit her lip, wondering if Midnight was just trying to make her feel better.

Midnight narrowed her eyes again at the younger woman, then looked to Joe's right hand. The ring Jordan had given him was exactly where it had been last time she saw him.

"Has he taken that off?" Midnight asked, nodding at the ring.

"No," Jordan said. "But that doesn't mean—"

"Yes, it does," Midnight said. "Jordan, Joe doesn't take his relationships lightly. Like I told you at the wedding, he wouldn't have brought you there to meet his family if you didn't mean a lot to him. Joe takes things very seriously, and if he tells you he loves you, he means it. Talk to him, you'll see," she added, knowing that her partner had likely never explained to Jordan his ways of thinking.

Joe wasn't like most men; he didn't really do casual lays. The woman either meant something to him, or he didn't sleep with her. It wasn't his style.

There was a light knock on the door then, and Randy Sinclair walked in. Her eyes went to Joe instantly, and relief flooded her features. She glanced up at Jordan.

"Hi, Jordan," Randy said, her tone friendly.

"Hi, Randy."

"How's he doing?" Randy asked both women.

"Better," Jordan said.

"They're getting ready to give him antibiotics," Midnight supplied.

Randy nodded approvingly. "This hit him fast, Christian said."

31

"Yeah, that's what he told me," Midnight said.

"I think that infection last year did more damage than they thought," Randy said, sounding worried.

Midnight nodded.

A nurse walked in carrying a glass bottle, and moved to the IV hanging next to Joe's bed. Randy watched the woman put the needle into the bottle, withdrawing some of the medication. She narrowed her eyes at the label.

"Wait!" Randy said loudly, moving to the woman's side and re-reading the bottle. "Don't use that."

"What?" the nurse asked, befuddled.

Midnight and Jordan watched Randy with surprise on their faces as well.

Randy took the bottle and held it up to the woman. "This is a penicillin derivative, isn't it?"

"Well, yes…" the nurse said, still not sure why Randy was questioning it.

"Well, I wouldn't advise you give my husband this, unless you're trying to kill him," Randy said sharply.

Midnight had closed her eyes when she heard the word *penicillin*.

"What? Why?" the nurse asked, not liking Randy's tone at all.

"He's deathly allergic to penicillin," Randy said. "That should be noted on his chart."

"We don't have his chart—his doctor is on vacation."

"Jesus…" Midnight said, shaking her head.

"I'm sorry, ma'am," the nurse said as she backed out of the room "We had no idea. I'm sorry. No one said anything. We had no idea."

32

"Just get him something else," Randy said wearily. "Tetracycline usually works best."

"Yes, ma'am. I'll check with the doctor. I'm sorry."

Randy nodded to the woman as she walked out.

"Well, that was close," Midnight said.

"Is he really that allergic?" Jordan asked, stricken.

Randy nodded. "Yes, he is. I swear to God, I'm going to have it tattooed to his forehead one of these days."

"He never said anything to me," Jordan said, her voice small.

"Jordan," Randy said, "it's not your fault. Joe needs to get some kind of medical bracelet that says that, but he refuses to wear one. It's not the first time I've had to stop them from giving it to him." She shook her head. "One time I literally had to knock the pills out of his hand, because he was just going to take whatever they handed him in a bottle. He didn't even bother to look."

"Jesus Christ," Jordan said. "He's that bad?"

Randy rolled her eyes, grinning. "He can be. If his mind is on one of the million things that he worries about all the time, he doesn't pay any attention to little things like what could kill him."

"Important safety tip," Jordan said, nodding.

Randy and Midnight looked at each other, then at Jordan, and started laughing.

"I'll go let the Gang know how he's doing," Midnight said a couple of minutes later. She left.

Randy glanced over at Jordan, and noted how tired the other woman looked.

"You should try to get some rest," she said.

Jordan nodded. "It's been a rough few days."

33

"I'm sure," Randy said, knowing well how many nights she'd spent awake doing her best to make Joe feel better.

"How's your house doing?" Jordan asked, referring to Sinclair House.

Randy nodded. "We're doing alright. Everything's hectic with the holiday season, a lot of kids getting sent to us. There's never enough staff to handle them all. And the money just never stretches as far as I'd like it to."

"But I thought…" Jordan began, then realized she might be talking out of turn.

"You thought what?" Randy asked, her tone still friendly.

"Well," Jordan said carefully, "I thought that Joe kind of took care of the funding…" Her voice trailed off as she grimaced, hearing the way that sounded.

Randy grinned. "Well, he actually sneakily set it up so that my funding comes from one of his father's companies, so I wouldn't balk at accepting money directly from him. But I try to keep that to a minimum. I've applied for lots of grants, but since it's a really unique situation, I'm having a hard time convincing them to give me the money. So I make the rest up with my own money." It was Randy's turn to grimace. "Of course, that comes from Joe too."

"But that was the divorce settlement, right?" Jordan asked.

"Yes, the divorce settlement that he was far too generous on," Randy replied, still feeling very sensitive about it.

Joe had been extremely generous, and Randy had been overwhelmed by it. There had been no words to truly thank him. She just sincerely hoped that in finally letting him go, he'd finally find the happiness he really deserved. It was Randy's genuine intention to help him in any way she could to achieve that.

34

"Would you mind if I came down there sometime?" Jordan asked.

"To Sinclair House?" Randy said, surprised.

"Yeah."

"No, I wouldn't mind at all, but why?"

Jordan shrugged. "Joe told me what you do down there, and I would love to see it in action. I think it's a very original idea that will benefit a lot of people in the long run."

Randy was surprised by Jordan's obvious interest. "Well, I'd love for you to come down. I'm sure the kids there would be thrilled to meet a superstar. If you wouldn't mind signing autographs and things."

"No, I wouldn't mind at all," Jordan said honestly.

"Well, just give me a call when things calm down for you two, and we can make some arrangements," Randy said, smiling.

"Great."

"What's great?" asked a gravelly, English-accented voice.

"Joe!" Jordan exclaimed, smiling brightly as she squeezed his hand.

"Yes, I know I'm great, but..." he said, grinning. His eyes trailed to Randy. "Hey, Rand."

"Hey," Randy said, smiling down at him. Then she raised an eyebrow. "You forget something, hon?"

"What?" he asked, sounding very English.

"Starts with a *P*, could have killed you if they'd given it to you..." Randy said sweetly.

"Oh," Joe said, grimacing. "Oops."

35

"Oops my ass, Joe," Randy said, grinning all the same. "I'm going to tattoo you yet, I'm telling you."

"Yeah, yeah," he said, waving his hand at her dismissively and grinning. He looked to Jordan then. "I'm sorry," he said. "I forgot to tell you that."

"It's okay, at least Randy was here to stop them," Jordan said, her voice indicating how much it had scared her that something that simple could have killed him.

Randy left a little while later, reminding Jordan to call her when she wanted to come to the house.

"What's up with that?" Joe asked Jordan.

"I'm going over to Sinclair House—I want to see it."

Joe grinned. "Why?"

Jordan gave him a dirty look. "Because I think what she's doing is really great, Joe, that's all."

Joe nodded, still grinning.

"Stop that!" Jordan said. "Seriously, babe, I just want to see how she does it. I'm thinking I might want to do something to help out."

"Something?"

"Yeah, you know, like I did in London for London Society."

"A concert?" Joe asked, surprised.

"Yeah, maybe during my break between tours. The publicity wouldn't hurt Randy's program. And it sounds like she could use the funding."

Joe's brows furrowed. "She's having trouble with funding?"

"Joe," Jordan said, putting her hand on his arm. "I think she wants to make it on her own now. She seems pretty embarrassed that you're still paying her way on this."

36

"I'm not."

"No, one of your father's companies is. She knows, Joe."

"Shit," Joe said, looking chagrined.

"I honestly think she could get funded for this, she just needs the publicity," Jordan said. "The concept she has is great—it's very personal, and it not only saves these kids a lot of social problems, but it probably saves law enforcement some grief, don't you think?"

Joe looked back at Jordan for a long moment, not realizing she'd really thought about what he'd told her about Sinclair House, but indeed she had.

"You're incredible, you know that?" he said.

"Why do you say that?" Jordan asked, smiling in spite of herself.

"Well, this is my ex-wife we're talking about."

Jordan nodded. "But I'm talking about her program, not her."

"That program is her, Jordan."

Jordan nodded again, then bit her lip as she gazed at him for a long moment.

"What?" he asked, noting the hesitation in her eyes.

She reached down, taking his hand, touching his wedding band. Joe continued to look at her. "What is it, Jordan?"

She stared back at him for a long moment, canting her head to the side. "Do you even realize you're still wearing your wedding ring?" she asked, remembering what Midnight had said and noting that he'd just said his "ex" wife.

Joe glanced down at his hand in hers, and looked a little surprised. He grinned self-consciously. "Actually, no, I hadn't realized that." His light blue eyes met hers directly. "Jordan, it's been part of my wardrobe for thirteen years. I don't even think about it anymore.

37

Hell," he said, reaching down to tug at the ring. "I don't even know if I can get it off anymore. I think it's melded to my skin." He grinned.

"I can fix that," Jordan said, grinning back.

"Oh, can you?" he asked, staring back at her.

She lifted his hand and put his ring finger in her mouth seductively, while he grinned at her. Then she proceeded to slide the ring off.

"Nicely done," Joe said, still grinning.

Jordan laughed. "Thank you, I thought so."

# CHAPTER 2

Donovan had just arrived home when he got word from Spider that Rosa's trial had been scheduled. She'd pleaded not guilty, and had predictably claimed that she'd been framed. She asserted that Sergeant Curtis had wanted to have sex with her, and when she wouldn't betray her husband, he had threatened to frame her. She claimed that all the evidence was planted. She didn't seem to realize that they had everything on tape and that Christian had an ace in the hole on this one. She'd find out soon enough.

Donovan was sitting at the sliding glass window, staring out at the setting sun. That's where Jeanie found him.

"Hey," she said, moving to look around the back of the chair. "You okay?"

Donovan glanced up, then nodded. "Rosa's trial starts in two weeks."

Jeanie nodded, gently taking the shot glass out of his hand then bending to pick up the bottle of tequila. There wasn't much left, and she recalled it being almost full last time she saw it.

"You had anything to eat?" she asked gently.

Donovan shook his head.

"But you'll eat if I order in, right?"

Donovan looked up at her, as if seeing her for the first time. She could see then how drunk he really was.

"Oh, babe," she said, kneeling next to the chair and pulling him close. "It'll be okay. Nick says he's keeping the press totally out, since we're undercover—they can't be putting our faces out there. You know Midnight'll protect you on this one."

"She shouldn't have to," Donovan grated out.

"You didn't do anything wrong," Jeanie said, tightening her hands in his hair. "You broke the case, Donovan, and that bitch could have killed you. She's the criminal here—she is."

He nodded against her shoulder, but she knew he was just assuaging her again. He'd agreed with her a million times before. But she knew he wouldn't be this drunk right now if he honestly believed he hadn't done anything wrong. More than anything in the world, he didn't want to embarrass the department with his mistake.

They'd talked to Nick Kopanke, the lawyer who had defended Randy Curtis for so many years and had since rejoined the prosecution, feeling his talents for setting things to right would be better served on the law's side. Nick had agreed that Donovan had not made a mistake. He'd been taken in by Rosa's game, but mostly because he'd been looking for a different kind of drug, and no one could imagine someone sinister enough to actually give out product for free to hook her dealers.

Nick was, however, proceeding with caution, not wanting to rain down any more bad publicity on Midnight's head. The lies and accusations in an anonymous letter that had made it into the paper the year before had caused Midnight enough grief. Nick, who had the utmost respect for the blond fireball of a Chief of Police, was determined to keep it from happening to her again.

He'd already received numerous calls from the Attorney General, the Governor, and the chief of the Bureau of Narcotic Enforcement, Phil Griffith, all indicating their support in this case. BNE had offered their best narcotics expert, the AG had offered his own experience, and the Governor had offered to have Rosa and her husband deported to whatever country would take them. John Davies, formerly the chief of BNE and the Attorney General, had of course laughed right after the offer. Nick had gotten the distinct impression, however, that Davies was quite serious. Midnight had a lot of supporters. People that she'd helped out over the years, or whom she'd just plain impressed. Nick couldn't help but respect that.

Jeanie eventually managed to get Donovan to eat something, then took him to bed, holding him close until he fell asleep. She was worried about the case; she knew Donovan would get raked over the coals by Rosa's attorney. She knew he was strong enough to handle it, but also that she needed to convince him that he'd done nothing wrong.

The next day, she went to see Dave Dibbins. She found him in his cubicle, working on his computer.

"Dave?" she queried.

He looked up, his sky blue eyes glowing as ever in his tanned face. "What's up, Jay?" he asked, using the nickname Donovan had coined for her.

"Can I talk to you?"

"Sure," Dave said, moving to stand. "Let's go grab some coffee." He gestured for her to precede him.

Once settled at the coffee shop, she looked at him seriously. "I need your help."

"Okay..." Dave said, always willing to help. He considered Jeanie and Donovan both very good narcs. He thought they made a

41

great team, both possessing qualities that could be honed into excellent instincts.

"Well, it's Donovan," Jeanie said. "He's so convinced that he screwed up on that Rohypnol case that I'm afraid he's going to just cave at the trial. I'm afraid that defense attorney is going to turn him inside out about screwing that bitch, and then I'm going to have to shoot the bastard myself."

Dave looked back at her for a long moment, noting the way she was gripping her coffee. His eyes went to her hands, then back to her face, and he remained silent until Jeanie realized what she was doing.

"Oh, oops," she said, grinning self-consciously.

"Do you want me to talk to Donovan?" Dave asked.

"Would you, Dave? I think you're the only one he'll really listen to—he respects your opinion." She grinned. "Ultimate narc and all."

"Oh yeah, that," he replied, without a spec of ego.


That afternoon, Dave called Donovan and told him to meet him down in the parking lot. Donovan found him there, leaning against his car, ankles crossed, arms on either side of him, his hands on the hood.

"Hey, man, what's up?" Donovan asked, moving to lean next to Dave, facing him.

"You think I'm a good narc, Donovan?" Dave asked, canting his head to the side.

"You're the best there is," Donovan said sincerely.

Dave nodded slowly. "Think I ever screw up?"

"I don't think you've ever screwed up as bad as me," Donovan said, realizing what Dave was trying to do.

Dave nodded again. "About five years ago, I had this case. It was a pretty simple one, really. Some guy was selling coke at some junior college; it was causing some serious problems for the school. So I went in. I bought from him a couple of times, and got in contact with a few of his regulars, telling them that I was taking over his turf. That, of course, got him pissed at me." Dave paused, reaching up to rub the bridge of his nose. "One of the girls that I'd contacted as one of his regulars called me. She asked me to come over to her place—she wanted to talk about making a deal with me. So I went. I get over there, she starts telling me how good-looking I am, how she really thinks we could party together. I tell her I don't use my product, she gets all pouty. So she says we could still have some drinks together. So I figure what the hell. She starts handing me beers and chasing them with shots of tequila, and inside an hour I'm feeling no pain. I must have blacked out at one point, because the next thing I know she's under me with her clothes all torn open. I start to pull away, and she reaches up and grabs my neck, garnering me a nice little scratch to go with a few more on my chest."

Dave paused, his expression wry. "Next thing she does is shove me away from her and start screaming rape. She makes a racket, the cops come, I end up having to identify myself as a cop to keep from things getting out of control. In the end, I find out that she's the girl-friend of the dealer, and he set me up to get arrested for rape charges—that way I'd be out of his way. She'd slipped me a mickey, and I had no clue, so convinced I was of my own irresistibility that I never even thought she was playing me. I still won the case, because I had the history of buys from him and the tape on it. And she had nothing on the rape because she hadn't actually gotten me to have sex with her, but she would have. So, see, Donovan, everyone fucks up, even the best."

43

"Yeah, but I've been doin' this a while, Dave," Donovan said, not ready to give in.

"How long?"

"Three years," Donovan replied with chagrin.

"I'd been doing it four then," Dave shot back.

"Oh," Donovan said, taken aback.

He hadn't really thought about how long Dave had been doing narcotics work. He just knew that Dave Dibbins was the best there was in the business. If Dave could be allowed a mistake like that, especially having known the woman was a drug user and definitely in some way associated with the suspect...

Maybe it wasn't as bad as he thought. He hadn't, in fact, had any idea that Rosa was involved. He'd thought she was just a man eater, and he'd needed something that casual and sexual at that point. It had been total coincidence that she was the woman dealing drugs. And in fact, Donovan had never been under the influence of any drugs, so he'd had no idea what the effects of Ecstasy would really feel like. It wasn't even a drug he'd been familiar with until he'd found out she'd been giving it to him. Sure, he had textbook knowledge of it, but he'd never really studied it, since it wasn't even a narcotic they usually went after.

When Donovan looked at Dave, he saw the older man watching him. Dave had indeed been watching Donovan, and knew the moment he had exonerated himself of the crime of being inexperienced. Dave's lips curled in a knowing grin, his sky blue eyes twinkling in amusement.

"Not too long of a trip, huh?" Dave said, indicating the route Donovan's mind had taken to get to that conclusion.

Donovan shook his head. "What sucks is it's the same things

44

Jay's been saying to me all along."

Dave shrugged. "Sometimes you just need someone not so close to it to confirm it, man."

Donovan nodded. "Jay asked you to talk to me, right?"

"She's worried about you, Pony. It comes with the territory of loving you."

"Yeah," Donovan said, nodding and grinning too. "Think we'll win this one?"

Dave pursed his lips contemplatively. "With my three best narcs and my newest prodigy on the final take down, yeah, I think we'll beat 'em."

Donovan nodded again, taking mental note of being called one of his three best narcs. Dave didn't give compliments lightly; if he said it, he meant it.

Extending his hand, Donovan said, "Thanks, man. Thanks for getting my head screwed back on straight."

"Anytime, Pony, anytime," Dave said, shaking his hand.


That night, Donovan made Jeanie a special dinner, by way of thanking her for helping him get things straightened out in his head. They ate companionably, and then sat on the couch drinking wine and cuddling.

"So, you're okay with all this now?" Jeanie asked.

Donovan kissed her temple, taking a drink of his wine and nodding. "Dave told me a story about how he screwed up even after four years of doing this. I guess we're all human."

"Yeah, go figure," Jeanie said, grinning.

"Watch it, Franco," Donovan said, narrowing his eyes.

"It's Curtis, thank you very much," she replied, her brown eyes sparkling mischievously.

"No hyphen?" he asked, raising an eyebrow at her.

"Well, maybe…" she said. "Franco-Curtis? I don't know, sounds funny."

"Sounds like a can of ravioli."

Jeanie elbowed him, making him cough and laugh at the same time. "Maybe I'll just be Franco on the job and Curtis off, like Midnight is."

"Midnight had a reputation under Chevalier," Donovan pointed out.

"You're saying I don't have a reputation?" Jeanie asked with mock haughtiness.

"Well, you have one, but we won't talk about that…" Donovan said, grinning.

"Oh, shut up!" Jeanie said, swatting his arm. "I know, I have the reputation for being the dumbest broad alive for letting you go twice."

"See, now that's not what I was talking about…"

"What were you talking about?" she asked, giving him a dirty look.

"That you're a good narc," he replied innocently.

"Oh, you are so full of shit, Curtis, you know that?" she said, laughing.

Donovan laughed too. "Seriously, though, Dave referred to you, me, and Stevie as his 'three best narcs' today."

"He did?" Jeanie asked, surprised.

"Yup."

"Wow," Jeanie said, as impressed as Donovan had been. "Dave doesn't just say things like that…" she added, by way of requesting confirmation.

"No, he doesn't."

"Wow…"

Donovan smiled, knowing that Jeanie was feeling the same sense of awe that he'd experienced that afternoon. It felt good.

That night, they made love and fell asleep comfortably, Donovan's mind finally allowing him to rest again.


The next day was New Year's Eve. Jeanie, Donovan, Stevie, and Christian went to see Joe in the hospital. It was obvious, from the moment they walked in, that he was feeling a great deal better. He was sitting up in bed, wearing sweats and a dark blue bathrobe. He was clean-shaven, and looked like he'd just taken a shower. He was engaged in a good-natured debate with the nurse, while Jordan looked on in amusement.

"Well, if you served anything halfway decent in this place, I wouldn't have to beg my girlfriend to smuggle me in food, would I?" Joe was saying with a grin.

"You know the rules, Captain—you've been here often enough," the nurse said, wagging her finger at him.

"Yeah," Joe said, giving her a mock disgruntled look. "And the menu has never improved."

"So buy the hospital and improve it," the nurse shot back, grinning at him.

"I just might," Joe threatened.

"Promises, promises," the nurse sing-songed as she walked out.

Joe looked at his visitors, smiling widely.

"You guys bring me any food?"

Christian grinned. "No, but I got a cigar if you want one."

"Oh, hell no," Jordan said, standing from her chair and narrowing her eyes at Christian.

Christian grinned unrepentantly. "Your lady speaking for you now, man?"

Joe smirked back at his cousin. "Only till I'm out of here. She's my only supply of real food right now."

"Hey!" Jordan said, swatting his arm.

Joe laughed. "So what kind of no good is the Rogue Squad up to?"

"Heard that, huh?" Donovan asked.

"Midnight tells me everythin', Pony, you know that."

Donovan nodded.

"Speaking of tellin'…" Joe said. "You tell your sister yet what you two did?"

"Uhh…" Donovan stammered, as Jeanie looked ashamed.

"I'm taking that as a definite no," Joe said.

"Well, we were going to, but with you getting sick and all, we didn't, well… we didn't get a chance," Donovan said, knowing how guilty he sounded.

"She's gonna kill ya," Joe said. "And every day that you go without telling her you eloped is one more hour of pain she'll level on your head before she kills you."

"I know, I know."

"And come to think of it…" Joe said, his eyes narrowing ominously. "She's gonna kick my ass for not telling her. You get your ass

48

over there and tell her, Donovan, before I get any more heat than I'm already going to get."

"Jeez, okay!" Donovan said, holding his hands up in surrender. "It's Jay's fault—she said she wants to see Randy kick your ass." He said the last grinning, getting elbowed in the stomach for it.

"Jeanie wouldn't do that," Joe said, winking at her. "She loves me."

"Sir, yes sir," Jeanie said, winking up at Donovan.

"Come on, Donovan," Stevie said. "Christian and I'll go with you, so she can't kill you without witnesses."

"She'll yell at me too," Christian said, making a face.

"Ah, poor baby," Joe said, grinning.

"Keep it up and I won't bring you any tequila for New Year's…" Joe scowled. "Oh, that's low."

"And?" Christian asked, looking unaffected.

"Yeah… and fuck you," Joe growled, his grin ruining the effect. "So what are you guys up to tonight?"

"Party at Jeanie's parents' house," Donovan said. The other three nodded.

"Big deal, huh?" Joe asked, raising an eyebrow.

"My parents have a huge house," Jeanie said. "They raised five of us there—they had to!"

"Cool," Joe said, nodding. "So I can safely assume you'll all get home alive, yes?" he asked, sounding fatherly all of a sudden.

"We'll probably all stay over at Mom's," Jeanie said.

"Speaking of the party," Christian said, looking over at Jeanie pointedly. "You make sure Erin's coming?"

"She'll be there," Jeanie said, looking mischievous.

49

Donovan glanced between his wife and Christian. "Alright, what's up, you two?"

Jeanie shrugged, grinning all the while.

"What did you do?" Donovan asked her, narrowing his teal blue eyes.

"I invited Mace to the party," Jeanie said with a smile.

"Oh man…" Donovan said, shaking his head.

"Hey, it was my idea," Christian said. "You have no idea how unhappy she's been since you two got back together permanently."

"She said she was happy for us," Donovan pointed out.

"Yeah, man, what else was she gonna say?" Christian asked, his tone bordering on accusatory. He felt Stevie's hand in his squeeze slightly, reminding him to ease up. "Look," Christian continued, sounding calmer again, "she's lonely, and she's not the type to go out and look for guys, so… I figured Mace might be a nice distraction."

"Who's Mace?" Joe interjected.

"Kevin Elmasian—he's new to narcotics, a T and D from Seattle PD," Christian said.

"Yeah, and we don't know anything about the guy," Donovan said. "He doesn't exactly look like Erin's style."

It was true. Kevin Elmasian, at first glance, looked like the classic narc. His dark blond hair was worn down to his collar, and usually with the top part of it swept back off his face in a short ponytail at the back of his head. He sported a full goatee around frequently quirked lips. He wore a diamond stud earring in each ear, and had a second stud of black onyx in his left ear. He was tall and lanky, with a casual, laidback look to his clothes. There was a definite sensation of cool calculation about him. His bright moss green eyes were frequently

50

hidden behind mirrored Ray-Bans. Everything about him spoke of easy confidence with an underlying threat of a very dangerous man. That was his "look."

When Stevie and Christian had met him the first time, Kevin—or Mace, as he'd been nicknamed in Seattle—had been leaning against the building smoking a thin cigar. Spider had led Stevie and Christian over to him, introducing the three. Kevin had straightened, dropping the cigar and stubbing it out with a black hiking boot.

"Kevin Elmasian, this is Stevie O'Neil-Collins and Christian Collins. You'll be working with them a lot in the next few months," Spider had said.

Kevin's eyes had taken in the black-haired, appallingly handsome man standing just behind the fantastic-looking redhead, his face showing nothing of what he thought of them. His eyes were still hidden by the ever-present shades. He'd extended his hand to Stevie first, without a hint of a come-on.

"O'Neil-Collins?" Kevin asked, his stare flicking to Christian then back to Stevie.

"Just married, haven't decided on the whole hyphen thing yet," Stevie said, grinning engagingly. "You can call me O'Neil for now."

Kevin nodded. "Mace," he said, indicating himself as he extended his hand to Christian.

"Blue," Christian replied, shaking Kevin's hand.

"Mace?" Stevie asked, never one to leave her curiosity unsatisfied.

"Yeah. Short version of my last name."

"Ah," Stevie replied, nodding. "Good thing we use pepper spray now, huh?"

51

That garnered a grin from Kevin, showing perfect straight white teeth. "Probably."

Stevie had already decided to like him, and Christian felt a kindred spirit in the outward rebel of Kevin Elmasian. Once Jeanie and Donovan had met him, Christian suggested to Jeanie that she invite him to the party.

"You should introduce him to Erin," Christian had further suggested.

"Ya think?" Jeanie had asked, surprised. She'd shaken her head and thought much like Donovan. "I don't know if he's really her type..."

"You aren't arranging a marriage, Jay," Christian had said. "They're big kids—they can decide if they like each other or not. Erin needs something or someone to take her mind off you and Donovan."

Jeanie had bit her lip, nodding. She'd known Erin wasn't taking their being together as easily as she'd tried to make it seem. Erin was happy for her and Donovan, but she was sad for herself. She had really loved Donovan, as far as she could, considering he hadn't been in love with her in return. All the same, she didn't think Kevin Elmasian was the answer either, just like Donovan had just mentioned.

Christian raised an eyebrow at Donovan. "So, how 'bout you let Erin meet him and decide for herself?"

Donovan shrugged, looking away from the Englishman. "Fine with me."

Jordan watched the conversation, noting that Joe did as well. Donovan was Joe's brother-in-law, and Christian was his cousin. What both men did and how they acted was important to Joe. He had

52

always walked a fine line with having his relatives working for the department, and now both indirectly for him. He knew people watched avidly to see if he'd treat Donovan or Christian any differently than he would any other officer, especially if they made a mistake. Joe was careful to remind both of them that his ass was on the line with theirs when they messed up.

Jordan read a lot of pride in Joe's appraising look of each of these young men. She knew things must get really complicated for him at times. Joe's personal life and work life were so deeply intertwined, Jordan wondered how he ever held it all together.


Kevin Elmasian sat comfortably in a chair in the corner of the spacious living room of the Franco home. His legs were crossed casually at the ankles, and his eyes tracked the people around him with mild interest. He held a mug of coffee, procured for him by the hostess. His longish hair was still damp from the wet walk up the drive; it was raining like mad outside. He wore black jeans, with black Nike hiking boots and a khaki green shirt. The two silver rings he wore on his right hand glistened in the light as he sipped from the mug. He wore a silver watch on his right wrist and a black banded bracelet on the left. He was a contradiction of wild and tame in one package. It was hard to pinpoint just which he was. Which was exactly how Kevin Elmasian wanted it. His hair was back in its customary tail at the back of his head, the lower part curling at his collar damply. Jeanie's mother approached him, looking anxious.

"Is the coffee alright, Mr. Elmasian?" Alma Franco asked.

"It's great, thanks," Kevin said, nodding.

"You sure you don't want something to eat?"

"I'm sure, ma'am, thank you."

Across the room, Jeanie nudged Erin. "Oh God, we need to go rescue Mace from my mother. Come on," she said, taking Erin's arm and tugging her along as she crossed the room.

"Mom, quit bugging the poor guy," Jeanie said, smiling at her mother all the same.

"He needs to eat," Alma said. "He's too skinny."

Jeanie shook her head. "That's what you said about the boys, Ma, and look how big they are now."

"And I was right," Alma replied confidently.

"You're always right," replied Jaime, one of Jeanie's four brothers, from behind Alma.

"See?" Alma said, grinning at Kevin. "I got 'em trained."

Kevin chuckled, nodding. "Yes, ma'am, you do."

"Mace," Jeanie said, "this is Erin. Erin, this is Mace. He's just joined the department from Seattle PD. Right, Mace?"

Kevin looked up at Erin, noticing the shy way she dropped her eyes from his. She was pretty, in a very sweet way. Her eyes, when she would look back at him, were a china blue. Her blond hair, much lighter than his, looked soft and wavy, and it framed her face attractively.

"Yes, right, Seattle," Kevin said. "It's nice to meet you, Erin."

"It's nice to meet you too," Erin said, looking everywhere but at him.

Kevin sensed easily that Jeanie was trying to set them up. He could tell by the way she was watching them expectantly. He shook his head slowly, wanting to roll his eyes. Not in town two weeks, and someone was already trying to set him up.

"I'll be back," Jeanie said, not bothering to look innocent as she drifted off, leaving the two of them feeling uncomfortable.

"So you're from Seattle?" Erin said after a long silence.

Kevin nodded. "Yeah, born and raised there."

Erin nodded. "So what brought you here?"

"Well, it wasn't the weather," Kevin said, grinning.

Erin smiled, then laughed softly. "Well, maybe we just wanted you to feel at home here."

"Is that it?" Kevin asked, liking the sound of her laugh.

"I said maybe," Erin said. "Then again, it could be the second coming of Noah and the Ark." Her grin was infectious, and Kevin found himself smiling back at her.

"Let's just pretend that it's for me, then."

"You, you, you..." Erin said, laughing again.

"See how I am?" he said, enjoying the banter.

"Yes, I see," she said, giving him a stern look, her grin spoiling it.

Donovan walked up then, hugging Erin from behind and kissing her on the top of the head. She glanced up and back at him and smiled.

"I see you met our newest colleague," Donovan said, nodding at Kevin.

"Yep, we were just discussing the weather," Erin said, grinning.

"She's boring the hell out of you?" Donovan asked Kevin, raising an eyebrow.

Erin elbowed him in the stomach. "Shut up!"

"Usually, weather discussions are for bored people," Donovan explained.

"I see," Erin said, making a face at Donovan, scrunching up her nose.

He made the same face back at her, then glanced at Kevin.

"What're you drinking, man?" he asked, looking pointedly at the mug Kevin still held.

"Coffee," Kevin replied.

"Just coffee?" Donovan asked, looking horrified.

"Yeah." Kevin nodded. "Just coffee."

"It's a party, Mace—you're allowed to cut loose," Donovan informed him.

"I know," Kevin replied, unfazed.

Erin watched the exchange, noticing that Kevin's hand had tightened slightly on the mug. She wondered at that.

Donovan shrugged, and said, "I'll see you two later. I'm going to go find my wife."

Erin and Kevin were silent for a few minutes, both looking around at the people milling about. Kevin drained his coffee and moved to stand.

"Think I'll go seek out a refill," he said, looking down at Erin.

She was about half a foot shorter than him, at five feet, six inches. She looked up at him and smiled shyly, and Kevin thought he saw a little bit of regret in her eyes as she nodded.

"Okay," she said. "Good luck."

"Thanks," he said, smiling at her.

An hour later Kevin found himself sitting in the same chair, his empty coffee mug at his feet. He watched people pass by. There was music playing in another room. He tuned in to the song playing; it was Matchbox Twenty, "Bent." His fingers moved on imaginary guitar chords as the solo began. Realizing what he was doing, he leaned down and picked up the coffee mug, moving to stand again.

"Hey, Mace, how's it going?" said an English-accented voice at his side.

Kevin turned, seeing Christian Collins and Stevie standing together. "Hey, Blue, O'Neil," he said, inclining his head.

"Hey," Stevie said, grinning at him. "What are you drinking?"

Kevin shook his head. "Does everyone here ask the same questions?"

"Someone else ask you that?"

"Yeah—Curtis. I'm drinking coffee—yes, just coffee," he replied succinctly.

"Okay…" Christian said, giving Kevin a lopsided grin. "Issues much?"

Kevin dropped his head, shaking it and grinning. "Sorry, man. I'm just on edge."

"No prob," Christian said.

"So what are you drinking?" Kevin asked Stevie, tilting his head to look at her glass.

"Tequila, with occasional shots of beer," she said, grinning.

Kevin laughed. "José and I don't get along anymore."

"José Cuervo?" Christian asked, grinning.

"That would be the one."

"I so hate when that happens," Stevie said, laughing.

"Yeah, me too. I think I threw up for three days," Kevin said, shaking his head.

"Holy shit," Christian said, looking suitably impressed. Kevin

57

laughed.

"Hey, any of you seen Erin?" Jeanie asked as she walked by.

"Nope," Stevie replied.

"Negative," Christian said.

"Not for an hour or so," Kevin put in.

Jeanie nodded, perplexed. "She wouldn't have left without saying anything, would she?"

Christian shrugged. Stevie simply shook her head.

"Well, I'm headed to the kitchen," Kevin said. "I'll watch for her."

"Thanks," Jeanie said. "I just worry about her, you know…"

"Why?" Kevin asked.

"Uh…" Jeanie stammered.

"Long story," Christian put in.

"Oh," Kevin replied, nodding. He knew he wasn't being told the story on purpose, but wasn't sure what that purpose was. "Well, if I see her, I'll let her know you're looking for her."

"Thanks, Mace," Jeanie said, smiling at him.

Kevin did more than keep an eye out for Erin; he went looking for her. He found her in the fourth quiet room he checked on the second floor of the house.

Pushing open the door, he gave a suitable impression of being surprised.

"Oh, sorry," he said, as if he'd just walked into the wrong room.

Erin was lying on the bed with her back to the door. She glanced around, and Kevin distinctly heard a sniffle. He stepped into the room, concerned.

"You okay?" he asked solicitously.

Erin sat up, wiping at her eyes and nodding. Kevin walked around the bed, watching her.

"You don't look okay," he said softly.

Erin bit her lip, feeling foolish for having been caught crying like a baby. And worse still, by this handsome new narcotics officer. Could she be more humiliated? No, she didn't think so.

Kevin sat down on the bed, bending one knee as he turned to face her. His eyes searched her face. "Want to tell me what's wrong?"

"Um..." she said, pressing her lips together. "I'd rather crawl under the bed in humiliation."

Kevin grinned. "I'll bet there are dust bunnies under there that'd scare a cat."

Erin grinned in spite of herself.

"So what's wrong?" he asked gently.

Erin shook her head, sighing as she glanced at him. "I'm just feeling sorry for myself."

"Over what?"

"My love life."

"What's wrong with it?"

"I don't have one."

"Oh," he said, looking appropriately sober.

"Well, I did have one, but that was a while ago, and, well, things are just not back on track yet."

"What was your last one like? Bad?"

"Well, since it ended up with him marrying someone else, I think that would be classified as bad," Erin said, sounding chagrined.

"Damn, and I thought I knew how to pick 'em," Kevin said, shaking his head. "So who was the jerk?"

"Donovan," Erin said, stunning Kevin.

"Donovan, like Jeanie's Donovan?"

Erin nodded. "Yes, that one."

"And you're here why?" Kevin asked, thinking he wouldn't be here in her situation.

"We're all friends," she said simply.

Kevin looked back at her for a long moment, perplexed, then leaned his elbow on his knee, his chin resting on his fist. "Explain this one to me, please."

Erin smiled slightly, realizing that it probably did sound really strange.

"Okay, Jeanie and I were friends first. Then she introduced me to Donovan, her fiancé at the time."

"Okay…" Kevin said, thinking this wasn't getting any less weird.

"We all three hung out together for a while—it was fun. But then Jeanie decided to take a job in San Francisco, and ended up leaving Donovan to do it."

"Not cool," Kevin said.

"No," Erin agreed. "Donovan was hurt badly. So as his friend, I tried to do everything to help him feel better…" she said, trailing off, still hating the way it sounded.

"And one thing led to another…" Kevin continued for her.

"Yeah," Erin said, chagrined.

"Okay, so then what happened?"

"Well, Donovan was very honest about still being in love with Jeanie. But my heart didn't want to hear that, so I fell in love with him. I think I was long before that anyway. He just seemed so sweet and all… Anyway," she said, shaking her head, "Jeanie ended up coming back, and things got harder."

"They got back together?"

"Well, no, not right away," Erin said. "Donovan kind of dated us both. We both knew he was doing that too, though. He wasn't ready to trust her again yet, but he didn't really love me like he did her. I just wanted what was best for everyone."

"Except you," Kevin put in.

"What?"

"You didn't seem to worry about what was best for you."

"I get what I want too," Erin said, knowing even as she did that she was lying.

"Do you?" Kevin asked, staring directly into her eyes.

"I knew the situation," Erin explained. "I knew Donovan was in love with her." She shrugged helplessly.

"Yeah, he knew it too."

"It's not his fault."

"It's not yours either then."

Erin was silent for a long moment, never having thought about it quite like that. She'd always figured she was to blame, knowing what she'd known, so she'd deserved what she got.

"Okay…" she said, narrowing her eyes in thought. "But it isn't like there's any penance to be paid here."

"True," Kevin agreed. "But you can see why they're trying to help you out."

"Help me out?"

Kevin's grin was sardonic, his green eyes twinkling in the dim light of the bedroom. "You think it was coincidence that we were introduced?"

Erin's eyes widened as her mouth dropped open. "They're trying to set us up?"

"I wouldn't doubt it."

"Yeah, but…" Erin began, but realized she was about to make a major mistake and shut up quickly.

Not quickly enough, however. "But what?" Kevin asked, his eyes already dancing with humor.

"I, uh…" Erin stammered. "Never mind. Nothing."

Kevin's grin widened. "But I'm not your type."

Erin's eyes widened again as she bit her lower lip, afraid she'd offended him.

Kevin shook his head. "Don't worry about it, doll. You're not exactly my type either."

Erin's eyes dropped from his. "I'm sorry," she said, shaking her head. "I didn't mean to be rude like that. I don't really know you. I just… You seem very… You just seem like the kind of guy that would like wilder girls."

Again Kevin smiled, nodding. "You nailed me. I confess, most of my dates usually have more tattoos than I do."

"How many do you have?" Erin asked, curious in spite of herself.

"Three."

"Wow," Erin said. "Don't they hurt to get?"

Kevin shrugged. "Depends on where you get them."

"Should I even ask where yours are?" Erin asked, looked embarrassed.

Kevin chuckled. "You're safe. One on either arm, and the third on my chest."

"Any of them say *Mother*?" Erin asked, grinning.

"Nope," Kevin replied, grinning too.

"Well, that's no fun. Everyone has a mother."

"I was hatched."

"Like a chicken?"

"Like a dragon."

"Ohhhh…" Erin intoned. "Intriguing. Do you breathe fire too?"

"On occasion," Kevin said, liking that she definitely had a sense of humor.

"Well, when my son grows up, I want him to get a tattoo that says *Mother*."

"You mean *when* you have a son?"

"I already have one."

"No way," Kevin said, shaking his head. "You aren't old enough."

"That's what my parents said," Erin replied blandly.

"How old is your son?"

"Steven is seven."

"Wow…" Kevin said, shaking his head. "How old are you?"

"I'm twenty-two. I'll be twenty-three in two months."

Kevin blew his breath out, shaking his head. "Young," he said. "And Steven's dad is… where?"

Erin shook her head. "I don't know, and I don't want to."

Kevin looked back at her for a long moment, then moved to sit next to her, leaning against the headboard. "Explain," he said simply.

63

Erin looked back at him for a long moment, surprised that he wanted to know about her son's father, and also pleasantly surprised that he'd moved closer to her. His arm rested on the back of the headboard, just behind her, as he waited for her explanation. So she told him.

"I met Tyler when I was just barely fifteen. He blew into town, the consummate James Dean, or so I thought. He swept stupid little innocent me off my feet. Before I even considered the consequences, we had sex, and the next thing I knew, I was pregnant and my parents were forcing us to get married."

"Oh shit," Kevin said, knowing how that would go over.

"Exactly," Erin agreed. "Tyler played it cool for a while, but as soon as he could, he dragged me out of my home town and away from everything I knew. When I had Steven, he dropped me off at Emergency at some strange hospital, and picked the two of us up two days later. Things just got worse and worse, and eventually he let all his pretenses drop and started hitting me whenever I disagreed with him. I learned to stay out of his way. But when he started getting violent toward Steven, I had to leave. And that's what I did."

Kevin nodded, looking serious. "You were brave."

"I had to be, for Steven's sake."

"A lot of women aren't though," Kevin pointed out.

"I guess not," Erin said. "I just couldn't bear the thought of Steven growing up afraid of everything. That wasn't how I was raised. We never had much, but my parents loved me."

"So has Tyler seen either of you since then?"

"Well, yeah, he tried," Erin said, grinning.

"Why do I know this is going to be the part where he gets his?"

"Because it was," Erin said, laughing. "He'd been calling me and threatening me at the office. Donovan had Steven and me move into his place with him so he could keep an eye on us. Donovan finally told the girls at the front desk that if Tyler called again, to give them Donovan's number. They did, and he called the house. Donovan set up a meeting with him. Tyler was sure he was going to kick Donovan's butt. But when he showed up, it wasn't just Donovan waiting for him. It was the entire Gang."

"The entire Gang?"

"Yeah," Erin said. "The Gang is, well, they're this group at the department—you'll hear about them. They're the people that everyone in the department, or almost everyone, looks up to and wants to be like. The Gang is made up of the chief, the Assistant Chief, Captain Sinclair, Lieutenants Debenshire and Nguyen, Sergeants Dibbins, Ako, Sorbinno, O'Neil, and Collins, and of course Donovan and Jeanie."

"That's a lot of people," Kevin said.

"More than that, trust me," Erin said. "Once you know all of them, you'll realize how important they are in the department. They're the best of the best. And no one crosses them unless they want to have a rough life."

"So this Gang met up with your ex?"

"Yep," Erin said, grinning. "And Tyler was stupid enough to come on to Midnight, the chief, in front of her husband. Rick laid him out flat."

"And the chief's husband is who?"

"Lieutenant Debenshire."

"That would explain the Chevalier-Debenshire hyphen for her name, wouldn't it?" Kevin mused.

65

Erin chuckled. "It only gets more involved from there. Captain Sinclair is best friends with the chief and with Lieutenant Debenshire. Christian Collins is Captain Sinclair's cousin. Donovan is Captain Sinclair's brother-in-law—well, was..."

"Was?"

"Yeah, Joe—Captain Sinclair—was married to Randy, Donovan's sister. But Joe and Randy just got divorced, so I guess Donovan isn't legally Joe's brother-in-law anymore."

"You people keep things close here, don't you?" Kevin marveled.

"You have no idea," Erin replied, grinning as she realized how it would look to someone new to the department.

They were silent for a while, and Erin found herself liking the feeling of his closeness. He wasn't inappropriately close; he was at a personal conversation distance. She could smell his cologne and wondered what it was. It had kind of a woodsy scent to it. She wondered about him—was he as much of a bad boy as he seemed? A real bad boy would have tried something by now, her mind told her. He was, after all, a police officer, and Midnight Chevalier herself had interviewed with him and hired him. She was what Erin considered the ultimate judge of character.

Erin thought like most of the Gang did—if Midnight approved of someone, then they must be okay. Of course, that didn't mean Midnight thought Kevin Elmasian would be right for someone like Erin Shandley. But Erin had found herself quite comfortable in this stranger's presence. She didn't know if it was because she was ultimately among friends, and that if Kevin Elmasian tried anything he shouldn't, she could call down some serious hellfire on his head. Erin didn't think she would be brave enough to do that, but Kevin Elmasian didn't know it.

"You feeling better?" Kevin asked, bringing her out of her ruminations.

She looked over at him, smiling. "Yes, I am. Thanks."

Kevin inclined his head, a grin playing at his lips.

From downstairs, someone loudly announced that New Year's was just five minutes away. They looked at each other and grinned.

"Guess we're kinda missing the party..." Erin said hesitantly.

"Kinda," Kevin agreed, making no move to leave.

"You don't mind?"

Kevin shrugged. "I'm not much of a party person anymore."

"Anymore?" Erin asked, sure there was something to that statement.

"Since I quit drinking."

"Oh," Erin said. She wanted to ask more questions, but didn't want to pry. "Is that why you were drinking coffee?"

Kevin nodded. "Yeah."

Again they were silent. Erin wondered what had prompted someone who was so obviously a wild child to stop drinking. She wanted to ask, but knew it wasn't her place to. Kevin found himself wanting to tell her, which was strange, since he'd left his old department basically to get away from the whole thing of everyone knowing his business.

They heard the call that it was one minute to midnight, and glanced at each other again.

"You better get out there if you want to score that New Year's kiss from some handsome stranger..." Kevin said, grinning.

Erin looked back at him for a long minute, and was stunned to hear herself say, "And I thought I might get lucky and score one from the handsome stranger I'm sitting here with."

Where had that come from? She couldn't believe she'd said it! Was he going to laugh at her? She took a chance and looked at him, and saw that he was smiling.

"And I thought you'd never ask…" he said, his voice lower, but with a note of humor to it.

Erin bit her lip as they waited, staring at each other. She searched his eyes, and her mind raced. Was he a good kisser? Was he humoring her? Like a child? Did he really want to kiss her? But he'd said she wasn't his type! Was she? Or was he just playing? *Oh, Erin, stop overthinking everything!* her mind screamed at her.

They heard the countdown.

"Ten, nine, eight…" the crowd downstairs was yelling. Kevin's hand touched Erin's waist.

"Seven, six, five…" He pulled her closer, his arm encircling her shoulders.

"Four, three, two…" Erin couldn't breathe. She was sure time would stop right there.

"One! Happy New Year!"

His lips touched hers. His kiss was strong, but not demanding at first, his hand at her waist pulling her closer. She kissed him back, responding to the pressure of his lips and not wanting the moment to end. Her head was already spinning. Could he kiss? By God, Kevin Elmasian could definitely kiss! Her arms encircled his neck as he gathered her even closer, his lips urging hers to open. When his tongue touched her lower lip she moaned—she hadn't meant to, but it slipped out. He groaned in response, his hands grasping at her, pulling her onto his lap, kissing her deeper, his hands at her back, pressing her close.

68

They kissed for what seemed like hours, both becoming quite breathless in the process. He broke away, trailing his lips over her jawline and down to her ear.

"Happy New Year," he whispered, his voice husky.

Erin shuddered slightly at the effect it had on her. Her body was alive with sensations. She found she was shaking. She couldn't bear to look at him and see if he thought she was some silly girl. Instead she buried her face against his shoulder. She felt his hands at her back, holding her to him. It felt really good, and she was afraid to do anything or say anything and break this spell.

Her mind kept telling her over and over that this was crazy. She didn't even know this man! But here she was, lying in his arms, after having kissed him like some brazen slut. My God, did he think she was easy? It wasn't like she'd shown him anything else. Did he assume she'd sleep with him now? *Was that an altogether bad idea?* her body seemed to be asking, but her mind warned her, *Of course it's a bad idea!* But why, really? She was an adult. He was an adult. Why did everything have to mean true love?

Hadn't she learned anything from being with Donovan? She had known he didn't love her, but she'd wanted to be with him, so she was. She'd dated a few guys since Donovan, but none of them had really sparked any interest. She knew she just needed to get Donovan out of her system. Having sex with other guys hadn't done it either. They just didn't do anything for her.

Kevin Elmasian did a lot for her—at least, that kiss sure had. She remembered the first time Donovan had kissed her. It had been a totally innocent thing, when he'd been trying to prove a point with Jeanie about his goatee, but it had set off all kinds of sensations in her. And now Kevin Elmasian's kiss had done that too, and a lot

69

more. She was ready to abandon her honor and just have fun. *I'm losing it.*

"Are you?" Kevin asked, his voice a low rumble in his chest, where her cheek rested.

Had she said that out loud? Oh, Jesus!

"I, um, huh?" Erin said, without lifting her head.

"You said you're losing it," Kevin said, grinning in the semi-darkness of the room.

"Oh, I meant to say that in my head," she said, feeling so stupid.

"Oh," he said, nodding. He was silent for a full minute, and she thought she'd gotten away with it. She was wrong. "So what are you losing?"

Erin sat up, her legs straddling his waist, her knees to either side.

"I, uh…" she stammered, trying to think of a suitable reply. "My mind?" she said, giving him a comical grimace.

"For kissing me?" he asked directly.

"For…" she began, then hesitated, amazed at how easily he could get her to admit things. How did he do that?

"For what?" he asked, not letting it go.

"For wanting to do more than kiss you," she said, staring directly into his eyes.

Kevin was silent for a moment, staring back. A slow smile spread over his lips. "And that's losing it?"

"Yeah," she said, curling her lips in self-disgust. "I'm not usually that easy."

Kevin nodded, chewing at his lower lip in thought. "And you think because I made you want to do more than just kiss me, that makes you easy?"

Erin gazed back at him for a long minute, trying to unravel what he'd just said. Finally she shook her head.

"No, but I'm afraid that it'll make you think I am."

Kevin nodded again. "I don't."

Erin narrowed her eyes at him for a long moment, trying to decide if he was bullshitting her or not. "You don't?"

"No, Erin, I don't," he said, his voice very serious, his eyes on hers.

Erin contemplated that, then looked up at him again. "Why?"

Kevin grinned. "You seem very sweet, very honest, and very cautious. Three things that don't add up to easy in any book."

"Then why did I kiss you?" she asked.

"I kissed you."

"Then why did I let you?"

"Because you wanted me to."

Erin gave an exasperated sigh. "Why doesn't that add up to easy, then?"

Kevin chuckled outright. "Do you want me to think you're easy, Erin?"

"No," she said, already looking like a child scorned.

"Then why are you trying to convince me that you wanting me to kiss you makes you easy?"

She dropped her head to his shoulder, shaking it. "I don't know."

Kevin grinned as his hands smoothed over her back. "Don't know what you want, do you, little one?"

She lifted her head, looking at him, her eyes searching his. Then she shook her head. "I guess not," she said sadly.

71

His hand touched her cheek, his fingers lacing through her hair. "Do you want me to kiss you again?"

Erin closed her eyes for a moment, feeling a shiver go through her just at his question. When she opened them again, he was watching her, waiting for her answer.

"Yes," she replied.

His lips were on hers not a breath after she'd said it. Again, he kissed her until they were both breathless. His hands slid under her shirt, touching her bare back. She moaned against his lips. His kiss deepened, his tongue sliding across her lips, spurring her on to greater action.

She unbuttoned his shirt, pulling the shirt tails out of his pants, her hands touching his chest making him groan. She could feel his muscles ripple as she caressed them, and she found herself dying to see his chest.

It was her that broke the kiss this time, pulling back to look at him. And what a glorious sight greeted her eyes. His chest was well defined, with every lean muscle outlined in perfectly smooth skin. Her eyes trained on the tattoo on his left pectoral muscle. It was about two inches square, a heart, a blood red heart, with a thickly linked yellow-gold chain around it and a gold-and-black padlock in front. The chain was made to look tight, squeezing the heart in its grasp. It was a very definite statement.

Her fingers traced the heart, her eyes trailing back up to his. He was watching her.

"Your heart is locked up tight?" she said.

He said nothing for a long moment, then nodded.

"Who hurt you so badly?" she found herself asking.

72

"My daughter's mother," he said, reaching up to pull her back to him. His kiss erased any more of her questions for the moment.

When they finally parted again, she was ready to ask questions again.

"Tell me," she said, moving back to sit on his lap, her hands at his waist.

He stared at her for a long moment, and once again found himself wanting to tell her. *What the hell,* he thought.

"When I was in the academy," he began, "I used to party all the time. My friends and I were always out drinking. I got so blasted half the time, it's a wonder I ever made it through the academy. Anyway, one night I met this girl. She was wild. She was willing to do anything, anywhere, anyhow. We started hanging out, and it became a thing," he said, his tone monotone, as if reciting it from memory but not feeling any of it. "Six months later, she tells me she's pregnant. She had told me she was on the pill, so I hadn't bothered to use any protection. I know, stupid, but I didn't really care in those days," he said, grimacing.

"What happened?" Erin asked, knowing there was a lot more to this story.

"Well, I asked what happened with the pills. She said they'd made her sick, so she stopped taking them a few months back."

"And she didn't tell you?"

"No," he said, his grin sarcastic. "Guess she didn't think to tell me that part. So, here she is pregnant, and I'm damned if I'm marrying her. But I cared about her, so I told her I'd stick it out with her, and we'd work things out."

Erin nodded, watching his face.

73

"Well, this girl was the ultimate drama queen anyway, and pregnancy only gave her more reason to throw fits and scenes. Which she did, all too often," he said, rolling his eyes. "By the time the baby was due, I was ready to give up. There was no way I could stay with her when she was acting the way she always was. She'd throw things, take off in my car, going on shopping sprees, whatever she chose to do. I couldn't keep up with all of it."

"What happened when the baby was born?"

The most rapturous smile crossed his lips then, and Erin felt tears behind her eyes at the sight.

"When I saw my daughter for the first time," he said, his smile still lighting his eyes, "I was in love. There was nothing I wouldn't do for her. I didn't care what hell Stacy put me through, she was the woman who had brought this perfect little human being into my life."

"What's your daughter's name?"

"Emily," Kevin said with a wistful smile.

"So what happened?" Erin asked, not entirely wanting to know, because she could just tell it was going to be painful to hear.

"Stacy and I stayed together, for the sake of Emily, is what I told myself. I even managed to convince myself that I loved Stacy for giving me Emily, at least for a while. But before long Stacy was right back to her dramatic scenes. She constantly used Em against me. She kept threatening to leave and take Emily where I'd never see her again. When I'd hate her the most, she turned into this sweet, loving woman. She'd pamper me, and do almost anything to make me happy. It was a constant roller coaster. She told me she loved me, that she just wanted everything to be perfect for Emily. I wanted that too, so we kept working at it…" His voice trailed off as he shook his head.

"What happened, Kevin?" Erin asked, watching him closely.

"Well," he said, his voice taking on a caustic tone, "her demons finally pushed mine too far one night. I started drinking, and didn't stop until I was so drunk I couldn't see straight. Then she told me to get out. That she wouldn't put up with a drunk around her child. I took my keys and left."

"Oh God," Erin said, shaking her head.

"No, God wasn't involved, honey," he said, his tone still caustic. "A 5.0 Mustang and a brick wall were, however."

"Kevin…" she breathed, shaking her head again.

"Oh, wait, it gets better," he said derisively. "Three broken bones, a concussion, and a number of cuts later, they got to asking me questions. Things like, 'How many drinks do you have in one day?' What? Ten to twelve isn't normal? Having a drink to get started every morning isn't normal? Drinking till I pass out at night isn't normal? Wow, go figure. 'Guess what, Mr. Elmasian, you're an alcoholic.'"

Erin looked back at him for a long moment, not sure how to react to what he'd just said. She waited, wanting to hear it all.

"Well," he said, his voice taking on an angry, hurt tone, "apparently physical therapy was one thing, but having to babysit an alcoholic was more than Stacy could take responsibility for. So she carried out her threat and took Emily and herself off to live away from me."

"She left you?" Erin asked, surprised, although she wasn't sure why she was.

"Yup."

"When you needed her most," Erin said, nodding, her fingers tracing over the tattoo again.

75

Kevin nodded too. Then he shrugged. "In the end, it was probably better. Emily shouldn't have seen me the way I was in the days when I was getting sober, and I learned to do everything for myself. I couldn't depend on anyone but me, so I didn't."

"What about your family? Do you have family in Seattle?"

"My parents and one younger sister," Kevin said. "My other three siblings live here in California."

"Well, what about your parents? Couldn't they help?"

Again his grin was wry. "Well, they could, but see, the thing about alcoholism is that it's a disease, a hereditary disease…" His voice trailed off as he swallowed hard. "If they admitted that I was an alcoholic, it might mean they'd have to admit that my father is one too."

Erin stared back at him for a long moment, unable to formulate a response. My God, was there no good to be found here? No wonder the man's heart was shut off. Whose wouldn't be?

"I'm sorry, Kevin," was all she could think of to say.

"Don't be," he said. "I beat it, and I've been sober for three years. I did it by myself, and I'm pretty proud of that."

"You should be."

He gave her a small smile. "Now you know all my secrets."

"You know all mine too," she said, smiling back.

"Yours are pretty mild."

"Sorry," she said, grinning.

"The hell you say."

"So," she said, tracing her finger down his chest. "Do I get to see the other tattoos?"

He grinned. "You sure you want to see them?"

76

"Do they all have such horrible stories attached to them?"

"No."

"Then yes, I do."

He nodded, sitting up enough to remove his shirt and toss it aside. Erin found herself gazing at his shoulders—they were extremely nice. He was all lean, strong muscles, and she just wanted to run her hands over them. Giving in to that impulse, she put her hands to his shoulders and slid them down his arms. She saw the tattoos then, and was surprised that she was impressed.

The tattoo on his left arm was incredibly detailed. She wanted to see it better, so she leaned over and turned on the light, which had him squinting at her.

"Sorry, I wanted to see it better," she said, looking at his arm.

This tattoo was about twice the size of the one on his chest and nowhere near as simple. It was a picture of a gray wolf, with every hair detailed finely. In its mouth the wolf held the neck of a guitar. The body of the guitar, a classic round shape, red with orange flames licking out from the sides, was detailed as well, with knobs and strings. The wolf's eyes were the exact same moss green as Kevin's— she looked twice to make sure.

"What?" he asked, seeing her glancing at him, then at the tattoo, then back at him.

"The wolf's eyes are yours."

Kevin nodded. "My tattoo artist got carried away," he said, grinning.

"Did he?"

"She."

"Oh… Did she?" Erin asked again. "Or did she know you?"

77

Kevin looked back at her for a long moment, not answering. But she was right. The girl that had done the tattoo for him had known him for years. Finally he shrugged.

"A group of us used to hang out—we called ourselves the wolf pack. It just seemed to work for me."

Erin nodded. "It's really nice."

Kevin grinned.

"What?" she said, catching the glint of humor in his eyes.

"It wasn't meant to be nice."

"Oh," she said, grinning at him. "Sorry, it's really, um, manly."

Kevin chuckled. "I think I like 'nice' better."

"Have it your way," she said. "What about the guitar?"

"The guitar is mine. I have one like that."

"You play guitar?"

"Yeah, I wanted to be a rock star when I grew up," he said, smiling wryly.

"Oh, I see…"

She moved to his other arm then, and saw a green dragon. Again, this one was very detailed, with vivid colors and minute detail. It was the same size as the wolf. The dragon's wings were extended, done in variegated shades of green, blue, and purple. It had a blood red tongue licking out from the mouth, and flames. The dragon's tail was wrapped around a black cross.

"What is this?" Erin asked, touching the cross, thinking it looked familiar somehow but not able to put her finger on just what it was.

Kevin grinned. "It's an Iron Cross, but probably not what you're thinking."

"What am I thinking?" she asked, not sure they were on the same page.

"Are you thinking it looks like a Nazi symbol?"

She nodded; she'd thought it looked sinister.

"It's not—it's an Iron Cross, given by the German military for bravery in the face of the enemy. In 1939 Hitler added the swastika to the center for his own purposes. No true Iron Cross has a swastika."

"Oh," Erin said, intrigued. "So is your family German?"

"Yeah," he said. "And apparently my great-grandfather received the Iron Cross for bravery in battle."

"Wow," Erin said, suitably impressed.

"My grandfather always told me I was just like his father, so brave and ready to charge ahead no matter what lay in front of me." He grinned. "Usually a whole field of land mines, in my case."

Erin laughed softly. "And the dragon is you?"

"I guess," he said. "But the wolf is me too, so who knows."

Erin nodded.

They were both silent for a long few minutes. Erin was still straddling his hips. When she realized just where she was sitting, she immediately got embarrassed and starting biting her bottom lip. She couldn't think of anything to say. She glanced at him to see that he was watching her. Apparently, long silences didn't bother him at all. His look was contemplative, like he was trying to figure her out. She smiled self-consciously.

"What?" he asked, his eyes dancing with humor.

"I, uh…" she stammered, biting her lip again. "I don't know what to say right now," she finally said.

Kevin nodded. His eyes still on her, he reached over and turned the bedside lamp back off.

"I think that's enough light for now," he said, grinning. The room was still dimly lit by the moonlight coming through the window.

He reached out, touching her cheek and feeling her tremble. Was she afraid he was going to attack her? Hell, if he'd wanted to, he could have done it long before now. Sliding his hand to the back of her neck, he pulled her down to him, resting her head against the hollow of his shoulder. She settled against him, and he heard her sigh softly. He grinned in the dimly lit room.

Erin definitely had a way of making someone want to be gentle with her. Kevin's gentle side was usually reserved for his daughter, but at the moment, he sensed Erin's fragility. For some strange reason he couldn't put his finger on, he didn't want to shatter that.

Erin lay against his chest, listening to his heartbeat. She had no idea why she felt such a connection with this man, but there was definitely a feeling of companionship. Here she was, lying against a man she barely knew. Not only was she lying against him, but she was pressed against bare skin! But she wasn't uncomfortable; she didn't feel like it was wrong in any way. She knew that being with Donovan had made her much more comfortable with her own feelings about sex and sexuality. Donovan had a way of making her feel like nothing she did was really wrong. She'd always felt attractive with him. That comfort level, however, hadn't extended to the men she'd dated after Donovan. She had no idea what had possessed her to be so honest with this stranger, other than the fact that he'd been so gentle in asking her what was wrong. Then he'd been open enough with her to share very personal things about himself.

80

She felt his hands on her back, holding her, his fingers stroking her hair. She inhaled the scent of his cologne, and just relaxed against him. It was a very comfortable moment, and she was allowing herself to enjoy it, and trying desperately not to overthink it, as was her habit.

After a long while, she lifted her head to look at him. His eyes were closed, but opened to look at her when she raised her head. Their eyes met, and his hand touched her face as he moved his head forward to kiss her lips softly. Erin moved closer, kissing him back, her hands on his chest. His hand buried itself in her hair, pulling her in, the kiss intensifying. Both hands were in her hair then, holding her, his kiss deepening further to passion. He moved to sit up, taking her with him, his lips never leaving hers. His tongue slid over her lips, and she parted them, moaning at the feel of his hands sliding over her back.

He caressed her as they kissed, making her tremble, her hands grasping at his shoulders, and then his hair. He broke the kiss, moving his mouth to her neck, his lips brushing over her skin, kissing, sucking, even biting gently, making her gasp. His hands moved to her waist, his thumbs slipping up under the edge of her blouse, touching her skin. She wanted his hands on her, she knew that. Reaching down, she lifted the edge of the blouse, pulling it up and over her head, moving to kiss his shoulder as his hands slid up her back. His mouth moved down to her collarbone, his arms going around her waist, holding her close. She let her head fall back, feeling his lips move lower.

His arms were crossed around her back, his hands coming to rest on either side of her torso, his thumbs brushing against the underside of her bra, eliciting the most incredible sensations. His lips

81

moved over the top of her bra, down into the valley between her breasts. Erin couldn't even think. She grasped his shoulders for support, even though she didn't need it, his arms wrapped around her felt so strong. She felt the warmth of his tongue sliding over her skin and she was sure she was going to explode.

"Please... please..." she said, wanting him to do anything so long as she kept feeling like this.

He lifted his head, taking possession of her lips again, pulling her body flush with his. His hands moved to remove her bra, pulling it off gently and tossing it aside. Her skin touched his, and they both shuddered. His teeth nipped softly at her lip as his fingers moved to the button of her jeans. Before long they were both naked, and he was pulling her to him again, kissing her deeply and holding her against him. He leaned against the headboard, and her body lay over his. His hands slid over her skin and he kissed her, touching her gently but with enough strength to make her want to beg him to make love to her. She could sense his tension—she knew she wasn't alone in wanting this badly. Waiting was making her want him more, and she wondered if that was his purpose in still taking time to touch her.

"Kevin..." she began, his lips cutting off what she started to say.

He pulled her up, kissing her neck, biting it gently, caressing her nipples and setting her on fire instantly. She gasped loudly, and then cried out in sheer abandon as he slid her body down on his. Her body had been so ready for him that within moments an orgasm washed over her, making her reach blindly for something to hold on to. His hands were right there, his fingers entwining themselves with hers. His orgasm joined hers, making the sensations in her body double in intensity. It left them both gasping for breath. Erin laid herself against him, feeling his body shaking, just as hers was. He held her

82

for a long time as he tried to slow his breathing.

"My God," he gasped softly, his breath still coming in ragged gasps.

Erin smiled against his chest and nodded, agreeing with him wholeheartedly. It had never felt like that for her. She'd never felt anything that powerful before. Donovan had been a very good lover, ten times better than her husband had ever been. But Kevin had just surpassed Donovan by miles. She hadn't thought she could ever feel anything like that. Her head was still spinning!

She felt him shaking his head, and glanced up at him. The look on his face was bewildered.

"What?" she asked.

He was quiet for a moment, then looked down at her. "Anyone ever tell you that you're hell on a guy's self-control?"

"Self-control?"

"Yeah," he said, grinning. "The ability to keep from coming the second you touch a woman's body."

"Oh," she said, widening her eyes. "What was wrong with your self-control? I thought that was timed rather perfectly."

He chuckled softly, nodding. "Well, yeah, it was, but usually I can hold out through a couple of orgasms. Your first one nailed me."

Erin smiled widely, before pressing her lips together in an attempt to appear apologetic. But her ego was jumping up and down jubilantly.

Kevin narrowed his eyes at her, as if trying to discern who she really was. He had definitely underestimated this woman, at least sexually. His response to her had been so forceful he couldn't have stopped it if he'd tried with every ounce of willpower in his body. No

83

woman had had that kind of effect on him since he'd been a teenager trying out sex for the first time.

He couldn't help but smile at the way her eyes were dancing happily. It was apparent he'd just told her something she'd never heard from any other man. She was such a compelling presence. She made him want to tell her things she'd never heard, she made him want to make her smile like that over and over again. *Jesus Christ, who is this girl?* his mind asked him vehemently.

They lay together quietly for a long time, finally falling asleep a while later. Neither of them moved from the position they lay in. Erin still rested over him, her head in the hollow of his shoulder, his arms wrapped around her.

\*\*\*

Stevie could see that Christian was drinking heavily, but he was enjoying himself and she wasn't about to stop him. The week that they'd been married had seemed unreal—being in Monaco, Joe getting sick, having to rush him back to the States. She hadn't felt like she was married during that time. Christian had continued to be the same as he'd always been. He always kept up the cool facade around other people. It was his way, and Stevie respected it. With her he was warm, passionate, but always with a level of control that kept him just out of her reach. She hadn't seen the weak, wide-open man he'd been after the suicide attempt again. He was back to his confident, strong self. She found that it was comforting to her that he be the strong man she'd known all along. It felt good to know that she was one of the few people he'd show any weakness to, however.

Stevie sat back on the stool, leaning against the bar. She was

84

watching her husband and Rick Debenshire; they had commandeered the stereo and were playing Motley Crüe. At that moment they were belting out the words to "Wild Side."

"The boys are going to town, I see," Midnight said, leaning against the bar next to Stevie.

"Oh yes," Stevie said, grinning.

"Blue's drunk off his ass."

"And how," Stevie said, laughing this time.

"Rick's not far behind," Midnight added, smiling indulgently at her husband as he winked at her.

Stevie nodded. It never ceased to amaze her that she was on such a casual basis with her once idol. Midnight Chevalier was almost impossible not to respect. She had everything together. Her career, her marriage, her life. She had a heated, passionate romance with her husband, and held one of the largest departments in the country in the palm of her hand. Yet she never seemed to let any of it go to her head. She was always down-to-earth.

"So, how are things?" Midnight asked.

Stevie glanced at her. Midnight was still watching the guys singing.

"Things are alright," Stevie said, shrugging. "We haven't really had a chance to be a normal married couple yet."

"Eh," Midnight said, grinning. "Normal isn't all it's cracked up to be."

Stevie laughed. "I guess you'd know, considering you and Rick are about as far from a normal married couple as they get."

"Oh, we're normal," Midnight said, still grinning. "We just can't seem to stay that way for too long."

85

Stevie smiled. "You two just seem so perfect for each other."

Midnight rolled her eyes. "We are perfect for each other. We're also perfect for the insane asylum sometimes."

"How do you two hold it together?" Stevie asked, sincerely curious how two such fiery personalities such as theirs kept from killing each other half the time.

Midnight stared at Rick for a long moment, her eyes tender. Then she looked back at Stevie.

"We found out that we weren't right for anyone else," she said, then shrugged. "We know that we love each other, we know that we belong together. That sees us through the fights. We know we're always going to be together. So we also know we have to get through whatever life throws at us. It makes us work harder."

Stevie thought about that for a minute, then nodded, understanding what she was saying. She envied them for having gotten there. But she also guessed that it took a lot to get to that place in their relationship. They'd been married for over thirteen years. Stevie looked at Christian then, and caught him watching her. She smiled at him, prompting him to walk over. He put his back to her, leaning against her. She parted her legs and pulled him closer, putting her arms around his shoulders and kissing his neck. He glanced at Midnight, nodding to her.

"Chief," he said, grinning.

"Narc," Midnight replied, grinning back.

"Change your mind yet?" he asked.

"Didn't you just get married?" Midnight replied, laughing.

"Oh yeah," he said, laughing as Stevie bit his neck playfully.

"Watch it, Collins," Stevie said. "Unless you'd like to check out

86

the accommodations in the Franco dog house."

"So tough…" Christian said, his voice trailing off as he straightened and turn around to face Stevie.

He leaned down, taking possession of her lips, kissing her deeply, pulling her close to him.

She bit his lip as she kissed him. "You better believe I am."

"Oh, I believe, I believe," he said, smiling down at her wickedly.

She shook her head. "You ready to pass out yet, handsome?"

"Not quite yet," he replied, reaching behind her for the tequila bottle he'd been drinking from most of the night.

Stevie sighed and shook her head, glancing at Midnight. Midnight shook her head too, and laughed.

Pushing off the bar, Midnight walked over to where Rick was talking to Dave. She came up behind him, putting her arms around him and resting her head against his back. Rick continued to talk to Dave, but his hands came up to cover hers.

Susan was standing next to Dave. His arm was around her shoulders, his hand on her arm, stroking her. Susan was leaning against him, listening intently to the two men talk.

Stevie watched the whole scene, feeling happy about everything at that moment. She knew she was a bit drunk herself, but she couldn't help but feel like her life was finally getting back on track. She loved the people she worked with. She was thoroughly enjoying her job now, and on top of that, she'd get to work with Christian on cases too. How much better could things get? She watched with a wistful smile as the music on the stereo changed to a slow song, Def Leppard's "Goodbye." Rick took one of Midnight's hands from his chest, turning around to face her, pulling her close. He kissed her tenderly, then whispered in her ear. She smiled and put her arms around his shoulders. They began dancing, and it was obvious they were lost in each other. No one else existed for them. Stevie watched Rick sing the words to her. The lyrics were about love and commitment, and how they'd never say goodbye to each other.

It was exactly what Midnight had been saying. They knew they loved each other and that they belonged together. They'd never have to say goodbye. Stevie could see how that would make it safer for them to fight. They knew no matter how much they fought, they'd always be together. It made it okay.

Stevie looked at Christian, who was also watching Rick and Midnight. He glanced at her and smiled warmly.

"What?" he asked, seeing her wistful smile.

"I love you," she said, feeling so good at that moment.

His look changed as he stared into her eyes, and she could see that he was feeling exactly what she was. His hand touched her cheek, and he pulled her to him, hugging her close, kissing the top of her head.

"I love you too, Stevie," he said against her hair.

They stayed that way for a while. Finally Stevie moved back to look at him. He smiled at her, but she could see he was definitely feeling the effects of the alcohol. His expression was almost sad. Suddenly she knew they needed to get out of that room. She took his hand, pulling him with her. She headed upstairs to the room that Jeanie's mom had given them for the night. Dragging him inside, she closed the door behind them. She could feel his reluctance all of a sudden. Turning to face him, she saw the shadowed look on his face. Before he said a word, she knew what he was thinking about.

Taking his hand, she led him over to the bed, sitting him down and kneeling down to take his boots off. His eyes stayed on her. She remembered the last time she'd dragged him away from one of his drinking binges. It had been the time she'd thought he was upset over losing Susan to Dave. It had set off a really rough period in their relationship. Stevie had been so hurt over the thought that he loved Susan so much as to be shattered by her abandonment. She'd stormed out of his room and refused to talk to him for a long time; even when she did talk to him, it was with absolute ice in her voice. Christian had been at a loss.

This time was different, and Stevie just knew he was thinking about the affair with Joe. And everything that had happened after that. When she looked up at him, he was still watching her. She tossed aside his boots and stood up. His eyes stayed on her. She straddled his lap, taking his face in her hands and kissing him deeply. His arms went around her waist, holding her so tight she could barely breathe. After the kiss, she hugged his head to her, stroking his hair.

"If I ever lose you…" he said, his English accent thick, his words slurred.

"You won't," she assured him.

"But I did," he said, sounding so lost. "I lost you, and I couldn't breathe, I couldn't move… Steve…" he ranted, his voice growing almost hysterical.

"Listen to me," she said, taking his face in her hands again, staring into his eyes. "I love you. I'm not going anywhere without you. Do you hear me?"

He stared back at her, closing his eyes. Then he started shaking his head. "No… I believed that before. I can't… Steve, I can't…" he said, his voice growing thicker as tears started clogging his throat.

Stevie got up, moving to lie down on the bed, pulling him down

89

with her. She lay slightly above him on the pillows, stroking his hair. She knew he was letting the alcohol get to him, and letting his darkest thoughts run wild.

"Shhhh…" she said as he continued. "Christian, I'm here. I'm not going anywhere. Listen to me," she whispered into his ear. "I love you, I'm yours. I'll always be yours and you'll always be mine. I love you." She continued to talk to him, feeling him start to relax against her.

His arm moved around her waist, pulling her closer. He held on to her as she talked to him. She could feel his breathing become even, and she knew he'd passed out or fallen asleep. She lay in the darkness of the room thinking about what had just happened. She knew it was his own personal demons talking, and she knew that they'd come back to haunt them for a while. But they'd get through it—she had to believe that.

# CHAPTER 3

Joe lay comfortably in the hotel bed, watching as Jordan moved around the room, an amused grin on his lips.

"Are you planning on perching soon?" he asked.

"What?" Jordan said, her tone harried.

"You're making me tired just watching you, Jordan."

"Oh…" she said, grinning. "Sorry, babe, I just want to make sure you're going to be comfortable."

"I'm fine, babe, relax."

Jordan sighed, moving to sit down on the bed.

"Are you sure you should have left the hospital so soon?" she asked worriedly.

"Jordan, I hate hospitals. I do a lot better in a place I'm comfortable. Don't worry, okay?" he said, reaching out to touch her leg.

She looked down and saw the ring she'd given him. She smiled warmly, thinking of how much her life had changed since she'd met him.

"C'mere," he murmured, taking her hand and pulling her down to him gently.

She lay down next to him, snuggling into his arms as he wrapped them around her. She kissed his neck softly, enjoying the warmth of his body next to hers again.

"I've missed this," she said wistfully.

91

"Me too," Joe said, grinning. "Not exactly what I had planned on for New Year's Eve, however."

"What had you planned on?" she asked, wondering belatedly if he'd had arrangements with Randy.

He shrugged. "I at least hoped to be out somewhere drinking and having a good time."

"Oh, well, you can't drink."

"I know, I know," he assured her.

"So what else would you have been doing?"

"Oh…" he said, grinning evilly.

"Joseph Michael Sinclair!" she exclaimed, laughing.

"I know—I'm an old lech, aren't I?"

"You are not old," she said, narrowing her eyes at him.

"Okay, so you're saying I'm just a lech?"

"Yeah," she said, grinning.

Joe nodded, giving her a narrowed look.

She reached up, kissing his lips softly. "I don't think you should overexert yourself right now."

He sighed melodramatically. "I'll take that as a no then."

"A no to what?"

"Me."

Jordan stared back at him for a long moment, then shook her head. "I'd never tell you no."

"No?" he said, grinning again.

"No," she said. "I'm just—"

His lips on hers silenced her. He made love to her then, taking his time and reminding her easily why she craved him so much. Afterward, they lay together, feeling happy and sated.

They'd both dozed off when Joe's cell phone rang. He reached for it, feeling around on the bedside table. Picking up the phone, he stuck it to his ear, hitting the answer button at the same time.

"Yeah?" he said tiredly.

Jordan turned over to look at him. She could only hear his half of the conversation.

"Hey, Robert, how are you?" Joe said. He listened for a minute, nodding. "Yeah, and what did you find?" he asked, his eyes connecting with Jordan's. "Really? Great! How much?" he said, his eyes narrowing at whatever Robert had just told him. He nodded. "Yeah, do it. I want it taken care of," he said with conviction. "How long will it take?" A pause. "Well, we have till January fourteenth." He nodded, then exchanged goodbyes with Robert and hung up.

"What was that about?" Jordan asked as he lay back down.

Joe was silent for a moment, then turned on his side to look at her. "You," he answered simply.

"Me?" she asked, thinking he must be joking.

"Yeah, you and your contract with Mark."

She looked back at him for a long few moments, shaking her head slowly. "No, Joe, tell me you didn't do anything..." she said, trailing off when she saw from the look in his eyes that he had indeed done something. "What did you do?"

"Jordan," Joe said, "you need to get away from that guy. He's dangerous."

"I know that," she said edgily. "But I can't do it right now. It's not that easy, okay?"

93

"It's quite easy, as a matter of a fact," Joe said. "He has an out clause in his contract with you."

"An out clause?" she asked, her head still reeling.

"Yeah, you pay him so much money, and you're out of your contract with him."

"No, Joe, no," she said, shaking her head. "It's not that easy. You don't understand!" she exclaimed, moving to stand. "Call Robert back, and tell him to stop whatever he's doing."

"No," Joe said simply.

"Goddamn it, Joe!" she yelled. "Call Robert. This isn't a game here."

Joe sat up, leaning against the headboard, crossing his arms over his bare chest. "I'm not calling him."

"Fine," she said, striding around the bed and reaching to pick up his phone. "I'll call him myself."

Joe looked back at her passively. She hit the "call list" button so she could get Robert's number. She narrowed her eyes as the words "ID withheld" came up where the number should have been. She glared at Joe. His expression was still passive, but his eyes twinkled with subdued humor.

"Damnit!" she exclaimed. "Give me his number, Joe," she said, her teeth clenched in what was nearing panic.

"No, Jordan."

She let out a yell of frustration and threw the phone at him. He blocked it with one hand, while his other arm whipped out, grabbing her hand and pulling her down to him. She yelled again, not willing to be thwarted so easily. Her hands clenched, but his were faster, and he held both her wrists in one hand, his other arm an iron band

94

around her waist, her back against his chest. He'd had a lot of practice dealing with fireballs like her; he'd dealt with Midnight for over seventeen years. No one was as dangerous as Midnight Chevalier when she was mad. Jordan didn't even come close.

"Jordan, calm down," he said into her ear, his tone both commanding and soothing.

She struggled against his hold, realizing once again how strong he really was. He wasn't hurting her, but there was no way she was going to win this one. Finally her anger and panic gave way to tears of frustration. She leaned her head back against his shoulder, tears streaming down her cheeks. He let go of her wrists and brought his hand up to touch her face gently. His lips were pressed to the side of her head.

"Talk to me, babe," he said beseechingly.

"Please, please…" she said, her voice clogged with tears. "Just stop Robert, please, Joe."

"Tell me why, Jordan," Joe said softly.

Taking her hand, he pulled her around so she faced him. Her head lay against his shoulder again; she wouldn't look at him. His finger under her chin changed that.

"I just can't leave like this, Joe," she said, hoping it would be enough.

"Tell me why," he repeated, his eyes searching hers.

She dropped her head to his shoulder again, shaking it slowly.

"I can't," she said simply.

"Why?"

She raised her head, looking him pleadingly in the eye. "Please don't make me tell you," she begged.

"I need you to, Jordan."

Her eyes searched his, and then closed slowly. She nodded. Moving back, putting at least a foot of distance between them, she reached for a pillow, wrapping her arms around it as if it were a life raft. Joe recognized her need for defense again, and knew that she was about to tell him something important. He reached out, touching her cheek softly, waiting for her eyes to connect with his. When they did, he smiled warmly. She bit her lip as tears appeared in her eyes.

"I told you," she began softly, "that Mark and I had dated in the past. I've known him for twenty years…" she said, trailing off as she gathered her courage. "I've known him since I was fifteen, because…" Again her voice trailed off as she looked at Joe.

Her expression was wistful, as if she were looking at him for the last time. Joe reached out, tugging the pillow out of her arms and taking her wrist, pulling her to him. He held her close, her cheek against his chest.

"Tell me," he whispered.

Jordan swallowed a few times, feeling like her happiness was about to be ended forever. Finally, she pulled back, knowing he deserved to hear the truth.

"I know him because," she said, her eyes locked with his, "his mother married my father when I was fifteen."

The words fell between them, and Jordan waited, terrified, for Joe's expression to change to one of horror and disgust. It did change, but not to anything she'd anticipated. His eyes closed for a moment, then he looked back at her, his face perfectly calm.

"Jordan, I know," he said softly.

"You what?" she asked. Surely she hadn't heard him right.

96

"I know," he repeated. "I know he's your step-brother."

"But how?" she asked, stunned.

Joe took a deep breath. His turn to tell her the truth.

"When all that shit happened in England with the concert, I decided to have Mark checked out."

She looked back at him for a long moment. "You were spying on me?"

"No, Jordan," he said, his tone strong. "I was checking on Mark, trying to find out if he was cheating you—which he is, by the by."

"But..." she said. "You knew about him?"

"Yes," Joe said, nodding. "Part of the report I received was that Mark was your step-brother."

"When did you get this report?"

"While we were in Vegas."

"So you've known all this time?" she asked, still unable to believe it.

"Yes, Jordan, I've known."

"But... why didn't you ask me about it?"

Joe shrugged. "Well, it didn't really matter to me that he was your step-brother, and I didn't want to tell you about his cheating you until I had the evidence to prove it. Robert has that now."

"But..." she began, still shocked that the fact that she'd slept with her brother didn't bother Joe, or maybe he didn't realize the extent of her and Mark's relationship. "You do realize that Mark and I... well, we...," she stammered, unable to actually say the words.

"Slept together," Joe supplied.

She nodded mutely.

"Yeah, I realize that," Joe said, searching her face. Then it

97

clicked. "Jordan," he said, reaching out to put his hand to her cheek. "Is this what he has over you?"

She looked back at him for a long moment, still trying to get over the fact that Joe Sinclair didn't care that she'd slept with her own brother. Finally, she realized what he'd just asked her and nodded slowly.

"Oh my God..." Joe said, a look of total disbelief on his face. "That's it?"

"That's it?" she echoed incredulously. "Yeah, that's it. I slept with my own brother—isn't that enough blackmail material for a lifetime?"

"Jordan, you slept with your step-brother, a man that's not even your own blood," Joe said, his look telling her he thought she was crazy. "And it's not like you two grew up together—he was an adult already, for God's sake. Hell, if anything, he'd look like a bastard for taking advantage of such a young woman."

The relief that flooded Jordan's face was almost painful to see. All at once she was crying and laughing and hugging him. He held her close, feeling a little guilty about not telling her what he'd been told sooner. He'd had no idea that it was the fact that Mark was her step-brother that was bothering her so much. He'd started to suspect only when she was so reluctant to tell him.

"You have no idea how relieved I am," she said, shaking her head in wonder.

"Jordan," Joe said chidingly. "What did you think I was going to do?"

She pulled back to look at him, tears still on her cheeks. Her eyes searched his as she shook her head.

"I didn't know, but I definitely didn't think you'd still want me."

Joe shook his head disbelievingly. "I think you've been let down by too many men."

"Well, maybe. But Joe, I wouldn't expect any man to handle this kind of thing well. I just figured you wouldn't want to deal with this kind of garbage. It makes a casual relationship very complicated, real quick."

Joe lay back against the headboard, pulling her down with him. They lay together for a long time, neither of them talking.

"Is that what we are?" Joe asked finally.

"What?" Jordan asked, her mind still having been rejoicing over the fact that he now knew her deepest, darkest secret and was still there with her.

"A casual relationship."

"I guess…" Jordan said, not sure what he was getting at.

Joe nodded and was silent for a long time again.

Jordan sat up, looking down at him. "Aren't we?"

"Aren't we, what?"

"A casual relationship."

"If you say we are, then I guess we are," Joe said evenly.

"Like I have a choice here?"

"Why wouldn't you?"

Jordan was silent for a long moment, then shrugged, looking away. "I don't know, I just…"

"You just what?" Joe asked, his look piercing.

She glanced back at him. "I just don't want to assume too much where you and I are concerned."

"Why not?"

Jordan took a deep breath, blowing it out in a deep sigh as she shook her head. "Because I want too much."

"What's too much?" Joe asked, his head canting to the side, giving her a sidelong look.

"Everything," Jordan said. "Your time, your love, your heart, your body, your soul…" Her voice trailed off again as she shook her head.

"You want all that?" he asked her, his tone ambiguous.

Jordan didn't answer for a long moment, instead picking at invisible lint on the bed sheets, her head lowered, her chin on her raised knee. Finally she nodded, unwilling to see his reaction to her admission.

"And what did you think I want?" Joe asked. When she didn't answer, he started supplying her with possible replies. "A quick piece of ass? A star fuck? A trophy for my mantel?"

Jordan's head came up on the first comment, her eyes searching his and seeing his anger.

"No," she said hesitantly. "But I didn't figure you were looking for a commitment, Joe. You just got out of a thirteen-year marriage."

"I'm aware of that," he said evenly.

"I just figured you needed something in between…" she said, trailing off as he shook his head at her in disbelief.

"Do you think I tell everyone that I love them?" Joe asked.

"Well, no."

"No," he said. "Do you think I would have brought just anyone to Vegas with me for that wedding? A wedding where every person I consider family was going to be?"

"Well, no…" Jordan said, starting to see that he'd been telling her what she meant to him all along, and she hadn't really gotten it.

"No," Joe repeated.

"Joe, I just... I didn't know. I mean, I just didn't understand..." Jordan said, shaking her head.

"You're so used to being used, Jordan, you have no idea what to do with someone that doesn't want to use you."

She thought about that for a minute, then nodded. "You're right. I'm sorry."

"Don't be sorry," he said, his voice softening finally. "Just understand that I'm not in this because you're famous. I'm not in this because you're beautiful, or rich, or any of that." He reached out, pulling her back to him. "I'm in this because I want to be. I'm where I want to be, and I want to be with you. Okay?"

"Okay," she said, her tone pouty.

Joe shook his head, leaning down and kissing her softly. "I love you. Got it?"

"Got it," she said, the start of a grin on her lips.

"You, not your money, or your fame. Got it?"

"Got it," she said, then gave him a sidelong look. "Not my body either?"

"Well, I love your body too," he said, grinning mischievously.

"But you said—"

"Shut up, Jordan," he said, cutting her off, his lips further silencing her, until she couldn't think of anything but his body with hers.

They made love again, and Jordan felt like the whole world had suddenly been made right. She didn't think she could be happier. Then it occurred to her that she hadn't gotten any details about this out clause in her contract with Mark.

"How much do I have to pay Mark to get him out of the contract with me?" she asked.

"It's taken care of," Joe said simply.

They still lay with their bodies intertwined. Joe's body half covered hers, his arm as well as one leg over her possessively. Jordan pulled back, looking at him.

"What do you mean, taken care of?"

"I mean, I took care of it, Jordan. Don't worry about it."

"How much, Joe?" she asked, sensing that he was avoiding telling her that part.

He sighed, shaking his head, putting his face into the pillow.

"Joe…"

"Seven fifty," he said simply.

"Seven fifty?" she repeated, thinking that wasn't much. Then it hit her. "*Seven hundred and fifty thousand?*" she practically screamed.

Joe glanced at her with one light blue eye. Then nodded.

"Oh my God!" she exclaimed. "No way, no way," she said, shaking her head. "I can't afford that, Joe."

"I said it was taken care of."

"No," she said, shaking her head again. "You can't, Joe. That's too much. No."

Joe propped himself up on one elbow, looking down at her. "Jordan, I want you out from under that bastard, before I lose it and beat the shit out of him."

"But that's almost a million dollars. I can't let you do that!" she said, her tone bordering of frantic.

"It's already done, Jordan."

She looked back at him for a long moment, then shook her head slowly. "Then I'll pay you back. I'll sell the apartment in London," she began, trying to think what else she could do.

"No, you won't," he said. "I made the decision to pay Mark off, and I'm paying for it. Do you understand me?"

"I can't let you," she said seriously.

"You will," he said, his tone just as strong.

"Damnit, Joe," she muttered.

He simply looked back at her passively. It was obvious to her that he was very used to getting his way on things. She could see how that would be extremely attractive to a lot of women. But she was used to doing things for herself, and she didn't like that he was suddenly paying her way in and out of things.

"I'll pay you back," she said.

"Nope."

"Don't be a stubborn bastard, Joe."

"Why change now?" he asked, the hint of a grin on his lips.

"Don't laugh at me!"

"Shut up, Jordan," he said, not for the first time that evening. He kissed her.

She bit his lip, making him grin.

"I mean it," she said vehemently. "I'm going to pay you back."

"Fine," he said, sliding his hand up her skin, making her begin to tremble yet again.

"Joe…" she said. "I'm serious."

"So am I," he replied, kissing her neck softly.

She growled deep in her throat, but gave up her fight. Joe Sinclair probably did always get his way. She wasn't going to let him this time, but she couldn't fight his effect on her body anymore either.

103

\*\*\*

The dawn was just breaking when Erin woke up. She rubbed at her eyes, turning over in the bed. The memories hit her then, and she remembered the conversation with Kevin. Her body remembered well their making love too. It was then that she realized he wasn't in bed with her anymore. She turned over toward the window and saw him. He sat on the window seat, wearing only his black jeans from the night before. A plume of smoke curled up over his head as he blew it out. He held a thin brown cigar in his right hand, smoking it as he looked out the open window. Erin watched him. He had a handsome profile, and in the morning light, his body was even more appealing. She wasn't sure if she should say anything, so she didn't.

He glanced over at her, having heard her turn over. His eyes connected with hers and he smiled.

"Good morning," he said.

"Hi," she said, smiling back at him.

He took a couple of long drags on his cigar, then stubbed it out in the ashtray that sat in front of him on the window sill. Standing, he walked over to the bed, looking down at her. She sat up, and he sat down next to her.

"What time is it?" she asked, even as she glanced at the clock.

"Just before seven."

"Have you been awake long?"

"An hour or so."

"That long?" she replied, surprised.

"Yeah," he said, shrugging. "I'm not much of a sleeper."

"Oh…" she said, not understanding what he meant, but not wanting to question him too thoroughly. "Is anyone else awake yet?"

He shrugged again. "I've heard some movement downstairs, but not a lot."

Erin nodded. "Are you going to try to get some more sleep?"

"Nah," he said, shaking his head. "No point in trying once I'm awake."

"Oh," she replied, still feeling totally at a loss as to what to say to him.

Kevin watched her for a long moment, sensing her hesitation. Leaning forward, he kissed her lips softly, then, putting his hand to the back of her head, deepened the kiss. Within moments, Erin was holding on to him as he pulled her closer. Her hands moved over his bare shoulders, his back. She groaned as his tongue slid over her lips, making her shudder at the feeling.

Sitting back, he pulled her onto his lap, his hands sliding over her skin, touching her, caressing her, making her gasp and writhe. His lips continued their plundering of her willing lips. She gripped his shoulders as his fingers moved down between her legs, making her moan out loud, his lips covering hers again, lest she be heard outside the room. Within moments he was bringing her to a release, and she couldn't think straight. She strained against him as wave after wave of ecstasy washed over her.

"Oh God… God…" she whispered frantically.

When she'd quieted, he kissed her again. She looked up at him in wonder, and found that his eyes were even brighter green in the morning sunlight.

"You have the most beautiful eyes," she said in a hushed whisper.

Kevin grinned at her, then inclined his head. "Thanks."

Erin leaned her head against his shoulder, thinking she had to say something, but she couldn't even begin to imagine just what. She pressed her lips to his shoulder. She felt his hands tighten at her waist and hip. Moving her head in toward his neck, she kissed him again. Again his hands tightened slightly on her skin. She kissed her way up to his ear. She could feel his breathing had quickened, and his hands were caressing her back now. One hand slid up her back to hold her head, telling her without words that he wanted her where she was. Kissing his neck again, she moved her mouth to his ear, biting it gently, careful to avoid the earring. He groaned. He moved his head, his lips taking possession of hers, kissing her deeply, hungrily.

He lay back on the bed, pulling her down with him. Moving her onto her back and leaning down over her, he kissed her again. His lips moved over hers with tantalizing strength. His hands caressed her, as she touched his chest, moving up into his hair. He shifted away from her long enough to shed his jeans, then joined her once again on the bed. Her hands moved down his back, then to his waist. He groaned against her lips as she touched him.

"God, Erin…" he whispered, kissing her with hunger again.

His touch was almost frantic in his need. Within minutes her body was alive with sensation. He moved over her, sliding his body inside hers, causing her to gasp wildly as the sensations washed over her again. Her body reached its release as she grasped his shoulders. His body joined hers once again in orgasm. Afterward, he pressed his lips to the curve of her neck, shaking his head.

"That control thing again?" she asked softly, a grin on her lips.

"What control?" he queried, with a grin of his own. "I don't seem to have any anymore."

106

"I still say it's perfect timing."

"Mmhmm," he murmured against her neck.

They lay together for a while.

"God, I need a smoke," he said in almost a groan.

Erin bit her lip, smiling, liking that she made him feel that on edge.

He sat up, reaching for his shirt and the pack of cigars in the pocket. Then he picked up his jeans and put them on, pulling his lighter out of the pocket. Flipping it open and putting the cigar in his mouth, he lit it, closing the lighter with a loud click. Erin looked at the lighter as he tossed it onto the bed. She picked it up. It was silver, with a black Iron Cross emblem. She glanced at Kevin to see that he was watching her through the curling smoke.

She grinned, then tilted her head as she looked at the cigar. It was the size of a cigarette, but it definitely didn't look like one, nor did it smell like one. It smelled good, with a hint of sweetness to it.

"That's not a regular cigarette, is it?" she asked.

He shook his head as he took another long drag. "It's a cigar."

Erin nodded. "You don't inhale cigars, though, do you?"

Kevin grinned unrepentantly. "Well, most people don't, but I do."

"Why?"

He went to pick up the ashtray, which was still on the window sill, then sat back down on the bed, leaning against the headboard. Erin moved to sit next to him, facing him.

"Well," he said, looking down at the cigar, "I used to smoke cigarettes." He shrugged. "But when I quit drinking and tried to smoke again, I found that I associated the taste of cigarettes with the taste of alcohol. See, that's my big hang-up—I like the taste of alcohol. So as long as I don't taste it, I don't crave it too much. Well, the association between the taste of cigarettes and the taste of alcohol was just too strong, so I ended up switching to cigars. The taste is totally different, but it satisfies my need for nicotine."

Erin nodded, thinking this man never did get any more simple, did he?

"I guess that makes sense," she said, then looked at him for a long moment. "So it doesn't bother you to be around people who are drinking?"

He shook his head. "Nope, so long as I don't taste any alcohol. I'm pretty good about being able to avoid it." He grinned. "Just makes me a bit of a drag at parties, ya know?"

"You weren't a drag, Kevin."

"I'll bet Collins and Curtis wouldn't agree with you on that."

"Oh, please," Erin said, rolling her eyes. "Donovan isn't that big of a drinker either, and no one can keep up with Christian. Even he knows that."

Kevin grinned.

They spent the next two hours talking about whatever came to mind. Erin told him more about the department and how things worked and what she did. He told her more about his old department, and some of the people he knew in San Diego PD who'd transferred from Seattle before him. Before they knew it, it was 9:30.

"I guess we'd better get out there before everyone starts to wonder," Erin said.

"Probably should."

They both got dressed, grinning like bad kids.

108

"Think you'll shock them?" Kevin said as he sat watching her run a brush through her hair.

"Shock them?" she asked over her shoulder.

"Coming out of here with me."

"Oh," she said, not having thought about that. Then she shrugged. "I'm an adult. I can do whatever I want."

"Uh-huh," he said, not sounding convinced.

"God, don't make me nervous about this!" she exclaimed, grinning at him. "I can sleep with someone the same night I meet him if I want to."

"Right," he agreed, his eyes twinkling with humor.

"Shut up!" she said, laughing.

As it turned out, no one was around who would really be paying attention to who Erin was with. Most of the people up and moving about that morning were kids and Jeanie's family. There were children running around everywhere, asking for things, crying because they didn't get what they wanted. Video games were going in two rooms; both TVs seemed to be on max volume. Jeanie's mom was trying to fix breakfast, talking in quick-paced Spanish at top volume to be heard over the din.

When they walked into the kitchen, Erin didn't notice right away when Kevin stepped back. She turned to see that he was still standing in the doorway. He had a look on his face that was tense. She could see a muscle in his jaw jumping as he clenched his teeth. He ran a hand through his hair, then looked at her.

"I'll meet you outside, okay?" he said, then turned and walked quickly away.

Erin stared after him for a long moment, not sure what to make of his behavior. She was greeted by Jeanie's family then, so it took her a few minutes to make her way outside. She found Kevin leaning up against a dark green SUV out on the street. He was smoking, and as she watched him lift the cigar to his mouth, she could see that his hand was shaking.

"Kevin?" she queried softly.

His head snapped up, and she could tell he was still tense. She strode up to him.

"Are you okay?" she asked, not understanding what was going on.

He nodded, looking anything but okay. He took another long drag off the cigar.

"Can you leave now?" he said tersely.

"Leave?" she asked, thinking he wanted her to leave him alone.

"Yeah. I mean, do you need to go back to the house for anything, or can we just leave?" he asked stridently, but it was obvious he was trying to make it less so.

"Yes," she said, nodding. "We can leave. I took a cab over—Jeanie and Donovan were going to give me a ride home."

He nodded. "I can take you home, but right now I need coffee."

He turned and opened the passenger door of the vehicle he'd been standing against. It was a Dodge Durango R/T. Once inside she looked around. The seats were tan leather. It was a very nice vehicle, and it did seem to fit him quite well. When he got in on the driver's side, she could see that he was still tense. He started the vehicle, and music blared out of the radio. He changed CDs, and a song started that was very hard and driving. He pulled away from the curb, and reached into his pocket for another cigar as he pushed the lighter element in on the dashboard. Within moments the Durango was flying down the road, music blaring. Kevin was blowing the smoke out in long streams. Erin sat silently, watching him. He sang the words to the song, which were very angry. She wasn't used to such hard, driving music, even with men like Christian. She found she was fascinated with the way Kevin drove at breakneck speeds, but so casually at the same time.

By the time he pulled into a gas station that apparently served the kind of coffee he liked, he'd smoked five cigars.

"You want anything?" he asked, sounding a little closer to normal.

"No, thanks," she said with a smile.

He nodded and got out of the car. He reappeared a few minutes later, carrying a large coffee and another pack of cigars. As he pulled back onto the road, he lit up another cigar.

"Kevin?" Erin said.

He glanced over at her, seeing the worried look on her face, as if for the first time.

"God... Erin," he said, shaking his head. "I'm sorry."

"What's wrong?" she asked. "Did I so something?"

"No," he assured her. "No. It's not that. I'm sorry, I'm so used to everyone knowing. I just... I'm sorry."

"Everyone knowing what, Kevin?" she asked, trying to make sense of what he was saying.

He took a long drag on his cigar, tossed it out the window, then looked over at her.

"I didn't plan on spending the night there," he said.

111

"I'm sorry, I didn't mean to—" she began, thinking that was why he was mad.

"No, Erin, it's not your fault," he said. "It's just that… Well, if I want to be human first thing in the morning I need Adderall, coffee, and about ten cigars."

"Adderall?" Erin said. "Why does that sound familiar?"

"Well," he said, glancing over at her, "if you know anyone with ADD, then you'd know Adderall."

"ADD?" she said, surprised.

"Attention Deficit Disorder."

"I've heard of it," Erin said. "But I don't know much about it."

"It means that I can't concentrate on one thing at a time. My mind tries to pay attention to everything at the same time."

"That must be difficult."

"It is," he assured her.

"Like the kitchen this morning?" she asked, beginning to understand.

He nodded. "Too much coming at me all at once."

"I see. That's why you had to get out of there."

"Yep," he said, lighting another cigar.

"So what does the Adderall do?" she asked, curious now.

"It slows my brain down a bit, so I can handle things easier."

Erin nodded, looking over at him. No wonder he was so complex. "So last night, you were okay at the party…"

"Because I was still on Adderall."

"And this morning you were okay in the room with me."

"Yeah, because that was just you and me—there wasn't a lot of

112

other stuff coming at me."

Erin nodded again. "So once you take the Adderall, you're more able to handle that kind of stuff?"

"Right. In the meantime, I smoke, drink coffee, and listen to obnoxious loud music," he said, grinning. He knew she was probably totally freaked out by his choice of what he called "death metal."

Erin laughed softly, wondering if she'd given herself away on the music. It had indeed been loud and forceful, and she'd been surprised by it.

"Now," he said, relaxing in his seat. "Do you want me to take you home? Or do you want to go to my place with me so I can shower, get Adderall, and then we can go have some breakfast or something."

"I think I like option number two," she said with a smile.

"Good," he said with a wink. "I like option number two too."

They pulled up to his house a few minutes later. Erin was suitably impressed. It was a nice three-bedroom place in a decent neighborhood in Chula Vista. The inside was nice as well. The house itself was probably about fifteen years old, but it had been kept up well.

"Are you renting?" she asked, assuming he had to be.

"Nope, it's mine," he said as he laid his jacket on the island in the kitchen. Noting her look of surprise, he grinned. "I owned a condo in Seattle. I sold it and was able to sink a decent amount down on this one so my payments wouldn't bury me."

"Oh," Erin said, grinning self-consciously. "I didn't mean to be nosey."

"No prob," he said, laughing. "It's not like it's a national secret. You rent?"

"Yes!" she said. "I couldn't afford to buy if my life depended on

113

it. I rent with three other people in Pacific Beach."

He nodded, thinking that must be difficult with a small child. He showed her around the house then. And she was further impressed. It really was very nice, not too big but with plenty of space for him. A lot of his things were still in boxes, but his furniture seemed nice enough, very casual, like him.

"And this is my room," he said, leading her into the master bedroom.

He sat down on the bed as she looked around. This room had been totally unpacked. He had posters on the walls of rock bands— Metallica, Disturbed, and Matchbox Twenty. He also had a framed poster of a seascape, with waves crashing on huge rocks in the ocean. The sky above the rocks was dark and black, split by lightning. It was a very dramatic scene, and seemed to fit the turbulent man sitting on his bed, unlacing his boots.

"I like that one," she said, pointing to the seascape.

He glanced over his shoulder. "Yeah, me too," he said as he tossed his boots aside.

Standing, he pulled his shirt tails out of his jeans, unbuttoning his shirt, watching her look at the pictures on his dresser. She turned around and smiled self-consciously. He grinned.

"You gonna hang out while I take a shower? Or did you want to join me?" he asked, his green eyes twinkling mischievously.

Erin bit her lip, averting her eyes. Kevin laughed softly.

"Go make yourself comfortable," he said. "I'll be out in a little bit."

Erin went back out into the living room. She looked around at all the boxes, and noticed then that he did have a coffee table in

114

among them. Walking over to it, she saw a silver case and a rolled-up length of white paper. She sat down on the brown leather couch by the coffee table and looked at the silver case.

She was able to ignore her curiosity for a while. Gazing around at his living room, she saw a large TV sitting on an oak stand. He had an oak bookcase containing some videotapes and a large box next to it. Erin stood up and went over to look at the movies.

He definitely liked action movies. He had all the *Lethal Weapon* series, as well as the *Die Hard* series, *Young Guns*, *Tombstone*, and *American Outlaws*. He also seemed to like science fiction, since he had all the Star Wars and Star Trek movies, as well as *2001: A Space Odyssey* and its sequel. Glancing into the open box next to the shelf, she smiled, noting that it was full.

She went back over to the couch, sitting down and looking at the silver case again. Finally she gave up trying to ignore it, and reached out to open it. It was about two feet long and a foot wide, and about six inches in thickness. When she opened it, she was surprised to say the least. The case contained colored markers, colored pencils, grease pencils, paints, charcoal pencils—everything for artwork. And it looked well used. She glanced at the rolled-up piece of paper then, knowing she had to know what it was but not wanting to be that nosey.

When Kevin emerged ten minutes later she had closed up the case, but had her hand on it as she looked up at him. He was dressed in faded blue jeans, white tennis shoes, and a long-sleeved Quiksilver shirt in blue and white.

His eyes went to the case, and he grinned. "Guess you've discovered my secret, huh?"

"Well, part of it," she said, biting her lip, glad that he didn't seem

115

to mind.

Kevin nodded, sitting down on the couch next to her.

"Well, let me show you all of it," he said, picking up the rolled paper and removing the rubber band around it.

He rolled the paper out, and Erin was stunned. It was a rather large poster-sized piece of paper, and on it was the most intricate design she'd ever seen. It had a Celtic style to it, but was so complex it was impossible to determine exactly what it was. The drawing was in black, and it was obvious he'd started coloring it with colors that blended yet stood out at the same time.

Her eyes moved over the entire poster. Kevin was watching her. He knew exactly when her eyes fell on the initials at the bottom of the drawing.

"KJE?" she said, then looked at him.

He nodded.

"You drew this?" she asked, sounding stunned.

"Yeah."

"Oh my God, Kevin…" she breathed, looking the poster over again.

He grinned. "My doctor considers this therapy."

"Therapy?" she asked, tearing her eyes away to look at him.

"Yeah, it gives me something to practice training my mind on."

She nodded. "So you get used to concentrating on one thing."

"Yeah, and the sense of accomplishment when I've finished drawing it."

"So now you're coloring it, and that's a whole other project, right?"

"Right," he said, grinning.

She reached out, touching the initials. "So what does *J* stand for?"

"My middle name."

Erin gave him a look that said, *Duh.* "And what is your middle name, Mr. Elmasian?"

Kevin stared at her for a long moment, sensing that telling her his middle name was going to give her ammunition to use against him later. Finally, laughing at the look she was giving him, which reminded him a lot of his mother when she didn't get answers to her questions, he gave in.

"James. My middle name is James."

"Kevin James Elmasian," Erin said, testing out the sound of it. Then she nodded. "It sounds like you."

"Good thing," he said, smiling. "Since that's what they named me."

Erin laughed softly.

"You ready to go?" he asked, standing up.

"Sure."

He took her to a nearby restaurant for breakfast. She found that he didn't actually eat breakfast; he only ordered coffee.

"Is that your idea of breakfast?" she asked.

"That and a cigar," he said, grinning. "But since I can't smoke in here…" His voice trailed off as he looked around.

Erin shook her head. It went against her grain not to mother him and tell him how important it was that he eat. But she bit her tongue. She'd just met this man; she certainly didn't have any place hassling him about his eating habits. Kevin noticed how she clamped her mouth shut, and was amused by it. He could tell she wanted to

117

give him hell over not eating breakfast, but she'd decided against doing so. He found it amusing and endearing at the same time.

It had been a long time since a woman cared enough about him to hassle him about eating. Stacy had been so self-absorbed that she'd never cared what he did, as long as he could pay for what she wanted. Other women had never seemed to worry much about him—either that or because of the total tough-guy image he had going on, they were afraid to bitch at him. He didn't know which it was, but Erin hadn't really seen the tough-guy thing too much either. For some reason, he didn't want to play the cold, distant role with her. She was too sweet for her own good; he could sense that easily. He knew he'd warn her off him if he was a friend of hers. His demons were large in number, and he was far from suitable company for a woman like her.

Donovan Curtis definitely seemed like her type. Kevin had already heard Christian Collins' favorite term for Donovan—"Boy Scout." It did fit. Donovan didn't look like he'd ever been a bad boy, but whatever he did have, it seemed to work for him. He was successful in the narcotics field, maybe because he didn't come across as a narc, but as some good boy trying to be bad.

Now, Collins was definitely a kindred spirit in the bad-boy arena. Kevin had liked him from day one. There was no bullshit there. Collins was for all intents and purposes a down and dirty fighter. The amazing good looks didn't seem to hinder him at all, just making people want to be around him.

Kevin was still trying to figure out where he fit into the picture. It was obvious that Midnight Chevalier picked the best and the most trusted to be part of the narcotics team, so he knew that he fit in somewhere. He just needed to work out where.

"Kevin?" Erin asked, noting that he was far away suddenly.

118

"Hmm?" he murmured, then realized his mind had been wandering. "Sorry, just thinking."

"Can I ask about what?" Erin asked, picking up her toast and taking a small bite.

Kevin grinned. She definitely wasn't intimidated by him. "Just about the team. I'm not sure where I fit into all of it," he said honestly, surprising himself.

Erin nodded slowly. "Well, I don't know a lot about the narcotics team, other than the people I know on it, but I think you fit in pretty well."

"How so?" Kevin asked, curious about her take on it. She did, after all, know all these people much better than he did.

"Well," Erin said, "there's Donovan, who is able to get to people because he's so innocent-seeming. No one ever takes him for a cop—he's like the all-American good guy."

Kevin grinned, nodding.

"And then there's Jeanie, and she's got this sex appeal that guys react to, but she's able to play it because she really is a sweet person. Then there's Stevie, who basically exudes sexiness, so guys never even think they're being played—they think they're scoring big time. And then there's Christian, who is so drop-dead gorgeous, he just seems like some out-of-work movie star. People are so drawn into him, they wouldn't even care if they knew he was a cop."

"Okay, so I fit where?" he asked, feeling strange that he was asking her all this.

Erin looked at him for a long moment, then said, "Well, you're enough of a bad boy to fit the narc image, and you've got a quality of still water running deep. You remind me a lot of Dave Dibbins."

"I do?" he asked, surprised.

"Yeah," Erin said, nodding. "Dave seems like the coolest character you could ever meet. He's so passive, but with a look that tells you there's a lot going on in his head. You just never know what. And that's what scares people. They think he might be violent, or dangerous, and they just don't know."

"Metal under tension," Kevin mused.

"What?"

Kevin looked at her then, grinning. "That's what someone said I was once. Metal under tension, and at any moment I could snap and take anyone out."

Erin canted her head to the side, as if trying to decide if that fit him.

"I can see that," she said, nodding. "But you're also a really nice guy."

"Am I?" Kevin asked, his look skeptical.

"Yes."

"Maybe you're just seeing what I want you to see."

Erin was silent for a long moment, her blue eyes looking into his.

"And maybe I'm seeing what you don't want anyone to see," she said softly.

Kevin was taken aback. She was right. He rarely showed anyone the side she was seeing. She seemed to bring that out in him. Usually he was cool and calculated. Even his close friends weren't ever sure what he was thinking. But here this girl was, telling him that she knew what she was seeing.

They talked about other things then. Erin sensed easily that

Kevin didn't want to continue along the lines they'd been talking, so she changed the subject. They finished breakfast and he took her home. When he pulled up to the house she directed him to, she turned to him.

"Thank you," she said quietly.

"For what?" he asked, looking mystified.

"For everything," she said, smiling shyly. "For being so sweet and for listening to all my woes and not telling me to get over it."

Kevin laughed at the face she'd made when she said that. Then he nodded. "You're welcome."

"I hope I get to see you again," she said, biting her lip and praying she didn't sound too eager.

"I'm sure you will," he answered, his green eyes on hers.

He leaned across the seat, kissing her softly.

She reached up, putting her hand to his neck, her thumb brushing gently over the earrings in his ear. Turning, she got out of the car and went inside, not wanting to look back. Kevin watched her go, reaching into his pocket and taking out a cigar. Lighting it, he put the Durango into gear and drove off.

# CHAPTER 4

Kevin sat in the passenger seat of Donovan's Mustang. He could feel the other man's eyes on him, but refused to look guilty by asking what Donovan's issue was. Instead he continued to watch the street, waiting for the dealer they'd been tailing to come out of the store. It had been two days since the party, and they'd been working non-stop on this case since then. Kevin hadn't talked to Erin since New Year's Day. He'd wanted to call her a couple of times, but hadn't had the time to actually talk, so he hadn't bothered. No sense in calling her then saying he didn't have time to talk.

Donovan watched Kevin. He was very tempted to ask the other man what he'd thought of Erin, but he didn't want to push. Erin would kill him if she thought he was trying to talk Kevin into liking her. All Donovan knew was that both Erin and Kevin had disappeared on New Year's Eve. He assumed that Kevin had gotten bored and left, since he hadn't been drinking at all. Jeanie had told him that she thought Erin had gone upstairs to bed.

Jeanie had checked the room Erin had been staying in that night, and found that the bed had indeed been slept in, but Erin was gone long before Jeanie and Donovan had dragged out of bed at noon. Jeanie had called Erin, but she had been busy at the time, and had said she'd talk to Jeanie later. As usual, with Erin, she avoided the whole thing, and therefore Jeanie never got a chance to talk to her about her disappearance on New Year's Eve.

"So," Donovan said, itching to break the long silence that seemed to stretch between them. "What did you think of Erin?" he asked, almost wincing at how stupid that sounded.

Kevin looked over at him, his moss green eyes reflecting no emotion whatsoever, even as he raised an eyebrow at the other man. He pursed his lips, looking like he was considering the question.

"She's cute," he answered simply.

Donovan nodded. "Yeah, she is."

"Why do you ask?" Kevin asked, his look direct.

Donovan was taken aback for a minute. He thought it was obvious why he'd ask; it wasn't something he thought he'd have to explain.

"Well, I, uh…" Donovan stammered. "She's a really nice girl. I'd just like to see her happy…"

Kevin didn't help him out at all, simply watching him as he stumbled over an attempt to explain.

"Why are you so worried about her well-being?" Kevin asked, his tone perfectly guileless.

"She's my friend," Donovan replied, just a touch too defensively.

Kevin nodded, not looking convinced, his green eyes glittering in subdued humor.

Donovan looked back at the other man for a long moment, feeling really guilty all of a sudden. Damn! How did Kevin Elmasian manage to make him feel like shit without saying a word? Donovan sighed, turning his head back to the window. They were both silent for a full five minutes.

"She's in good hands," Kevin said simply.

Donovan snapped his head around. He didn't see any sort of emotion in the other man's eyes.

"What does that mean?" Donovan asked, a hint of threat in his voice.

Kevin's lips quirked in a sardonic grin. It was definitely easy to get Curtis going.

"You her keeper?" Kevin asked caustically.

"No," Donovan said, his teal blue eyes narrowing. "I told you, she's my friend. I don't want to see her hurt."

Kevin's look changed to one of mock surprise. "A few minutes ago, you wanted to see her happy, assumably with me. What changed your tune?"

Donovan gritted his teeth. He had just said that, and Kevin had called him on it. Jesus Christ, this guy was good. *Yeah*, Donovan thought, *good at making me look like a fucking idiot.*

"You're right, I did say that," he acquiesced. "I guess I'm just worried about her."

"Why?" Kevin asked tonelessly.

Again Donovan sighed. He was being nailed ten ways to Sunday during this conversation. Why hadn't he just kept his mouth shut? He put his hand on the steering wheel of the Mustang, looking at the pony in the center, picking at it edgily.

"Because I hurt her," he said finally, glancing over at Kevin. "Because I let her fall in love with me, when I knew I couldn't love her back the way she deserved."

Kevin nodded, not commenting.

"Look," Donovan said, "I'm sorry. I just need to know she's going to be okay."

124

Again Kevin nodded, looking considering. "I don't promise wine and roses," he said evenly. "But I don't plan on hurting her, either."

Donovan nodded, realizing that was the best he could hope for at this point. In truth, he still really didn't think Kevin Elmasian was Erin's type at all, but it wouldn't hurt her to start dating again. Her last couple of attempts had failed miserably, and she hadn't dated in six months. She was spending all her time with Steven, or with him and Jeanie.

\*\*\*

Across town, Erin was sitting in Christian's Viper as he drove to lunch. He'd dropped into her office—formerly his—to ask her if she was free. She'd happily agreed—anything to take her mind off the fact that Kevin hadn't called her. She kept telling herself to stop being a whiney schoolgirl, but it wasn't helping her mood much. She'd started to rethink everything she'd thought about him. Wondering if she'd just been an easy score for him was center stage at that point. She also kept wondering if she'd imagined her feelings of a connection. Just because they'd slept together didn't mean that it was a permanent match. He was a guy, after all, and guys were known for the ability to have sex and it not mean a damned thing to them. No matter what he'd said to her that night, his actions said more. He hadn't called. It had been two full days since then. He hadn't called.

"Hey," Christian said, glancing over at her.

"Hmm?" she murmured, pulling herself out of her thoughts.

"With me here?" he asked, a jet black eyebrow raised over Ray-Ban Predator II sunglasses.

125

"Yeah... sorry," she said, looking appropriately apologetic.

"So what's up, little one?" he asked gently.

Erin was one of those women that even the toughest of men wanted to be gentle around. Even Christian Collins, notorious hot-headed player, couldn't stand to hurt her feelings. The few times he'd flown off the handle at her, he'd felt like shit for months afterward. She'd never say anything, but she'd have that look in her eyes, like a puppy he'd kicked in his anger. And she still adored him, even if he'd been vicious in his fury. It made a man want to do anything to make her happy again.

Erin looked over at Christian, but she couldn't think of an answer. Finally she just shook her head, gazing back out the window and praying she wouldn't start crying. The very thought made tears sting the backs of her eyes.

"What happened?" Christian asked.

"Nothing," she said, unconvincingly. "I'm just being emotional today."

Christian nodded, reaching for a cigarette and lighting up. He opened his window and blew a stream of smoke out. Glancing over at her again, he saw that she was still looking out the window. Her way of avoiding his eyes.

"Who is he?" Christian asked evenly. "I'll kill him."

Erin laughed softly at the dramatic statement.

Christian grinned. He'd known that would lighten her mood.

She looked at him then, a question in her eyes.

"Ask," he said simply.

Erin took a deep breath and blew it out slowly. "What does it mean when you don't call a girl?"

"I never call."

"Okay, I meant for normal guys that can't get every woman they lay eyes on," she said, making a face at him.

Christian laughed, shaking his head. "How well do you know the guy?"

"I don't," she said, then grimaced. "Well, I mean… I kinda know him, but not really well."

Christian's eyes narrowed behind his sunglasses. He had the distinct feeling he knew who she was talking about.

"Mace?"

Erin's eyes widened. How did he guess so easily? She nodded, looking down at her hands.

"Did he say he'd call?" Christian asked.

"Well, no," Erin said. "I asked if I'd see him around. He said I would."

Christian nodded, not looking pleased.

"The thing is…" Erin said, trailing off as she began to look supremely embarrassed.

"The thing is what?" he asked, sounding extremely English.

Erin bit her lower lip, looking at him and wincing visibly. "I kinda slept with him."

"You what?" he roared, stunned.

Erin flinched at his outburst.

Christian was shaking his head. "Erin, Erin…" he said, over and over. "Have I taught you nothing? If not by anything but example?" His look was calculated, as if he were trying to discern what she'd learned from him. "Kevin Elmasian is a player. He's probably as good a player as me. What did he do to get you to sleep with him?" he

127

asked, thinking he might actually kill the other man.

"Blue, he didn't do anything," Erin was quick to assure him. "He was really nice. He kind of found me hiding out and feeling sorry for myself on New Year's Eve. He sat down and talked to me, and got me to tell him why I was so upset."

"Donovan and Jeanie?" Christian asked, knowing he was right.

Erin nodded, looking disgusted with herself. "Anyway, we talked for a long time, and before we knew it they were announcing midnight. So I kind of asked him to kiss me—you know, for the New Year…" she said, trailing off as she made a face at her assertiveness.

"And he did?"

"Yes, he did," Erin said, rolling her eyes in amazement. "And man, that guy can kiss!"

Christian grinned. "Like I said—player."

"Uh-huh," Erin said, winking at him. "But he didn't push for anything else. We'd talked about his tattoos, so I kind of asked him to show me them…" Her cheeks colored in embarrassment.

Christian shook his head, amazed at her blatant behavior. "Damn, that was one helluva kiss, huh?" he said, raising an eyebrow.

Erin bit her lip and smiled.

"So what tats does he have?" Christian asked, curious in spite of himself.

"He has a wolf, a dragon, and a locked heart," Erin named off.

"A locked heart?"

"Yeah, long story," she said airily.

"But he told you?"

"Yes."

Christian nodded, approving that Kevin had apparently shared some of his own secrets with Erin.

"And where are these tats located?" Christian couldn't help but ask.

"His arms, and one on his chest," Erin said quickly, still embarrassed.

Christian nodded again. "And you just couldn't resist the chest, huh?"

Erin laughed, sounding embarrassed, but shook her head. She shrugged. "I guess I just figured, what the hell, I've slept with guys I don't love before. And if the thing with Donovan taught me nothing else, it taught me that it doesn't always have to mean true love."

"Yeah, but you were in love."

"Well, yeah," Erin said, grimacing. "But I mean, I can just enjoy being with someone too. It doesn't have to mean marriage and a white picket fence, right?"

Christian nodded, surprised by her change in thinking. Erin was the original romantic. She thought love was the be all and end all of life. She'd been so happy when he and Stevie had finally reconciled and were getting married. She'd even been happy for Donovan and Jeanie getting back together, even if it meant she didn't have Donovan anymore. She loved "love." But here she was being realistic about sex not meaning love, and not having to mean love either.

"But you're not in love with Mace, right?" Christian asked, already having a bad feeling that despite her brave words, she really was emotionally involved with the guy.

"No!" Erin denied vehemently—almost too vehemently.

Christian looked over at her for a long moment, his stare assessing. He shrugged.

129

"Look," he said. "If you like the guy, and he does it for you, then call him."

"No way," Erin said, shaking her head.

"Erin," Christian said, reaching over and touching her leg. "Don't sit back and wait for him to call you. If he doesn't call, then call him."

"Yeah, but what if he just wanted another notch for his bedpost—how stupid will that make me look?" Erin asked, her true fear coming to bear.

"Then I'll personally kick his ass."

"Blue…" Erin said chidingly.

"I'm serious, Erin. No one plays the people I care about. Donovan's lucky I let him live with doing what he did with you."

Erin was warmed by his statement, even if she was sure she'd die of embarrassment if he went after Kevin for sleeping with her and not wanting her after that.

"Blue, I gave it to him willingly. It's not like he took it without permission."

"Yeah, well, he'd better learn real quick who not to fuck with in this department. I won't be the only one to nail him if he makes that mistake twice," Christian said, his tone quite serious.

Erin knew he was right. If Kevin made the mistake of trying to play too many women within the department and Midnight got wind of it, she'd probably personally kick his ass. Midnight didn't take the poor treatment of women lightly.

"Please don't do anything, Blue, okay?" Erin pleaded. "I don't know that he was just using me, I'm just second-guessing myself because he hasn't called. I'm being silly. I'm sorry I got you so riled up."

Christian looked at her for a long moment, then nodded slowly.

"Besides," Erin said, grinning mischievously, "I understand that ex-players make the best significant others."

"Shut the hell up," Christian said, grinning in spite of his words.

"How are you and Stevie anyway? Are you feeling all married and stuff?"

Christian shrugged. "Don't feel any different," he said, holding up his left hand. "'Cept for the new jewelry."

Erin grinned. "Isn't that good though? I mean, at least you're not feeling all trapped, right?"

"True," he agreed. "Stevie's not exactly the classic wife type, ya know?"

"And you're classic husband material?" Erin deadpanned.

"Point taken," he said, laughing.

They spent the rest of the lunch hour talking about anything and everything. He did ask her if she'd had a good time with Kevin, and she was abashed to tell him that yes, indeed she had. Christian had nodded, and chalked up another few player points for Kevin Elmasian.


Later in the day he ran into Kevin in the parking lot. Kevin and Donovan were headed in to file their paperwork on their surveillance; Christian was headed out to meet Stevie on their case.

"Mace," Christian said, his tone indicating he expected Kevin to wait.

Kevin stopped and turned to lean against the back bumper of Donovan's Mustang. Donovan continued into the building. Christian reached up and took off his sunglasses; Kevin had already done so, putting them in his pocket as he reached for a thin cigar. Lighting it, he waited for Christian to speak. Christian noted that Kevin Elmasian didn't have a problem with long silences. It was a good power play, Christian knew, because he'd used it often enough.

Kevin lit his cigar, taking a few long drags and blowing out the smoke. His legs were crossed casually at the ankles; everything about him said he was totally relaxed. There was nothing defensive about his appearance.

"How'd the surveillance go?" Christian asked.

"It went," Kevin replied, his look still casual.

Christian nodded. "Everything settling down for you here?"

"Well enough."

Christian's light blue eyes met Kevin's green ones. "You need to call her, man," he said without any further preamble.

Kevin's lips twitched slightly, the only indication that he understood what Christian meant. His look, however, was quite direct. Neither of them spoke for a long minute.

"What makes you think I didn't plan to?" Kevin asked evenly.

"Doesn't matter what I think, Mace," Christian said, his tone just as even. "It matters what she thinks."

Kevin dropped his eyes from Christian's then, knowing he had no response for that. Finally he nodded, taking another long drag off his cigar then tossing it to the ground and stubbing it out with his boot.

Christian nodded too, then continued toward his car. Kevin remained leaning against Donovan's car for a few minutes, looking up at the sky. Then he pushed off the bumper and strode into the building.

Donovan didn't intimidate him, but Christian Collins did. In Christian, Kevin could see a dark, dangerous man. He'd heard that Collins did his own thing and to hell with the consequences. Kevin wasn't afraid of Collins, but he did have respect for someone that exuded confidence like he did.

In the end it was another two days before Kevin had enough breathing space to call Erin. Even then, he called late at night, not even sure she'd answer.

"Hello?" Erin answered, sounding sleepy.

"Erin, hi, it's Kevin," he said smoothly.

He lay in his bed, wearing sweatpants and no shirt. His arm was up over his head, his hand holding on to the headboard. Erin sat up on her end, trying to calm herself from the thrill that had gone through her when she'd heard his voice.

"Erin?" he queried when she didn't respond right away.

"I'm here," she said, biting her lip, praying she wouldn't say something really stupid. His next words, however, left her speechless for a few moments.

"I want to see you," he said simply, his voice deep and sensual in her ears.

A thrill shot through her. Her heart started beating faster.

"When?" was all she could manage to breathe.

"Now."

Erin all but dropped the phone, gripping it tightly as she tried to calm herself enough to think. Could she go now? She needed to make arrangements for Steven. Could she see him now? Oh God, she wanted to, more than anything at that moment.

133

"Erin?" he said again. "Can you make it over? I know it's late…" He trailed off as he glanced at the clock. It was 10:30.

"I'll be there as soon as I can," she said, determined to find a way.

In the end it was much easier than she'd expected. Her roommate who quite often watched Steven for her agreed to keep an ear open for him, and he was already long since asleep. She also offered to get him up and take him to school in the event Erin couldn't make it home in time. Erin got a shameless wink on that comment. She laughed, praying she'd be that lucky.

She was at Kevin's door an hour later. Fortunately, she'd showered earlier that evening, so all she'd had to do was get dressed and put on makeup.

Kevin answered the door wearing sweatpants and nothing else. His eyes connected with hers immediately as he stepped forward, putting his hand to the back of her head and kissing her deeply. A thrill went through Erin as she reached her hands up to encircle his neck. His arms slid around her, dragging her body closer to his. Stepping back inside the house, still holding her to him, he kicked the door closed.

Erin grinned against his lips.

"Did you miss me?" she said, humor tinging her voice.

"Can you tell?" he asked, his arms still around her as he looked down at her.

"No, you're so good at hiding things…" she said, grinning.

"Uh-huh," he replied, leaning down to kiss her again.

Within minutes they were in his bedroom, making love. Erin

couldn't believe how easily and quickly she lost herself in abandon. She tried not to read too much into it, but she knew that her heart was already saying, *See? Meant to be!* She'd thought that too many times with Donovan. But even Donovan hadn't made her feel like this.

Afterward they lay together. It took Kevin about thirty seconds to reach for a cigar, after he'd caught his breath. Erin glanced up as he sat up, grinning at him.

"That intense, huh?" she said.

"Oh yeah," he said, grinning with the cigar in his mouth.

He leaned back against the headboard and put his right arm out in invitation to her to snuggle up to him. She did so gladly.

"So how are things going?" she asked.

"On what front?"

"Well, work," Erin said, not sure what other fronts he had.

"Well, other than being grilled by my co-workers about one cute little blonde I'm seeing, just the usual."

"Grilled?" Erin asked hesitantly, then bit her lip. "About me?"

"No," he said, grinning down at her. "The other little blonde I'm seeing." When he saw her face fall, he touched her under the chin, making her look at him. "Yes, Erin, you. I was just kidding, babe."

"Oh, God, Blue didn't..." she began, looking frightened suddenly.

"Didn't what?" Kevin asked, canting his head to the side.

"Well, he threatened to kick your... well, you know," she said, still looking worried.

"Well, he didn't kick my you know, but he did tell me that I needed to call you," Kevin said, not sounding rankled in the least.

135

"He did?" Erin asked, already beginning to wonder if Christian had threatened Kevin and that had been why he'd called.

"Yes, and before you let that worried mind of yours get too wrapped up, no, that's not why I called you," he said, his green eyes looking down into hers. "In fact, he told me I needed to call you about two days ago."

"Oh," she said, grimacing at the interference her friends were causing. "I'm sorry, Kevin. Blue's kind of protective like that. I'm sorry he bugged you about it."

"Don't worry about it. Donovan tried to nail me too."

"Oh Lord…" Erin said, rolling her eyes and wondering if it could get worse.

Kevin chuckled. "Not to worry, little one. Donovan doesn't even sort of intimidate me."

"Yeah, but still…"

"Good God, woman, will you relax?" Kevin said, exasperated. "Your friends are just looking out for you. I get that. I'm glad you have friends like that. And nothing they can do or say to me will dictate what I do. I make my own choices, no matter what. Okay?"

Erin bit her lip and grinned. "Okay."

Kevin stubbed out his cigar. Leaning down, he took her face in his hands, pulling her up to him and kissing her again. Within minutes she was forgetting everything, including her friends who were trying to help her. It was another couple of hours before they once again lay in bed catching their breath.

Kevin glanced over at her and shook his head. Once again she'd made him lose all control. She just grinned, looking quite pleased with the outcome.

136

"You're a witch, I just know it," he muttered as he once again reached for a cigar.

Sitting up, he put his feet on the floor, lighting the cigar. Erin impulsively reached out to slide her hand up his back, and then back down, letting her nails skim his skin.

"Mmm…" he murmured contentedly.

Erin moved to sit behind him, running her nails over his shoulders, down his back, then back up, over his shoulders again. He stubbed out his cigar and leaned against her, his happy sigh loud. Erin put her arms around him, holding him against her, his head resting on her shoulder. She ran her nails lightly over his chest, grazing the skin on his stomach and abdomen. As she moved upward again, he turned his head and his lips touched her neck. His teeth subsequently grazed her neck when her nails skimmed over his nipples as he sucked in a sharp breath.

"God, what are you doing to me?" he asked huskily as he continued to kiss her neck, his hands coming down to hers to guide them over his skin.

Again they became intertwined. Kevin marveled at the fact that he couldn't seem to get enough of her. Erin was surprised by how willing she was to try or do anything with him. She'd usually been so shy in bed, but Kevin was bringing out something totally different in her, and she liked it.

Later they went to his kitchen to find a snack. They ended up back in his bedroom, on the bed, with the radio on in the background. They brought with them cans of soda, a jar of peanut butter, and Ritz crackers. Once again leaning against the headboard, Kevin watched as Erin spread peanut butter on a cracker then held it out to him. He leaned forward, taking the cracker with his mouth. While he

137

ate his, Erin made one for herself. Kevin reached out, moving the jar of peanut butter, and turned himself to lie with his head in her lap. She laughed at the fact that he put his bare feet up on the wall to be able to have his head there. She proceeded to feed him crackers.

Naturally, peanut butter got on her fingers, and Kevin took his time licking it off. A few smudges had gotten on her bare thigh—he turned to slide his tongue over that spot as well. Erin melted instantly, her hands touching his hair, then moving over his back. Kevin continued his exploration and within minutes had Erin writhing and pulling at him. They made love again, and throughout the night off and on, leaving them both exhausted in the early hours of the next morning.

"Oh my God," Erin groaned as she glanced at his clock. "I'm supposed to be at work in an hour and a half."

Kevin chuckled contentedly. "I don't have to work today."

"Lucky!" Erin said with mock scorn.

Kevin propped himself up on his elbow, looking down at her as she lay on her back.

"Call in sick," he said, his eyes delving into hers.

"So I can stay here with you?"

"So I can have you all to myself all day," he replied, making her shiver.

Erin thought about the idea of spending all day with him. It was a very attractive offer. She didn't want to turn him down, but she knew it wasn't a very responsible thing to do, calling in sick when she really wasn't. She usually reserved her sick days for when Steven got sick, which he did often, like any other child in a public school. If she didn't have sick days, she'd end up off payroll, and that would mean even less of her already too small pay check.

138

Kevin dropped his head, his lips touching her bare shoulder, moving to her neck, then to her ear.

"Please?" he asked softly.

Every bit of reason left her then. She'd make it up somehow. She wanted this, she was enjoying the time with him, and to hell with the consequences for the moment. She had days to regret it later.

"Okay, I'll call," she said, and was rewarded with a deep but very sweet kiss.

"Thank you," he said, sounding very sincere.

Erin worried for the next half hour as to what to say to her boss. She didn't like the idea of lying to Rhiannon. In the end she didn't, not really. She called and told Rhian that she'd been up most of the night, and was just feeling really fatigued at that point. Rhiannon told her to get some rest and they'd see her tomorrow. Simple as that.

Erin hung up the phone and snuggled back into Kevin's embrace. He was already half asleep. She felt his lips pressed to the side of her head, and fell into a deep sleep thinking how good all this felt.

She woke hours later. Turning over, she noted two things. It was 12:00 in the afternoon and Kevin wasn't in bed anymore. Getting up, she pulled on her long shirt from the night before and went looking for him. She found him in his living room, sitting on the floor at the coffee table, with his back against the seat of the couch. He had a cup of his favorite coffee and an ashtray with a number of stubbed-out cigars next to where he was working on the table. The sliding glass door was open, and it was raining, but it still wasn't really cold in the room. He was working on his art. The radio was on, although the volume was low.

Standing behind and to the side of him, Erin was able to observe him without him seeing her. He looked extremely content. She

139

watched his hands move over the poster he'd shown her the first time she'd been in the house. She also noticed what she hadn't before. He'd managed to unpack all the boxes that had previously been stacked. She hadn't had a chance to notice last night, so intent was she on kissing him that she saw nothing.

Sensing that he was being watched, Kevin glanced to his side.

"Good morning," he said smoothly.

"Good morning," she said, moving to kneel next to him.

He pulled her closer to kiss her lips softly.

"How long have you been up?" she asked, her eyes moving over the poster and seeing how much detail he was putting into the coloring.

Kevin glanced at his watch, then shrugged. "'Bout three hours."

"Kevin, we didn't go to sleep until about seven a.m.," she reminded him.

"I know," he said, not looking surprised.

"That's only two hours of sleep."

He nodded in agreement. When he looked up at her, he could see she didn't understand.

"I don't sleep a lot, Erin."

"How can you not?" she asked, knowing that going all the time would have to be a major drain on his system.

"I go like this for a while, then I crash and sleep for a few days," he said, shrugging. "It's how I've always been. I wake up and I can't go back to sleep because once my mind starts it's hard to shut back down."

"God," she said, shaking her head. "So how do you cope?"

Kevin indicated the poster in front of him. "I work on stuff like

140

this, turn on the music, that kind of thing."

Erin nodded. She gestured for him to continue what he was doing. He grinned at her, then did as she bid. She watched him for nearly an hour, finally moving to lie down on the couch behind him, watching him color in minute detail over his shoulder. She reached out her hand, running her nails over his back as he worked.

"Mmm…" he murmured.

Turning his head, he kissed her softly, then went back to work. After another hour he stood up and stretched, glancing down at her. She smiled up at him, and he extended his hand. She took it and got up off the couch. Pulling her to him, he hugged her, then led her back to the master bedroom, where he pulled off her shirt and underwear, and then his own clothes. He then led her to the shower.

He took his time washing her hair and running soapy hands over her skin. Erin exalted in the feeling of his hands on her. She also determinedly pushed him to the wall of the shower and did her own exploration with soapy hands. The water had run cold by the time they were through. They dried off quickly, jumping back into bed and under the covers to warm up with each other's body heat.

Erin was giggling at how funny it was that they were freezing because they'd played in the shower for too long.

"What's so funny, pretty girl?" he asked, grinning down at her.

Erin smiled up at him, liking what he called her. "I was laughing about our long shower, handsome man."

He nodded, still grinning. He kissed her softly, reminding her of her previous excitement. She wrapped her arms around his neck, pulling him down to her as she kissed him deeply. His hands slid up her sides as he moaned against her lips. They made love again, and

141

then spent the next couple of hours talking. They talked about Steven.

Erin told Kevin all he wanted to know about her pride and joy. Kevin found that he liked the way she lit up when she talked about her son. It was very endearing to him, considering the way Stacy, the mother of his daughter, never seemed to care about how Emily was doing in school, the cute things she said, or whatever. Erin was the kind of woman Kevin would have wanted for Emily's mother. She was the kind of mother that would save every little drawing her child did, and wear a macaroni-and-popcorn necklace because her child made it for her.

He was thinking along those lines as she talked. She noticed his wistful smile.

"What are you thinking?" she asked, reaching up to touch his cheek gently.

Kevin looked back at her for a moment, realizing how good it felt to have someone treat him so sweetly. It was a definite change from what he was used to. Maybe this was what he'd been missing while he was dating the tough girls from the wrong side of the tracks.

"I was thinking how nice it would be if you were Emily's mother," he said honestly.

Erin stared back at him. It was such a wide-open, candid statement. Most men wouldn't be so open with their feelings. And she knew immediately how altruistic that statement was for him to make. She already knew how much he loved his daughter, just from the look on his face when he talked about her.

She smiled, shaking her head.

"What?" he asked.

"I just…" she said, biting her lip, not wanting to sound silly but

142

not wanting such an incredible statement to go by uncommented on either. "Thank you," she said sincerely.

"Thank you?" he asked, surprised at her choice of words.

"You saying that it would be nice if I was her mother means you think I'd be a good mother to her, right?" she asked, wanting to make sure that she'd read his statement right.

Kevin nodded. "Yeah."

"Then thank you, because I know how much Emily means to you. It was a very sweet thing to say."

Kevin grinned, shaking his head. "You know, Stacy would take it as an insult."

"That you'd want her to be the mother of your child?" Erin asked, shocked.

"Yeah. She'd think I was wishing a curse on her or something."

Erin shook her head, unable to understand that. "I never really thought about being a mother. I mean, I was still barely a child when I had Steven, but since I have him, I can't imagine my life without him."

"Stacy's still trying to figure out how to salvage her life from having Emily."

Again Erin shook her head, unable to fathom that kind of attitude.

They spent the remainder of the day together talking about whatever came to mind. It was a nice day. He took her home at the time Steven got back from school. Before she got out of his truck, she leaned over and kissed him, thanking him for the evening before and the day. He grinned at her, reminding her they hadn't really done much.

"We spent time together," she said. "That was fun for me."

Kevin nodded with a knowing grin. "Okay, babe."

"Call me sometime," she said, smiling.

"Maybe," he said, winking at her.

She laughed. "You better, or I'll sic my friends on you again."

He rolled his eyes and laughed too. "In that case, I'll call you."

He leaned over and kissed her again, caressing her cheek as he did. "I'll see you soon."

Erin got out of the truck and headed inside, feeling very good about this new relationship.

Kevin thought about her as he drove back to his house. He still wasn't sure what had him so attracted to her, but he was starting to suspect that it was an irresistible force. The prospect both intrigued and worried him. He hadn't been in a real relationship since he'd stopped drinking. He wasn't sure how he would handle tension, fights, and issues in a relationship without being able to drink. That was why he'd avoided relationships for so long. They'd told him in therapy that he needed to avoid emotional entanglements while he got sober. That any setback might hurt him and send him back to the bottle.

Now he didn't know what he wanted from Erin. All he knew was that she fascinated him. The more time he spent with her, the more he wanted to spend time with her. She treated him with the gentleness of a mother, but the sweet tenderness of a lover too. For Kevin, who had never been treated that way, not even by his mother, it was something to crave, and he did, much more than he wanted to crave anything again.

# CHAPTER 5

Jordan lay in Joe's arms, staring up at the ceiling. Joe was fast asleep. She glanced over at him and couldn't help but smile. These days she didn't seem to be able to stop smiling. Ever since she'd told Joe about Mark, she felt so much better about everything. She'd been imagining that Joe would stop seeing her once he found out. That hadn't happened. He'd known all along. Who would have thought? Certainly never her.

Today she was going over to Sinclair House to find out what it was all about. Joe had told her that it had been Randy's brainchild. A house where kids could be placed when their parents were arrested during search warrants and callouts. Joe told her that it was a much warmer, more kid-oriented environment than the usual clinical surroundings of child services.

"Good morning," Joe murmured next to her ear.

Jordan smiled, turning her head so she could lean up to kiss him. "Good morning."

"What time are you meeting Randy?" he asked, glancing at the clock. It was 6 a.m.

"Not till ten o'clock," she said. "You still going into the office today?"

"Yep," he said, getting out of bed and stretching.

Jordan admired the view. He definitely had a nice body—there was no denying that. She couldn't believe how deeply she was in love with him. She never seemed to get enough time with him, or enough of looking at him, or making love with him. It was just crazy, she kept telling herself, but she was happier than she'd been in years, and there was no denying that he was the reason.

Joe canted his head to the side, seeing her watching him. "You buying or just shopping, babe?" he asked with a grin.

She laughed. "Oh, I'm definitely buying."

Getting up on her knees, she slid her hands up his chest. His light blue eyes looked into her gold ones.

"Yes?" he asked.

"Oh yes," she said, kissing him.

His hands slid around her back, pulling her closer as they kissed. After a few long minutes, he groaned against her lips, pulling back to look down at her.

"You're gonna make me late," he said, his eyes reflecting his desire for her.

"Would I do that?" she asked, in her best imitation of innocence.

Joe narrowed his eyes. "And then some."

Jordan laughed. "Can I come to work with you?"

"You'll be bored," he said as he walked toward the bathroom to take a shower.

"No, I won't," she said, getting off the bed to follow him.

"I'm gonna spend the day catching up on a ton of paperwork, love. You'll be bored."

"I want to see where you work," she said, her hands on her hips.

Joe looked at her for a long moment, then shrugged. "Okay, babe, but don't say I didn't warn ya."

Two hours later, not only was she not bored, she was fascinated with this side of him. The fascination had started when he'd put on the shoulder holster at the hotel. She'd watched him as he loaded the ammunition clip, then slid it into the gun and pull back the slide to chamber the first round. He'd explained anything she'd asked about as he settled the holster on his shoulders.

Now, sitting in his office and watching him deal with phone calls and paperwork, he just astounded her. He was so different here. He had a lot more authority than she'd thought he did, but he used it sparingly.

She'd already checked out all the plaques, posters, and weapons he had hanging on his walls. The weapons included a Daewoo automatic assault rifle and an AK-47. "Taken off some dealers and useless to us," Joe had said. There was a poster of men in black SWAT team outfits, with their guns up as if tracking a fugitive. The caption on the poster read, *When the smoke clears, only the best will be left standing.* Another sign had a picture of a handgun and said, *Gun control is using both hands.* He also had a couple of small bumper sticker-sized signs, with *We risk our ass to protect yours* on one and *I still miss my old partner, but my aim is improving every day!* on the other.

The one that had her raising a brow at Joe and actually needing an explanation was the framed silhouette target hanging on the main wall. When she glanced at him, she saw he was watching her and grinning. Jordan turned back to the target. The caption at the top of the frame said, *Captain Joseph Sinclair, San Diego Police Department's TOP GUN.* The small metal plaque at the bottom of the target was inscribed. Jordan moved closer to read it, expecting the words to be serious. It said, *Caution: this man is a licensed lethal weapon, and*

147

*could hit a gnat at 1,000 yards.* Jordan looked back at Joe.

"Really?" she said.

"Really what?" he replied, not remembering exactly what the plaque said.

"Are you really that good of a shot?"

"Oh, that," Joe said, shrugging. "I'm pretty good, yeah."

"So is this a real target?"

"Yeah, it's from my last requal before I left the department a few years ago."

"You left?" she asked, surprised.

"Long story," he replied airily.

"So, what score is this here?" Jordan asked, pointing to the target and making a mental note to ask about the "long story" later.

"It's a three hundred."

"Is that a good score?" Jordan asked, knowing nothing about shooting.

Joe grinned. "Pretty good, yeah."

"My ass it is," said an English-accented voice from the doorway.

Jordan looked over and saw Rick standing there. "It's not a good score?"

"It's a bloody perfect score," Rick said. "Don't let this guy bullshit you, Jordan."

"Shut up, Debenshire," Joe said, narrowing his light blue eyes at the other man.

"You don't scare me, Sinclair," Rick said, grinning unrepentantly.

"So he's a good cop?" Jordan asked, glancing over at Joe then back to Rick.

"He's one of the best," Rick said.

"Ah-ha…" Jordan said, nodding and giving Joe a narrowed look.

"I never said I wasn't good," Joe said, grinning.

"You never said you were either," Jordan countered.

"Good is presumptive," Joe said.

"Shut the hell up, Sinclair," Rick said, leaning against the doorjamb. "You're one of the best in this place. You've made more cases than any of us, and you've taken more fire and come back from it than any cop I've ever met. So just take the bloody compliment and deal."

"Fire?" Jordan asked, almost afraid to hear the answer.

"He's been shot, cut, had the crap beat out of him, burned, wrecked—you name it, Joe's had it. And it's never kept him down for long," Rick said, giving his best friend a "so there" look.

"What the hell is this? *This Is Your Life*?" Joe asked, rolling his eyes.

"You've been shot?" Jordan asked, surprised.

"Four times," Rick answered for Joe.

"At least I didn't step in front of a bullet," Joe said, his eyes dancing with mischief.

Jordan turned to look at Rick, whose deep blue eyes had narrowed at Joe.

"Don't start with me…" he warned.

"Oh, who doesn't like the boot on the other foot now?" Joe said, grinning.

"Fuck you," Rick said, his grin still in place.

149

Joe laughed, shaking his head. "Sorry, man, you're not my type."

"The hell you say," Rick said, chuckling too.

"So what is it you want, Lieutenant?" Joe asked, raising an eyebrow at his best friend.

"I want your okay on a search warrant," Rick said, walking forward and handing Joe the folder he was holding.

Joe looked it over and nodded, signing off on the warrant.

"Use Judge Connolly if you can. He's into getting these guys off the street, and he likes three-strikers."

"Sounds good. Thanks, man," Rick said, winking at Jordan as he walked to the door.

Jordan turned to look at Joe. "So when were you shot?"

"Which time?"

"Maybe I don't want to know," she said, shaking her head.

She knew he was a cop, but it had never really occurred to her that he actually got shot at, and actually hit on occasion. *Oh my God!* was all she could think.

Later in the day, there was a knock on the door. Joe said, "Come."

Spider Nguyen walked in, glancing at Jordan and smiling.

"Jordan, you remember Spider, right?" Joe asked.

"Of course," Jordan said, smiling at the other man. "How are you?"

"Fine, Ms. Tate, thanks," Spider said, moving to sit in the chair next to Jordan's.

"Okay, so let's hear it," Joe said, sitting back in his chair.

"Well, we picked up a new narc while you were gone—besides your cousin, that is."

150

"I heard he was changing careers," Joe said, nodding.

"Who told you?" Spider asked, not totally surprised that he knew.

Joe grinned. "Oddly enough, my ex-wife."

Spider nodded. "Randy must've heard it from Curtis."

"Yeah, she said Donovan thought Christian had the instinct for the job."

"Well, he's a Sinclair, right?" Spider said. "I'll have to let you listen to the wiretap from the case—the guy is scary, he's so good."

"Probably comes from having to use his looks his whole life," Joe said, looking disgusted that people would only see his cousin for his appearance.

Spider nodded, thinking along the same lines.

"Okay, so who's the new narc?" Joe asked.

"Kevin Elmasian," Spider said, handing Joe the file folder he'd brought. "He's good."

"I heard Rogue Squadron talking about him on New Year's Eve," Joe said, flipping open the folder. "They were wanting to introduce him to Erin…" His voice trailed off as he glanced up at Spider.

"Alcoholic?" he asked, surprised.

"Recovering, man," Spider said. "He's been sober going on three years."

Joe nodded, thinking that must be a very difficult thing to handle as a cop. Alcohol was most cops'—including his—fail-safe. Something to take refuge in when reality became too much for a while.

"You talk to him about it?" Joe asked.

"No," Spider said, shaking his head. "Midnight and Masters hired him, and she said it was discussed in the interview."

Joe nodded again. If Midnight was comfortable with Elmasian's answers, then he was too. Like everyone else in the Gang, Joe trusted Midnight's judgment implicitly.

"Dave know?" he asked. Dave Dibbins would be training the younger man.

"He knows," Spider said. "He's going to talk to Mace about telling the rest of the team, just so they can be aware and help him if he needs it."

"So where does this nickname, Mace, come from?" Joe asked.

"Elmasian's nickname—short version of his name."

"Who's he working with?"

"Rogue Squadron," Spider said, grinning.

"Ah." Joe nodded. "Probably a good choice."

Spider laughed. "And apparently they did introduce him to Erin, and things have gotten interesting from there."

"Really now?" Joe asked, curious.

"Yup, but you'll have to get the update from your cousin on that one."

"Okay, give me the rundown of everything else going on in narcotics."

Spider proceeded to tell him about every case that had been started and made while Joe had been away. Jordan was astounded to hear about the phenomenal amount of cases they handled. She was also surprised that Joe seemed to know everything about all of them. He was like a computer—he kept it all in his head—and yet she hadn't seen any of this in the time that they'd been together. She made a note to ask him how he kept it all together like that.

Kevin sat on the stone table in the department quad. He was smoking a cigar and waiting for the rest of the team to show up. Dave Dibbins, their lead, had called a meeting of "Rogue Squadron." Kevin was now considered part of that team, the fifth wheel as it were. He sat with both feet on the table's bench. He was wearing faded jeans, brown boots, a black shirt, and a weathered-looking brown bomber-style jacket. His shades were in place, even though the day was overcast. His dark blond, collar-length hair wasn't bound at all, falling around his face, making him look even more sinister.

"Looks like the consummate dealer, huh?" Christian murmured to Stevie as they walked toward the table.

"Looks comfortable," Stevie replied.

Stevie was, in fact, impressed with how comfortable Kevin Elmasian always seemed in his surroundings. Even if he was the new guy, and in totally foreign territory, he always appeared totally at ease. Kevin reminded her of Dave in that way.

"Looks can be deceiving," Christian said, noting that Elmasian's hands were shaking as he smoked.

As soon as Christian said it, Stevie noticed the shaking hands too. She looked up at Christian, and he nodded, just as they got to the table.

Christian turned his nod into a greeting to Kevin. "Hey, man."

"Collins," Kevin said, inclining his head to the Englishman. "O'Neil," he said, turning to Stevie.

"Heya, Mace," Stevie said, smiling. "How's it going?"

Kevin took a long drag on the cigar, blowing the smoke out a few moments later.

"It's goin'."

153

Dave walked up then, greeting all of them. "Where are Pony and Jeanie?" he asked.

"Pony?" Kevin said.

"Donovan's nickname," Dave replied. "He grew up loving Mustangs with the pony on the front, plus the whole Curtis thing—you know, from that movie *The Outsiders*?"

"Ah, yes," Kevin said, nodding.

Donovan and Jeanie walked up a few minutes later. Donovan was dressed in a dark suit, and looked very distinguished.

"Wow, Curtis, you didn't need to dress up for us," Christian said, grinning.

"Trust me, I didn't," Donovan said, making a sour face.

"He had to give another deposition," Jeanie supplied.

"Oh, and Collins, you'll be next, so don't get too smug," Donovan cheerfully informed him.

"Fuck," Christian said, as Jeanie, Stevie, and Donovan chuckled.

"With that said," Dave put in, grinning, "let's get started here."

They discussed current cases, trying to decide which direction to take on them.

"How's the Stevens case going, Mace?" Dave asked, making a point of involving Kevin in the discussions. He wanted to get a good feel for the younger man's instincts.

"It's going, but I think we need to push him," Kevin said as he lit another cigar, pointedly blowing the smoke away from the group.

Dave nodded, noticing the way Kevin's hands were shaking, as Christian had.

"You sure you want to push this guy?" he asked, his voice cautionary.

154

"Well, I've spent a week trying to get around to a deal, and he's so busy playing with his new boat he's not dealing," Kevin said. "I think he just needs a push."

"How do you plan to do that?" Christian asked, curious about Kevin's style.

"I was thinking along the lines of dropping the 411 that I have to go catch up with a friend of mine to make a score," Kevin said confidently.

Dave nodded. "So nothing directed at him."

Kevin shook his head. "And have him screaming entrapment after I bust him, nope."

Dave grinned, pleased.

"Not to mention the competition factor," Christian said, grinning too.

"Always a good motivator," Stevie added.

"So what about the Stanford case?" Dave asked, looking at Christian.

"I think I'm gonna have to kill the guy soon."

"That wouldn't really help our case much," Dave replied calmly.

"Yeah, well, he lays his hands on my lady one more time, and he's gonna lose them," Christian said. "Other than that, it's proceeding nicely."

Stevie rolled her eyes. "Dave, we've got a deal set up for this week—probably looking at Thursday or Friday, depending on when he can get his connection."

"So we want to set up a trace when?" Dave asked.

"Tuesday at the latest," Stevie said.

"But if the deal's not till Thursday, why that early?" Jeanie asked.

155

Stevie grinned. "'Cause Barnes and Noble over on Xbox team lost the shot at the source twice because he gets his stuff early."

The pair were really Barnes and Nabel, but since they were partners, everyone called them Barnes and Noble after the bookstore. And Xbox was really X-Strike, but since there was constant competition between the narcotics teams, that was Rogue Squadron's name for them.

Jeanie nodded in response to Stevie's statement.

"So we're gonna do it a bit earlier," Christian said. "Personally, I'd start tailin' his ass today."

Stevie nodded her agreement. "If he didn't manage to get to his source this weekend."

"Nah," Christian said. "He was hunting this weekend, so unless he got his shipment off the back of some stag, we're probably safe."

"Preppy boy hunting?" Stevie asked, rolling her eyes.

"Yeah," Christian said. "We'll be lucky if he didn't manage to shoot himself."

"Well, no," Kevin put in. "It'd save the taxpayers' money on a trial, right?"

Christian laughed, as did the rest of the group. "Good point."

"Okay, so I think we're all set," Dave said, calling an end to the meeting. "Stevie, get that tail set up on Stanford today."

Stevie nodded. Everyone stood to leave.

"Mace," Dave said. "Hang back a second. I want to talk to you."

Kevin sat back down, reaching for another cigar as he did.

Dave's eyes took in the shaking hands. "You okay?" he asked, moving to sit on the bench near Kevin's feet, his legs extended in front of him casually.

"Yeah, why?" Kevin asked, already ready to kick himself for sounding defensive.

"Well," Dave said, staring off into the distance. "I noticed your hands are shaking a bit…" He glanced back at Kevin.

Kevin nodded. "I didn't get home last night. I worked straight through."

Dave nodded slowly. "So you're saying you're tired?"

Kevin looked down at Dave for a long moment. He knew that Dibbins knew more than he was letting on. Then it hit him that Dave more than likely thought he was shaking because he needed a drink. Moving to sit next to Dave on the stone bench, Kevin turned to the other man.

"Look, Dibbs, it's not what you're thinking."

"What am I thinking?" Dave asked, his tone calm, his appearance composed.

So composed that it had Kevin thinking twice about what Dave might be thinking. It also had him wondering if a lot of people ratted themselves out to Dibbins because of his steadfast composure. Dave Dibbins was the best for a reason.

Kevin debated for a long minute, trying to decide how much he should confess, but in the end, he decided that Dave, as his lead, had a right to know even if he didn't already.

"Look, I don't know for sure what you're thinking, but if you're worried about my hands shaking, it's because I haven't taken my Adderall this morning."

"Adderall?" Dave asked, surprised.

Kevin grinned. He'd actually shocked the master. "Yeah, I have ADD, and if I don't take my Adderall, I get pretty edgy."

Dave nodded. "That I can live with."

"But you thought I was craving a drink, right?"

Dave looked back at him, his sky blue eyes gauging, then nodded.

"I don't really crave alcohol," Kevin said. "I'm fine so long as I don't taste it." He shrugged. "I'm kinda lucky in that way."

Dave looked thoughtful. "Anyone else on the team know about any of this?"

"Not unless you've told them," Kevin replied evenly.

"Nope," Dave said. "Not my place to tell them." He pinned Kevin with a look then. "But it's my suggestion that you tell them."

"Why?" Kevin asked, already feeling defensive again.

Dave leaned back, his face turned up toward the sky, his eyes closed. "Mace, these people are your lifeline, whether you like it or not." He looked straight at Kevin then. "And if you don't learn to trust them, you'll never be as good a narc as you could be."

"You work alone a lot—that doesn't seem to deter you," Kevin pointed out.

"Yeah, but I've been doing it a lot longer than you," Dave said. "And I worked with a partner for years before that."

"And you trust them?"

"With my life."

Kevin nodded. "I'll think about it, okay?"

"Fair enough," Dave said, moving to stand. "I think once you get to talking to them, you'll find out they have just as many faults as you think you do."

Kevin looked at him for a long moment, then nodded again. The two walked back into the building together.

158

Later that morning, Joe drove Jordan over to Sinclair House. Jordan was blown away by the size and magnitude of Randy's operation. The house itself was incredible. She spent the day being even more impressed with Randy Sinclair. It was much easier for Jordan see why Joe loved her. There was nothing fake about the woman. She was indeed beautiful, but she also seemed very sincere in her desire to help the children in the center. At one point, Randy and Jordan sat down in the kitchen to have a cup of coffee.

"Randy, what you've done here is fantastic," Jordan said sincerely.

"Thanks," Randy said, smiling. "I could never have done this if it weren't for Joe."

Jordan nodded, not sure what to say.

"He supported me through all of this. He even bought me this house to have the center in—did he tell you that?" Randy asked.

"I heard about him giving you the house for Christmas."

"Yeah, he's like that," Randy said, shaking her head, still ever amazed by Joe.

They were both silent for a long few moments, neither able to think of anything to say.

"When do you go back on your tour?" Randy asked.

"I have to meet up with them in Rome on the fourteenth."

"It must be exciting to do what you do."

"It is," Jordan said. "But it gets hard sometimes too."

"How?" Randy asked, curious.

"Well…" Jordan said hesitantly. She'd just realized that what she was about to say may not be welcome information to Randy Sinclair, and she didn't want to hurt her feelings.

Randy waited, canting her head to the side. "It has to do with Joe, I take it?" she asked, her voice devoid of any anger.

Jordan grimaced. "Yeah, I was just going to say that now that I've found this guy I want to spend time with, I have to go off on a tour for the next two months."

Randy nodded. "I can imagine that would be difficult."

"It's never been a problem before," Jordan said, again ready to kick herself for revealing too much.

"Oh," Randy said. "First time you've been in love?"

Jordan looked back at Randy for a long moment, surprised. "How..."

"Oh," Randy said, waving away Jordan's surprise. "For one thing, Joe's the kind of guy women fall for. He's the classic knight in shining armor of all of our dreams. Besides, I saw how you were at the hospital with him. You were worried sick. That's love."

Jordan nodded, surprised by Randy's candor, and her obviously well-adjusted attitude about Joe. "You're okay with all of this?" she said, realizing that it was a little late to ask that.

Randy shrugged. "I can't say it's the easiest thing I've ever done, but I know that if I need Joe, he'll be there. I love him enough to want to see him happy. He wasn't happy with me anymore. I gave him plenty of reason to want out."

"What happened?" Jordan asked, having been curious about what would make Randy let Joe go.

Randy shook her head. "I don't know, really," she said, still not sure what had changed. "I got so involved in this center, and we just

160

grew apart. I think Joe got to the point where he needed more than I could give him. He seems to have gone back to what he craved before he and I ever met."

"What's that?" Jordan said, wondering if she was asking a loaded question.

"A woman with more fire than he can handle," Randy said, grinning.

Jordan laughed. "Let me ask you this—does he always have to get his way?"

"Oh yes," Randy said, laughing too. "It's Captain Sinclair's highway or nothing at all."

"Ugh!" Jordan said, shaking her head. "He's going to be hell on my independence, then, isn't he?"

"Oh yes," Randy said. "Expect to fight with him a lot."

"Great…" Jordan said, making a face that belied her statement.

"Joe is one of those men that honestly want to help but forget that we women tend to like to do things for ourselves now," Randy said, looking a little bit wistful. "I think he fell in love with me because I didn't have that independent streak that drove him crazy with Midnight." She grinned impishly. "Course, being around Midnight didn't help to squelch that independent streak for long."

"Midnight sounds like a force of nature."

Randy laughed. "She is. She's the strongest woman I know. Nothing keeps her down for long."

Jordan nodded. She could see what Randy was saying about Joe. If he'd been in love with Midnight, and having to deal with Midnight's radically independent nature, Randy would have been a huge change. It was in essence what Joe had said—Randy needed him,

161

while Midnight didn't need anyone.

*The question is, where do I fit in here? Or do I?*

Randy watched Jordan for a few moments, seeing that she was worried about how Joe would take being with her. Randy herself didn't know, so she couldn't offer any assurances. It was hard to tell. Joe and Midnight had survived numerous battles, from what they'd both told her. They might have still been together to this day if they hadn't met other people and fallen in love with them.

"So," Jordan said, ready for a change in topic, "Joe said he'd mentioned to you the idea I had for raising money for Sinclair House. How do you feel about it?"

"I'd be grateful for the help," Randy said. "Joe told me about the concert you did in London, and how well it went over. I could use any and all help I can get." She grimaced. "I hate the idea that Joe's still having to support my fanciful ideas. He shouldn't have to anymore."

"Well, I don't think he feels like he's supporting any fanciful ideas. I think he honestly believes in what you're doing here."

"You're right," Randy said, nodding. "He does. I just don't want him to be stuck taking care of me forever. I'd like to give him some peace, you know?"

Jordan looked back at Randy for a long moment, seeing how hard it must be for her. Here she was, sitting in a house her husband bought for her. She'd been supported by him for years in school, and now in her center that she'd wanted to start. It must be very difficult to be in that kind of position. Jordan couldn't help but respect that Randy wanted to make the center self-sufficient, so as to free herself of the feeling of being dependent on her soon-to-be ex-husband.

Jordan couldn't imagine how that would feel, being so reliant on anyone. She also knew that it would be very difficult to handle for a woman that had in essence decided to let her husband go. On the one hand, Randy was letting him go. On the other, she was still tied to him.

Jordan left the house a few hours later, after having signed a number of autographs and taken pictures with some of the kids, and even with a few of the staff members who loved her music too. She promised Randy to work out the details of putting on a benefit concert. Randy thanked her for her willingness to do it.

\*\*\*

Two days after her hooky day with Kevin, Erin was sitting at her desk, working on the computer. She didn't notice Kevin leaning against the doorway to her cubicle for a while, so intent was she on solving the problem she'd encountered in the system.

Kevin watched Erin make faces at the computer, and heard her mutter things like, "Come on, don't do that," and "Fine, be that way." He chuckled at that one, which got her attention.

"Oh, hi," she said, her face lighting up like the sun.

"Hi," he said, smiling.

His moss green eyes were bright, since the morning sun was still hitting the windows outside her office area.

"How are you?" she asked.

"I'm good. You?"

"I'm fine."

They were both silent for a moment. Then he straightened, glancing over his shoulder at Rhiannon, who was working away on her computer. She was trying to ignore the conversation so as not to eavesdrop.

"So, I was thinking…" he said, looking back at Erin.

"Yes?" she queried, wondering if she was being too eager again.

"If you and Steven would like to have dinner with me tonight."

Erin was taken aback. He wanted to include Steven? Then again, why shouldn't he? It wasn't like he was foreign to having children.

"That would be great, as long as you're sure you want to be around an exuberant seven-year-old after working all day," she said, wanting to leave him an out if he was simply offering to be polite.

"You do it, right?" Kevin asked, a smile dancing in his eyes.

"Yes, but I'm used to it." She smiled. "You're not as weathered as I am."

"You have no idea how weathered I am, baby girl," he said, grinning.

Erin bit her lip at the endearment. She liked that he was so sweet with the way he talked to her. She'd heard a lot about him in the last few days. A few people had started calling him the Ice Man because of his cool facade. He was being compared to Christian, and coming out ahead in the chill factor. He never seemed that way with her though. She wondered at that.

"Then I'll put you to the test tonight," she said.

"I'll pick you two up at six—is that okay?"

"That's perfect."

"I'll see you then," he said, winking at her.

"Be careful out there!" she called after him as he turned and left the office.

Rhiannon grinned to herself at her computer; she'd heard Erin's sigh from where she sat. "All that, huh?" she couldn't help but say.

Erin rolled her chair out to the doorway of her cubicle, where she could see Rhiannon's desk.

"Ever just have that feeling?" she asked, her tone so wistful Rhiannon smiled.

"Yes, I have," Rhiannon said. "It feels good, doesn't it?"

"Yes, ma'am," Erin said, biting her lip again.


That night, Kevin picked her and Steven up right on time. He came to the door wearing black jeans, black boots, a steel-blue long-sleeved button-up shirt, and a long black duster jacket. Erin was still running around trying to get ready. She'd gotten Steven bathed and dressed and had begged her roommates to make sure he stayed clean.

Karen, one of Erin's roommates, answered the door. All three of the girls Erin lived with were very curious about this Kevin Elmasian who'd swept Erin off her feet. Erin had tried to describe him, but had only been able to tell them that he was gorgeous and that he had the serious "bad-boy thing" going on. As Karen opened the door, she saw Kevin flick the cigar he'd been smoking away. His moss green eyes met Karen's without a hint of nervousness.

"You must be Kevin," Karen said, sounding like a mother, when in fact she was only a year older than Erin.

Kevin nodded.

"I'm Karen. Erin's not quite ready yet, so come on in," she said, feeling nervous because he hadn't spoken yet.

Kevin stepped inside the house Erin shared with the other three women and her son. He was surprised at how small it really was. How did she do it? Before he got two steps inside, a small whirlwind made

165

its way up to him.

Steven stared up at the man from his three-and-a-half-feet height.

"Are you Kevin?" he asked, sounding like a cop doing an interview, his little face serious.

Kevin knelt down, putting himself at eye level with Steven.

"I'm Kevin," he replied, as if answering a cop. "Are you Steven?"

Steven giggled, liking the game they were playing. "Yep!" he shouted gleefully.

"Good information to have," Kevin said, grinning at the little boy.

He was a handsome little boy too. Kevin realized this Tyler must have at least been good-looking, for all the trouble he'd been. Steven had Erin's china blue eyes, but sandy-brown hair. He had an adorable mass of it, with curls at the ends. He also had an elfin-like, cute face that made people look at him wherever Erin took him.

"Are you a cop too?" Steven asked.

"I am," Kevin said, still using his serious voice.

"Got a badge, mister?" Steven asked, scrunching his face up in an imitation of a tough cop.

"I've got one, but do you?" Kevin replied doubtfully.

"Uh-huh," Steven said, nodding.

"Let's see it," Kevin said, his tough-guy voice coming out.

"You first," Steven said, standing on his tiptoes and putting his forehead against Kevin's in an attempt to be tough.

Kevin chuckled. "I never win these," he said, grinning as he reached under his jacket to pull his badge off his belt and hand it to Steven.

Steven took it with a look of reverence, touching it carefully. "Cooool."

Erin watched the exchange from the doorway, a warm smile on her face. It was so hard to watch her son with other people. She always worried that they'd hurt his feelings, or make him feel unwanted or like he was a bother. It hurt her to see his little face fall in disappointment. Ever since she'd gotten home that evening and told him they were going out with Kevin, Steven had been on cloud nine. He'd excitedly chattered all the way through his bath about how he was going to show "Kevin" his cars, and his train, and his LeapFrog Pad, and his room, and on and on. Erin had prayed silently that Kevin would at least pretend to be nice for Steven's sake.

What she saw, however, was a show of sincere attention, and it warmed her heart to this man even more.

As if he knew he was being watched, Kevin glanced up, and saw her standing in the doorway. He grinned, winking at her, then looked back at Steven.

"I'm gonna need that back, ya know," he said.

Steven handed the badge back. Kevin stood up, clipping it back on his belt. No sooner had he done so than Steven grabbed his hand.

"Do you want to see my room?" Steven asked excitedly.

"Steven…" Erin cautioned, not wanting him to overwhelm Kevin.

"Sure," Kevin said. "Since we have to wait for your mom, let's check out your pad."

Of course, "Steven's room" was actually Erin's room, so Erin had to move out of the way as Steven pulled Kevin determinedly inside. Kevin leaned over, giving Erin a quick kiss on his way by. Erin laughed and went back into the bathroom to finish getting ready. She

167

watched in the mirror as Steven pushed Kevin down to sit on the bed and started showing him all his treasures. By the time Erin was ready to leave ten minutes later, Kevin and Steven were happily entrenched in a discussion about whether or not the Dodge Charger was indeed better than a Trans Am.

"I'll tell you what," Kevin said, moving to stand as Erin joined them, "I happen to know people who have both of those cars. We'll ask them sometime."

"Really?" Steven asked excitedly. "Cool!"

Erin looked up at Kevin, astounded by his ease around her son. Kevin glanced at her, catching her little smile. He put his arm around her, looking her up and down.

"You look great, Mom," he said, winking at her.

"Thanks," she said, smiling up at him.

"You ready?"

"Yes."

"You ready, little man?" Kevin asked Steven.

"Yep!" Steven replied eagerly.

"Let's roll then."

They left the house. Kevin took them to dinner at a local hamburger place that had "the best milkshakes and french fries in the world," according to Steven. While they waited for their food, Kevin and Steven got into a heated game of Pac Man at one of the tabletop arcade games. Erin noted that Kevin "accidentally" got eaten by the ghosts a lot, making it so Steven won. After the third game, Kevin stood up, beckoning to Steven to follow him.

"We'll be right back," Kevin told Erin with a grin.

Erin watched as Kevin took Steven to the other side of the game

168

area. Their backs were to her, so she couldn't see what they were playing, but she watched as Kevin fed dollar after dollar into the machine. Finally both "boys" let out a whoop; Steven was jumping up and down excitedly. He came running back to the table with a pink stuffed teddy bear and handed it to Erin. Erin hugged Steven, then glanced up as Kevin walked back over to the table, a satisfied grin on his lips.

"Thank you to you too," Erin said, smiling up at him.

Kevin sat down next to her, leaning over and kissing her lips.

"You're welcome, but Steven won it for you."

"I know," Erin said, winking at her son. "That's because he's the master of the crane game, aren't ya, Steven?"

"Yep!"

Kevin grinned, nodding.

Their food came just then. Erin leaned over to whisper to Kevin, "How many cartons of cigars did that cost you?"

"I don't know what you mean," Kevin replied, his grin ever present. "Steven's a master of the crane game."

"Uh-huh, that and Pac Man," Erin said, winking at him. "Thank you, Kevin."

Kevin said nothing, only looking down into her eyes and smiling.

They ate then, sharing a big basket of fries with their hamburgers.

After dinner, Kevin drove them over to Mission Bay, Belmont Park, where he bought Steven an endless supply of tokens to play any and every video game that caught his fancy. Erin looked on, even getting herself involved in a shooting game with Kevin and finding out

169

rather quickly that he was indeed a master marksman, even with a fake gun.

By the time they left the park, Erin was sure Kevin had spent at least half a paycheck on tokens for Steven. It was nine o'clock, and Steven's eyelids were drooping, and he was having a hard time even walking to Kevin's SUV. Kevin bent down and scooped him up in his arms, and Steven's head dropped to Kevin's shoulder. He was asleep in an instant. Erin glanced up at the picture they made, and smiled. She knew she was letting her heart run away with her, but Kevin just seemed to get better and better.

They put Steven in the backseat, with his seatbelt on and Kevin's duster jacked rolled up and set against the door for Steven's head to lean on.

"Are you sure that's not going to mess up your jacket?" Erin asked worriedly.

"Nah, it's okay," Kevin assured her.

He opened her door for her, and once she'd got in, he stood there looking at her.

"Can you spare a couple of hours for me?" he asked. "We can lay Steven down in my extra bedroom, so you and I can have a little time together. Okay?"

"Okay," she said, thrilled that he wanted to spend even more time with her.

Once at his house, Kevin carried Steven from the truck while Erin used his keys to open the front door. They laid Steven down in the spare room, where he remained totally asleep. They stood in the dim light, watching him for a moment.

"He's so tired," Erin said, glancing up at Kevin. "You wore him out."

"That was my whole plan," Kevin said, winking at her.

"Oh, was it now?" Erin asked, reaching up to put her arms around his neck.

Kevin pulled her close, leaning down to kiss her deeply.

Erin sighed against his lips.

"I've been wanting to do that all night," he said.

"I've been wanting you to do that all night."

"Come on," he said, taking her hand and leading her out.

He made his way to his room, closing the door behind them. He pulled his gun out from the small of his back, setting it on his dresser, and took his badge off his belt and tossed it down next to it. Erin watched as he went to the window, opened it, and turned on a fan that stood in front of the window, pointing out. He proceeded to pull out a cigar and light it with shaking hands.

Erin smiled. "That bad, huh?"

"Arcades kind of put me on edge," he replied, grinning, with the cigar between his lips.

He sat down on his bed, unlaced his boots and kicked them off, then leaned back against the headboard, his legs stretched out comfortably in front of him.

Erin sat on the bed, facing him.

"Arcades put you on edge, and yet you took us there…" she said, trailing off as she shook her head.

"I wanted Steven to have fun," Kevin said, shrugging. "Not just do boring adult stuff."

"Well, I have to say, you were so incredible with him."

"He seems like a really good kid."

"He is, but I know he's longing for a male role model right now.

171

I hope you didn't feel too latched onto tonight."

"Nah," Kevin assured her. "I had a good time. I don't get to play much anymore."

Erin smiled. "So you had to use my son to get to play, huh, Mr. Elmasian?"

"That's right," he said, grinning

"Well, thank you," she said sincerely, looking into his eyes.

"You're welcome."

They sat in silence for a while. Erin watched him as he smoked. She realized she was getting used to his long silences now. They didn't seem nearly as uncomfortable to her anymore.

"I've been hearing rumors about you," she said after a few minutes.

"Oh yeah?" he asked, his tone lazy.

"Yeah, I've been hearing terms like 'stone cold' and 'ice man.'"

He grinned. "Metal under tension?"

"Nope, not yet," she said, laughing softly. "But someone did mention the whole 'still waters run deep and dangerous' thing."

Kevin nodded, having heard all those terms before.

"So why don't I ever see any of that?" she asked, curious as to why he didn't seem at all cold to her.

Kevin looked back at her for a few long moments, taking a long drag on his cigar and blowing the smoke out a few moments later. Stubbing out the butt before lighting another cigar, he glanced at her again.

"Damned if I know," he said finally, shaking his head. "No one I know would even recognize me when I'm with you."

"Really?"

Erin had assumed that he was just cool with people he didn't know, or people he worked with, or whatever. But no one saw this side of him?

Kevin nodded.

"Surely your family sees the warmer side of you," Erin said, to which he shook his head.

"Okay, but at least Emily, right?"

Kevin looked thoughtful for a moment. "She sees something like this, but I'm thinking in terms of adults."

"And no adult has seen this side of you?"

"No one."

Erin sat and thought about it for a long time, then reached out and touched his cheek. "Then I should thank you."

"For?"

"For letting me see this part of you."

His look was considering. "How do you know this isn't just another facade, though?"

Erin shook her head. "I don't think that's the case, Kevin. You've tried to convince me of that before, and like I said then, I think it's the real you. I just think that maybe you haven't been given the chance to be this part of yourself."

Kevin didn't answer, just shrugged.

"Do I ever want to see what the others see?" Erin asked, thinking that she probably didn't.

"I doubt you'd like it."

Erin nodded, thinking he was probably right.

Again they were silent as he finished his second cigar. He reached over, stubbing it out. With his other hand he took hers and pulled her to him, his lips taking possession of hers as soon as she was within reach. Erin was surprised by the action, and put her hands on his shoulders to steady herself. He pulled her onto his lap, deepening the kiss. His arms wrapped around her as the fire between them caught.

He caressed her through the material of her shirt, making her moan against his lips. She still wore her heels. She moved to take them off, but his hands stopped her.

"Leave them on," he said huskily.

Erin bit her lip, but nodded, kissing him again. He unbuttoned her shirt, but he didn't remove it. Instead he touched her through the lace of her bra, causing all kinds of thrills in her. His hands moved to where her skirt was drawn taut against her legs, since her knees were bent to straddle his waist. He slowly pushed the material up so that it was hiked up over her hips. His hands touched her bare legs as his lips left hers, kissing down her neck.

Erin reached down, unbuttoning his shirt, smoothing her hands over his chest, seeking to excite him as he was exciting her. When his fingers pulled aside the material of her bra, exposing a rigid nipple, she cried out, pressing her body down against him, causing him to groan. He gripped her hips, pressing her down harder on him, as his lips moved down to her nipple. Within moments she was ready to beg him for anything. In her desperation to reach her release she grasped at his belt, unbuckling it and pulling at the buttons on his jeans. He obliged her by lifting his hips so she could push his clothing down. Again he held her waist, pressing her against him, and it served to only excite Erin further. Kevin was breathing in ragged gasps too; it was obvious he was pushing his limits as well. His hands slid up her skin, one shoving aside the material over her other breast, his mouth

174

closing over her other nipple again. Erin couldn't begin to even think.

"Kevin, Kevin..." she chanted over and over again. "Please..."

His mouth moved up her neck to her ear. "Come for me, Erin, now," he commanded, his voice so deep and husky in her ear, she felt it throughout her body.

Within moments she was doing what he told her, grasping at his shoulders as she cried out. It took her a while to recover, her body still trembling as his lips captured hers again. He continued to touch her, keeping her body simmering with heat. His lips moved over her skin again, taking his time and exciting her all over again. Finally, he moved her body down onto his.

Because of the forceful orgasm she'd just sustained, her body was still simmering, so Kevin was able to control himself and take his time as he wanted to. Slowly, he slid off her shirt, pulling down the straps of her bra, exposing her breasts totally. His hands and lips made her writhe against him, which only served to excite him further. The buildup to their release was extended and seemed even more powerful this time.

"Jesus, Jesus..." he chanted, feeling her excitement build with his, into an impossible, pulsing heat. "Come with me, Erin... Come with me now, babe, now," he moaned, and felt her body contract in its release.

They both let out sounds of ecstasy, gripping each other as they did.

Afterward Erin lay against him, feeling so drained she couldn't even begin to think of moving. He lay much the same way, his hands on her legs. His head was back on the headboard, his eyes closed as he tried to catch his breath. He blew out a long breath, shaking his head as if to clear it. In truth, his mind was still trying to catch up.

175

Now he knew what people meant by earth-shattering orgasms.

Meanwhile, Erin was thinking about the fact that she'd just totally lost herself in this feeling with him once again. She didn't stop to think about "love"; she didn't care about that when she made love with him. She couldn't think beyond the way he made her feel. She didn't care what he did to her, how he did it, what he said, how he said it, as long as he made her body feel the way he did every time. The term "brazen slut" came to mind, making her grin.

"What are you grinning about?" he asked, feeling it against his chest.

She lifted her head, looking up at him. "I was just thinking of what a brazen slut I am with you."

"Are you?" he asked, laughing.

She nodded. "Oh yeah."

"What do you consider brazen slut behavior?" he asked as he moved to sit up and reached for a cigar.

Erin watched as he flipped open his lighter, lighting the end of the cigar and taking a long, deep drag off it.

"Just letting you do anything you want to me," she said, smiling almost shyly now.

"Anything?" he replied, his lips curling sardonically.

"Well... I mean, I don't care what you do, as long as it feels as good as it always does. You know?"

Kevin nodded, looking thoughtful.

"What?" she asked.

He didn't answer for a long moment. "You consider what we just did kinky?"

Erin shrugged. "It's not something I've really done a lot..."

176

"A lot?" Kevin echoed.

"Okay," she said, giving him a mockingly sour look. "Ever."

"Never?" Kevin asked, grinning.

"No," Erin said, embarrassed.

"The Boy Scout doesn't go for hot and fast, huh?" Kevin joked.

"Kevin!" Erin said, laughing in spite of herself.

"Sorry," he said, not looking like he really was.

"Donovan was a good lover," Erin said, feeling the need to defend the man she'd loved.

Kevin nodded, taking another drag off his cigar and blowing the smoke out. His eyes narrowed slightly, but he said nothing. It bugged him that she felt the need to defend Donovan, and it bothered him that it bugged him. Why? The last thing he needed was a woman to get under his skin right now.

"Kevin?" Erin said, sensing a change in his mood suddenly.

His green eyes shifted to hers. Still he said nothing.

"Are you okay?" she asked.

"Yeah, I'm fine."

Erin looked back at him, disbelieving. She leaned forward, kissing him softly. Then she pulled back slightly.

"I love the way you make me feel, Kevin. No one's ever made me feel like this," she said, the sincerity in her voice so strong he felt it.

He reached over to stub out his cigar, sitting all the way up. His hand went to the back of her neck as his lips captured hers again. He kissed her deeply and so thoroughly she felt fully possessed by him by the time he pulled back to look at her.

"Don't ever compare me to Curtis, Erin," he said simply, his tone even but with enough of an edge to make her realize he was very serious.

"I wasn't, Kevin," she said softly, shaking her head. "There is no comparison." She grinned. "Christian says you're what's known as a 'high-level player,' the best at everything you do." Her finger touched his lips then. "And you are definitely the best at this."

Kevin grinned, both for the comment she'd made and for the one that Collins had made.

"High-level player, huh?" he said. "Would that make him the master then?"

Erin laughed softly, nodding. "Oh my God, that man could seduce Mother Theresa."

Kevin laughed. Then he pinned her with a look.

"Has he seduced you?" he asked, not sure why he wanted to know.

Erin didn't answer for a long moment, looking straight into his eyes. "No, he hasn't."

"Has he tried?"

Erin shook her head. "No, he never has. I don't think I'm the type he likes to conquer anyway, but he also knows I have way too much respect for Stevie to do that to her."

"Besides the fact that she'd probably kill you, right?"

"Right," Erin said, grinning.

Kevin nodded, satisfied that she was being honest with him. And oddly relieved that she'd never slept with Collins. He glanced over at the clock next to his bed. It was already almost midnight.

"Why don't you and Steven stay here tonight?" he asked. "It's Friday, and maybe we could all hang out tomorrow or something…" he said, trailing off as she smiled at him.

178

"You want to hang out with us?"

"I want to be with you," he said. "Steven will just help me feed my need for play time," he added with a wink.

"Oh-ho, now the truth comes out," she said, laughing again. "I'm sure Steven would be thrilled."

"And what about you?" he asked, for some insane reason craving her response.

"I love spending time with you, Kevin. You have to realize that by now," she said, touching his cheek.

He didn't answer her. Instead he kissed her, hugging her close. No, he hadn't realized that, but it felt really good to hear.

In the end, Steven and Erin spent the entire weekend with Kevin. The three of them had a great time playing Xbox games, renting movies, chasing around in Kevin's backyard, going to lunch, getting Big Macs for dinner. Steven was in seventh heaven, and Erin was sure she was falling in love with this man. She made herself not say anything to him, knowing how terrified men were of "the *L* word." But she couldn't help but feel love for a man who would get down on the floor of his living room and push Matchbox cars around on a road that he and Steven had drawn on a piece of poster board Kevin had for his artwork.

# CHAPTER 6

Things settled down after Jordan went back to Europe. Joe fell into a routine at work and with his home life. He found and bought a large town house that had three bedrooms and a decent-sized backyard.

"It's bigger than most people's house, Sinclair," Midnight commented the first time she saw it. "But I guess it's a bit scaled back from the mansion you had before."

Joe shrugged. "Don't need all that now, it's just me half the time."

He had the kids on weekends mostly. It was easier with their schooling if they were with Randy in the evenings. Many nights, Randy would invite him to dinner, and he'd eat with them.

The divorce became final two weeks after Jordan went back on tour. She called him, and he sounded very somber. When he told her about it, Jordan got quiet, and had to go shortly after that. Joe hadn't thought anything of it; she was frequently busy with her tour.

***

The trial of Rosa Delario never ended up taking place, after Nick Kopanke showed Rosa's lawyer all the evidence against her, including the DNA taken from the beer bottle Christian had spit his shot into.

180

The evidence showed that there was indeed a large dose of the chemicals needed to make Ecstasy. The beer bottle had Rosa's fingerprints on it. Notwithstanding the transcripts from the wiretap of that night, in which Rosa implicated her husband as the chemist behind the scene and herself as the one giving Ecstasy to men without their knowledge. There was no way she was getting out of the charges.

In the end, Rosa pleaded guilty to the manufacture and distribution of narcotics, two counts of assault on a peace officer, and reckless disregard for the health and safety of a peace officer. Her lawyer told her to consider herself lucky they hadn't charged her with attempted murder of a peace officer. She was sentenced to fifteen to twenty-five years in prison. Her husband, Larry, pleaded guilty to the manufacture of narcotics, and received a lesser sentence of ten years.

Donovan breathed a sigh of relief that none of the dirty laundry was ever aired to the press, even though Midnight had assured him repeatedly that the press would have no chance to blow this out of proportion; since Donovan was an undercover peace officer, his name and/or likeness could not be used. In the end, it all finished quietly, which was better for everyone all around.

\*\*\*

Erin and Kevin were seeing each other regularly. Every time he got a break from doing case work, he would call her. Sometimes she, Steven, and Kevin would spend time together, other times just she and Kevin. One night, when he'd called her at nine o'clock, she'd come over. As usual, they ended up in bed. They were asleep a few hours later when his phone rang. He was lying on his stomach, Erin on her back, his arm around her waist, his face nuzzled against her neck. He

181

reached for the phone blindly, picking it up and tucking it under his ear.

"Yeah?" he said tiredly.

Erin opened her eyes, turning to look at him.

"Wait, wait," he said, coming more awake suddenly. "Mom, slow down. Is he okay?" he asked, listening for a moment. "Okay… uh-huh… okay, Mom. *Was* he drinking? Right," he said, sounding unconvinced with the answer. "Of course he wasn't drinking. Right… Yeah, I know, Mom, okay…" He trailed off as he turned over onto his back, running his hand through his hair. "I don't know," he said, sounding agitated. "No, I mean… I'm not with the PD anymore, Mom. I can't just—Okay, but I can't do anything." He shook his head, glancing at Erin. She'd sat up, her face showing her concern. "Mom, what did they say?" he asked, striving to keep his voice even. "Okay, and what did they say his blood alcohol was?" He listened again, closing his eyes and shaking his head. "And you want me to argue what with them?" he asked irritably.

Erin could see he was losing his patience. She reached out, touching his stomach. He glanced at her. His hand reached down to cover hers. "Okay, Mom, I'll come up there and see what I can do, okay?"

A few minutes later he hung up, breathing a frustrated sigh.

"What happened?" Erin asked.

Kevin sat up, reaching for a cigar in the same motion. He lit it, shaking his head. "My dad totaled his car."

"Oh my God, is he okay?"

"Oh, of course," Kevin said snidely. "He was probably too drunk to feel it."

Erin bit her lip. "What did your mom say?" she asked, aware that he was irritated with his mother at that point.

"As usual, she defended him. He said he only had a couple of beers at the bar before he drove home."

"And you don't believe that."

"Not with a blood alcohol level of point one five—that takes a couple of cases, not a couple of beers."

Erin grimaced. "And your mom wants you to come up there?"

"Yeah," he said sarcastically. "She thinks I can 'fix' it."

"How?" Erin asked, surprised that his mother thought it would be that easy.

"I have no idea," Kevin said, shaking his head. "She doesn't seem to get that evidence is evidence—it doesn't just go away because it's on the father of a former Seattle PD officer."

"What are you going to do?" Erin asked, seeing that he was very agitated. He was fast working his way through the first cigar and reaching for his second.

Kevin scrubbed his face. "I don't fucking know," he said, sounding desolate. "I'll go up there, but there isn't going to be shit I'm going to be able to do." He shook his head again. "Like they're going to listen to the fucked-up alcoholic ex-cop from their PD, right?"

"Kevin…" Erin said. "Please don't say that about yourself. You're not fucked up, and you've busted your butt staying sober for three years…" She trailed off as she reached out to touch his arm.

Kevin smiled sadly. "Not everyone thinks like you do, babe."

"Well, why the hell not?" she asked indignantly.

Kevin grinned, chuckling a moment later. "I don't know. Maybe I should send you up there to set them all straight, huh?"

183

"When do you want me to go?" she asked, smiling. She was glad she could make him feel at least a little bit better.

They were quiet for a bit, while he lit and smoked a third cigar. When he stubbed that one out, Erin moved to lie back down, pulling him with her. He lay on his back. She propped herself up on her elbow, reaching out to stroke his hair.

"When are you going to leave?" she asked.

"In the morning."

Erin nodded.

"God, I hate going back there," he said, shaking his head.

"Is it bad?"

He nodded. "I escaped from that house years ago. Going back there always makes me feel edgy."

"How will your sister take it?" Erin asked, remembering that he'd said that his little sister, Samantha, was only sixteen and still living with his parents.

"She's the one I'm worried about," Kevin said. "She's always been in denial about Dad's drinking too. Mom has her convinced."

Erin shook her head. "Will you be okay though?" she asked, worried about him being back in a place that obviously held so many bad memories for him.

"I don't have a choice, do I?" he said, glancing up at her.

"No, you need to be there for your family," Erin said, touching his cheek. "But please remember that your responsibility only goes so far," she said sternly. "Your father makes his own choices about drinking. You've fought your demons and won—it's up to him to fight his own."

Kevin looked at her for a long moment, then reached up to

184

touch her cheek. He pulled her down to him, kissing her softly—his way of thanking her for her words of encouragement. She stayed with him that night, and drove him to the airport the next morning.

At the gate, he turned to her, handing her his keys.

"Do me a favor," he said, leaning down to kiss her. "Take care of my place while I'm gone, okay?"

Erin nodded. "No problem."

She reached up and hugged him. He hugged her tight, then turned and walked toward the gate. Erin waited for the plane to take off, then went home to get ready for work.

It was two days before she heard from him the first time. He called her at 9:30 p.m.

"Erin, it's me," he said, sounding very tired.

"Kevin, how are you?" she asked softly, lying back down on her bed, careful not to wake Steven up.

"I'm okay," he said dully.

"How's your dad?"

"He's doing alright. He has a couple of broken bones and a strained ankle, so they're keeping him in for a while."

"How's your sister doing? Is she okay?"

"She's a little freaked out. But she's really sure I can fix everything," he said, sarcastically cheerful.

"Oh, Kevin…" Erin said, feeling for him. "Just do what you can do. They can't expect you to fix someone else's mistakes."

"Can't they?"

"No, they can't," Erin said stubbornly. "Even if they want to."

Kevin found himself grinning for the first time since he'd gotten to Seattle.

185

"No, huh?"

"No," Erin said, still sounding petulant.

Kevin nodded, turning over on his side as he lay in his bed. He stared out the window unseeing as they continued to talk. She told him about the mail he'd gotten in the last two days, making him laugh a few times when she told him how excited he should be that he "could already be a ten million dollar winner!" They talked for almost an hour. They hung up with her asking him if he'd had any sleep.

"Not quite yet," he said. "But I'll work on it and get back to you."

"Try to get some sleep, Kev, please?" she pleaded gently.

He smiled at her shortening of his name, and felt warmed by her concern. Once again, something he wasn't used to having bestowed on him.

"I'll try," he said. "I promise."

"Thank you," she said, smiling.

"Don't thank me yet, I haven't accomplished it."

"You promised me you'd try," she said, sounding like a mother. "And trust you to manage it."

He laughed softly, imagining easily the wink that had accompanied that comment. "I will, babe."

"Okay," she said, biting her lip. "Goodnight, Kevin."

"Goodnight," he replied softly.

They hung up, and Kevin lay in his bed feeling lonely all of a sudden. God, was he that addicted to her? At that moment he longed to pull her body close to his and revel in her warmth. He lay there thinking about how crazy it was that he wanted so much when it came to her.

His musings were interrupted by a light knock on his door.

"Yeah?" he called out.

"Kevin?" came Sam's tentative voice.

"Come on in, Sam."

She opened the door and poked her head in.

"Who were you talking to?" she asked, the usual nosey sixteen-year-old little sister.

Kevin looked at her for a long moment, wondering if he should even comment on the fact that she'd obviously been eavesdropping. Finally he let out a sigh, shaking his head. No point, she wouldn't care anyway.

"My girlfriend," he said, liking the way that sounded. "Why?"

Sam shrugged. "I was just curious." She grinned. "Is she pretty?"

Kevin stared back at her, having forgotten what it was like to be questioned by his little sister about everything. He'd left home when she was only seven, but even then, she'd been curious about everything. Every time he'd come home for holidays or whatever, she'd question him about everything under the sun.

"She's pretty."

"Is she a blonde?" Sam asked, sure that every female in California was.

"As a matter of fact she is," Kevin said, grinning. "With beautiful blue eyes too."

Sam moved to sit down on the bed, and Kevin gave up hope of being able to sleep for a while.

"What's her name?" Samantha asked.

"Her name is Erin."

"Erin?" Samantha echoed. "Not Butch or Slick?"

Kevin narrowed his eyes at her. "No, it's Erin."

187

Sam nodded. "So she have like every tattoo known to man?"

"She doesn't have any," he said, realizing what she was thinking now. "This girl's actually normal, Sam. No tatts, no piercings, except her ears. Normal-colored hair, wears normal clothes, has a job…" He trailed off as if to indicate the many wonders of having a job.

Sam stared at him for a full two minutes. She was obviously stunned.

"You mean, you're dating a *normal* girl?" she asked in an awed whisper.

"Yeah," he said, grinning. "Go figure."

"Oh my God, I can't believe it!" she said, laughing. Then she looked at him seriously. "Is she nice?"

"She's very nice," Kevin said, grimacing. "Probably too nice for the likes of me."

"Well, maybe she can make you nice too."

Kevin looked at her for a long moment. He knew his little sister hadn't meant it the way it sounded, but he was thinking about what she'd said all the same. Could Erin make him into more of a human being? For so many years now he'd felt totally disconnected from the rest of the populace. Cut off from people for various reasons—his drinking, his subsequent need to get sober, his temper, his constant need for movement and stimulation, the ADD, everything. He'd never felt like a "normal" person, so he'd never attempted to connect with anyone "normal." It was something to think about.

Kevin ended up staying awake the whole night. Even after Samantha wandered off, having no concept of the thoughts she'd haphazardly triggered in his head. In therapy Kevin had learned to be brutally honest with himself about his faults and shortcomings. He'd learned to take responsibility for his own actions. He'd also learned to lay responsibility at the feet of the person it truly belonged to, rather than taking in all the blame, so as to become a victim.

Growing up, he'd had two older brothers and eventually two younger sisters. In the way of the classic middle-child syndrome, he was often forgotten, or treated as if he wasn't as important as the others. As the third boy, his mother didn't have the time to support him in activities as she had her brothers. And when Amy came along when he was five, she was the only girl, therefore the center of everyone's attention. Kevin was quickly pushed aside for a sight on "the new baby girl!" Kevin was starting Kindergarten at the time, and really needed attention to succeed. It was all, however, shifted to Amy. He learned to cope.

When Amy started Kindergarten, the fanfare in the household was not to be believed. There were all kinds of new teaching toys bought, time spent with her doing her "homework," everything. Kevin retreated further into oblivion. It was at that point that he started to feel extremely frustrated and angry a lot of the time. There were outbursts and angry tirades in school, at home, and with his friends. That was when Kevin discovered the "curative powers" of alcohol. It started with sips of his dad's beer. Then it progressed to stealing full cans of beer from his father and then from the local store. Eventually, by high school, he was drinking hard liquor. He'd found that it took more and more alcohol to give him that feeling of well-being, that feeling of numbness.

In school he found that he was always bored. He couldn't stand to listen to his teachers drone on and on about things he didn't care about. His mind would always drift, and he'd end up missing something. It became a vicious cycle of boredom, inattention, and a constant struggle to just skate by. Passing just enough tests, turning in just enough homework to keep from failing. It continued until he was lucky enough to get JoAnn Prose for a home room teacher. JoAnn was intuitive enough to see that something more than just laziness was going on with Kevin. She observed him for half a semester, and decided that something needed to be done.

She attempted to contact Jean and John Elmasian. Neither parent seemed eager to come in and talk to her. There were many made and missed appointments, and phone calls that were never returned. Finally, after months of trying, JoAnn got Jean Elmasian in her room for a meeting. She set about trying to explain what she felt was causing problems for Kevin.

"Mrs. Elmasian, I think I might know why Kevin is having so much trouble with school."

Jean looked back at the young teacher blankly. "What trouble?" she asked sharply. "What is it this time? What did he do?"

"Ma'am, it's not that kind of trouble," JoAnn was careful to tell her, sensing easily that this parent wasn't exactly eager. "Kevin is a very intelligent young man."

"He gets Cs and Ds," Jean snapped, her tone indicating that she didn't think Ms. Prose knew what she was talking about.

"Yes, ma'am, that's the trouble I was talking about," JoAnn said, trying to keep from sounding condescending. "While Kevin is very intelligent, he's not getting the grades he could be getting."

"What makes you think he's so smart?" Jean asked, sounding as if the teacher were insulting her personally.

"I had the opportunity to test his IQ. He received a rather high score," JoAnn said, still astounded by it.

"That's just mumbo jumbo crap," Jean said dismissively. "It doesn't mean anything in the real world."

"Ma'am," JoAnn said, struggling to maintain her patience, "Kevin's IQ is 140, well above average—145 is considered genius level."

"That boy isn't that smart," Jean insisted.

"Well, ma'am, he will only realize his full potential if he's given the tools to succeed. The problem is, I believe he has Attention Deficit Disorder."

"He's got what?" Jean asked, looking as if JoAnn had mentioned a communicable disease.

"His mind works much faster than most people's. It works so fast, in fact, that he has a hard time focusing on one thing at a time."

"I thought you said he was smart?" Jean said snidely.

"He is, ma'am. This has nothing to do with intelligence—actually, people with ADD tend to be much more intelligent. They get things faster than you or I might get them. He needs to learn how to train his mind to get around his disorder."

"So what's that got to do with me?" Jean asked, looking at her watch. She needed to be at Amy's school in twenty minutes to take her to ballet class.

"First of all, I'd like to have Kevin formally tested for ADD. If he has ADD, it will take work to help him overcome it and give him a better chance at being successful in the future."

"So do whatever work you have to do with him," Jean said, thinking that she could be done with this now.

"Ma'am, you don't understand," JoAnn said, noting the way Jean was checking her watch. "The work that will have to be done will require work on all of our parts. Kevin, myself, and you at home."

191

"I don't have time for that!" Jean exclaimed. "I have five children!"

"I understand that, ma'am, but if Kevin doesn't start working on this, he's going to just continue to have problems."

"He's just fine," Jean said. "Why are you trying to cause problems? With your tests and your theories. You're wasting my time here. Maybe you have the time to sit here and worry that my son can't concentrate. He's a teenager, for God's sake! Of course he doesn't concentrate. Haven't you ever heard of hormones, Ms. Prose?"

"I'm sorry, Mrs. Elmasian, but I think this is a lot more than just hormones. I'd like your permission to evaluate Kevin for ADD," Jo-Ann said, persevering regardless of Jean's attitude.

"Fine, do whatever you want. Waste more of your time, so you can find out that he's just an average kid who's busier thinking about cars and girls than he is school."

JoAnn Prose went about evaluating Kevin. With the help of the school psychologist, she determined that Kevin not only had ADD but he was also borderline hyperactive. She attempted to contact Jean Elmasian to tell her the results. She also wanted to recommend that Kevin be seen by a doctor to perhaps get on medications that would help him cope with the disorder. Jean Elmasian refused to be engaged in another "ridiculous conversation" about her middle son.

In the end, JoAnn did as much as she could for Kevin. She sat him down and explained to him how his mind worked. She explained why he got frustrated and angry when he didn't understand things immediately. She tried to give him tools to use to better cope with the problem.

Jean Elmasian, however, never bought into the idea that her son

192

needed any kind of help or treatment for a problem she was convinced didn't exist. The end result was Kevin's hasty exit from under his parents' roof as soon as he graduated high school.

Kevin stayed in touch with JoAnn, garnering more and more insight into how to handle his disorder. He eventually got a doctor's referral to a specialist, who helped him with medication and therapeutic exercises to help him better learn to focus.

There were times when he allowed what he called his "demons" to run wild and loose. His drinking continued and often played hell with his control. He flew into rages all too frequently, usually causing himself more harm than anyone else.

It had been those demons that had been fed by Stacy's dramatic personality. She fed and finally freed them to the point that he could no longer control them. That had been when he'd driven his 5.0 Mustang into a brick wall. He wanted, in his head, to kill his demons. He'd almost succeeded.

***

Joe had taken to watching the news at night, since he was home alone most evenings. Whereas he had never paid any attention to the "entertainment" section of the news, he now found himself watching it, in hopes of catching a glimpse of Jordan and getting a better idea of what she was up to. She was in a totally different time zone from him, almost the opposite of his, so they had a hard time connecting. He'd often get a heads up on where she was from the stories on TV.

This particular night, his interest was grabbed right out of the chute; he was caught by the "hook."

193

"Is Jordan Tate already moving on?" was the question the anchor person asked before they cut to a commercial.

Joe sat back on the couch, feeling the need for a cigarette suddenly. He waited through the intolerable commercials. He waited through three more news stories before they finally got to the entertainment news. And of course, he had to sit through the latest on J-Lo and Ben, Catherine Zeta-Jones and Michael Douglas' new baby, and even the updates on what rap singer Eminem had done. Then the picture of Jordan flashed on the screen. It was a promotional photo. The woman who did the entertainment news seemed to be looking right at him as she said, "Is Jordan Tate already moving on from her new man?" A picture of Jordan walking into a club with a dark-haired man flashed up on the screen. Joe's hand tightened on the arm of the couch. "Jordan Tate was seen with bad-boy rocker BJ Sparks at a London hot spot, coming in and leaving much later that night. Is her romance with millionaire Joseph Sinclair IV over already?" A picture of Jordan and Joe kissing on stage at her Paris concert flashed onto the screen. "Jordan has dated rocker BJ Sparks off and on for the last two years. Now that she's caused the divorce of Joe Sinclair, is she bored?" The woman smiled icily. "We'll just have to wait and see."

Joe stood up, walking over to the TV and shutting it off. He went into the kitchen, reached above the stove, and pulled out a bottle of tequila. He took it out onto the small back deck of the townhouse. He sat down on a lounge chair and started drinking.

His pager went off an hour later. It was Midnight. He ignored the message. His pager went off again. It was Kyle. He ignored that. It took an hour, but he heard a knocking on his door. He shook his head, looking up at the night sky. It was cold out and he had no jacket on, and he didn't care.

194

"What the fuck are you doing?" Midnight asked from the sliding glass door.

Joe shook his head. "You picking locks now, Night?"

"Just get up and get in the house, Sinclair. Don't make me come out there," she said calmly.

"Got a cigarette on you?" he asked, glancing back over his shoulder.

"No, but I have a baton I'm about to use on your head. Get in the house," Midnight replied sweetly.

Joe shook his head. "Worthless," he muttered, even as he staggered to his feet.

He found that there were a few people in the house. Christian, Stevie, Rick, Kyle, and Dave all stood or lounged against walls or furniture, waiting for him to walk back in.

"Someone forget to tell me it's my birthday or somethin'?" he asked, narrowing his eyes.

"You do know better than to believe the news, right?" Christian said, right off the bat.

"What news?" Joe asked insolently.

Christian narrowed his eyes at his cousin, but Stevie answered for him.

"The news that has you out there on your balcony drinking and working on pneumonia again."

"I was havin' a drink. I can still do that, right?"

Midnight held up the bottle of tequila, which was nearly empty. "*A* drink?"

"The bottle was close to empty."

"Yeah, right," Rick said. "That's why you're three sheets, right?"

195

"I'm only one sheet, thank you very much."

Midnight glanced at Rick. He looked back at her, shrugging. Joe seemed in decent spirits, but he'd been known to fake it before.

"You call yet?" Dave asked evenly.

"Why should I call?" Joe asked, looking surprised.

"So you could get some clarification," Kyle put in.

"Clarification of what? Whether or not she let her sheets cool from us before she fucked him?" The hurt was in his eyes, even when his voice was full of venom, and everyone felt it. "Whether or not it's been fucking him that's kept her from calling me lately? What should I fucking call her about, Dave?"

He stood looking for all intents and purposes perfectly controlled. That broke when Midnight walked up behind him, putting her arms around his waist and leaning her head into his back. Joe's cheek jumped as he gritted his teeth, not wanting to break down in front of his friends. Stevie walked over to him, reaching up to touch his cheek, smoothing the twitching muscle in his jaw. He stared up at the ceiling, not wanting to see the look in her eyes, the sympathy, the worry. Rick joined them, reaching out to put his hand on Joe's shoulder, openly hurting for his friend. Christian came to stand behind Stevie, putting his hands on her shoulders and looking at his cousin. Dave and Kyle walked over too. It was like a human shield they were making around him. The alcohol in his veins didn't allow him to fight their effect for long. He dropped his head, shaking it and blowing his breath out.

"Fuck it, let's get plowed," he said.

They ended up sitting around drinking with Joe. They talked and eventually joked about Joe's "face value" having gone up from being "just a cop" to a "millionaire" in the press.

196

"Yeah," Joe said. "That and three bucks'll buy me coffee at Star-bucks, right?"

Rick nodded. "But look at it this way—you'll be recognized at Starbucks now."

"Fuck…" Joe said, shaking his head.

"So, who's on the hit squad?" Midnight asked.

"No hit squad," Joe said soberly.

Midnight stared at him for a long moment. "They could be full of shit on the news, Joe. It wouldn't be the first time."

Joe shook his head. "She's dated Sparks before. She told me that much."

"So?" Midnight said. "They could be friends, you know."

"Yeah, right," Joe said, giving her a highly skeptical look. "Have you seen her? Have you seen him? Friends, yeah, right, sure, my ass." He tossed back another shot.

"Uh… Sinclair…" Rick said. "Hate to point this out, man, but take a look at my wife and then at you. You've slept together, but you're just friends now, right?"

"Well, tha's what we tell you," Joe said, grinning.

"Fuck you," Rick said, grinning too.

"No, that's something we don't tell Night."

"Gad!" Rick said, rolling his eyes. "Someone sober his ass up. He's nothing but trouble when he's fucked up."

"Joe?"

Everyone turned to see Randy standing in the doorway.

"Randy," Joe said, surprised to see her but too drunk to see the concern in her eyes.

He stood up as she walked over to him. Her eyes searched his.

197

He looked back at her, his eyes bleary. Randy glanced around at the rest of the group.

"Drinking party?" she asked.

"We're here to be supportive," Christian said, grinning.

"Yeah, supporting him killing his liver even further," Randy said, narrowing her eyes at him. She looked back up at Joe. "That story couldn't have been true, Joe," she said, reaching up to touch his cheek. "She loves you. I saw that much in the little amount of time I spent with her."

Joe nodded, looking very cynical.

"Call her, Joe," Randy said. "I'm betting she can explain what you saw. There wasn't anything inappropriate with her going to a night club. There was nothing incriminating at all, except for what that woman was assuming. Don't let them screw this up."

Joe looked down at her, then shook his head miserably. Randy reached out, putting her arms around him, hugging him. He held her close.

"I just don't want to be played here," he whispered against her hair.

"I know, Joe, I know," Randy said, pulling back to look at him. "But don't let the press play you either, okay? If you love her, ask her for the truth. Don't assume what you've seen is right. Okay?"

Joe nodded, looking unhappy.

The rest of the Gang called it a night then. Randy stayed to make sure Joe got to bed okay. After everyone else was gone, she ushered Joe to his room, pushing him down on the bed and reaching down to unlace his boots and take them off. She pulled the covers up over him.

She was closing everything up when the phone rang. Without thinking, she picked it up.

"Hello?"

There was a long silence, then the line clicked and went dead.

Randy shook her head and hung up. She left the house a little while later. She didn't see the photographer clicking away with his camera.

The next day, it was all over the news that Joe Sinclair was reconciling with his wife. Of course, in London, Jordan had already seen the story. She threw things, she screamed at anyone that bothered her. Then she started drinking, and the cocaine started again. She'd been clean for a long time, but the idea of Joe going back to his wife made her want to hide from the world again.

# CHAPTER 7

In the end, it was BJ Sparks who dragged Jordan out of her stupor.

"Are you fuckin' nuts?" he snapped, shoving her into a cold shower to sober her up.

"Yeah, nuts for falling in love with a married fucking man!" she screamed.

"Oh, bloody fucking hell, Jordie, you know that story about him reconciling with the wife was pure bullshit, just like that story about you and me that you tried to call him about."

"Yeah, and his fucking wife answered!" Jordan yelled.

BJ shook his head. "I'm not doin' this with you. When you're sober, we'll deal with it."

Two days later, BJ strong-armed her into a car, which took them to the airport. He then threatened her with great bodily harm if she didn't get on his private jet. She cussed and fought and scratched him to keep from going anywhere; he picked her up easily, since he outweighed her by at least a hundred pounds.

Once on the plane, she asked where they were going.

"California," BJ said. "You have some shit to work out. An' I ain't watchin' ya do it by putting half of fucking Colombia up your nose, so sit there and shut up till we land. Or I'll fuckin' gag your ass and toss you in a closet. You got me?"

Jordan knew better than to test Brenden James Sparks on one of his threats; he'd carried them out often enough. She seethed the entire trip. Brenden got up at one point and went to the bedroom section. He lay on the bed and made a call.

"Yeah," he said, his cockney accent quite clear. "I need to speak to one Midnight Chevalier-Debenshire, please. It's important."

"I'm sorry, sir, she's not in at the moment. Can I take a message?" asked the ever-efficient secretary.

"Yeah, can you tell her that BJ Sparks called. I need to talk to her about her friend." He reeled off his number. "Got that, love?"

"Uh, yes sir," the woman said hesitantly, not sure if this was a joke or not.

All the same, she gave Midnight the message when she got back from lunch with Rick, during which they'd discussed at length what to do about Joe.

"BJ Sparks?" Midnight asked Cassandra. "The BJ Sparks?"

"Yes, ma'am. That's what he said, and his accent sounded real, but I don't know for sure…"

Midnight shrugged. "Well, I'll give it a shot."

Walking into her office and closing the door, Midnight picked up her phone even as she pulled her gun out from the small of her back and put it in her desk drawer. She dialed the number as she closed the drawer with her hip. She leaned back in her chair.

"'Ello?" answered a very authentic-sounding English accent.

"Mr. Sparks?"

"That would be me, love," Brenden said, getting up from his seat and heading back to the bedroom, where he lay down on his bed again.

"I'm Midnight Chevalier. I believe you called me?" Midnight

201

said, still not totally sure this wasn't a joke.

"Chevalier? What happened to the Debenshire?" BJ asked. He was always getting hung up on details.

"That's my married name, Mr. Sparks. What can I do for you?"

"You're not married then?"

"Yes, Mr. Sparks, I'm married."

"Bloody hell," he said, grinning.

"What can I do for you, Mr. Sparks?" Midnight asked again, though she found herself grinning at his tone of voice.

"Well, I have a favor to ask."

"What would that be?"

"Well, I have myself a hostage," BJ said. "And I need to get her to America and put her in a locked room with your Joseph Michael Sinclair."

"Is that safe?" Midnight asked, amused at the way BJ Sparks spoke.

"Probably not. But if she doesn't find out that he still wants her, she'll end up back in rehab, and I'll have to dry her ass out again."

Midnight nodded. "When will you be here?"

"'Bout ten hours."

"That'd be around seven p.m. You got a pen?"

"Not likely," BJ said. "Give me the info—I'll memorize it."

"Okay—1296 La Jolla Village Drive."

"Is that your place?" BJ asked, grinning widely.

"That's Joe's place."

"Damn!" BJ said, chuckling.

"Have Jordan there at eight. I'll make sure Joe is present."

202

"You got it, love," BJ said. "Now tell me," he added, his tone dropping an octave, "are you as beautiful in person as you sound on the phone?"

"I wouldn't know, Mr. Sparks. I can't hear myself on the phone," Midnight said with a rakish grin.

"Ohh…" He groaned dramatically. "I'm hopin' I'll find out."

"Uh-huh," Midnight said. "Let's just work on Joe and Jordan for now, huh?"

"Can we work on us later?"

"Would that be before or after my husband shoots you, Mr. Sparks?"

"God, before, I hope," BJ said, laughing suggestively.

Midnight laughed too. He definitely didn't give up, did he?

"See you tonight," she said.

"Count on it."

\*\*\*

Later that night, Midnight sat in a chair in Joe's bedroom, watching him drink himself silly yet again.

"Don't you have somewhere to be?" he asked.

"I have lots of places to be," she replied tiredly.

"So go, be there," he said, flicking his hand toward the door.

"So you can drink yourself unconscious again?"

Joe looked back at her for a long moment. "Maybe because I want to be alone in my senility."

"Don't start that shit with me again, Sinclair," she said, narrowing her eyes dangerously. "Didn't someone like Jordan Tate being interested in you in the first place repair that fucking ego of yours?"

"I was a nice diversion, I'm sure," Joe said evenly.

"You were a lot more than a fucking diversion," Jordan said from the doorway.

Joe's head snapped up, even as Midnight got to her feet. Joe's eyes touched on Jordan, then skipped to the man standing behind her. BJ Sparks. Joe's eyes widened, and he started to stand.

"Oh, hell no!" Midnight said, putting her hand out, pushing him back down.

Joe and Jordan stared at each other.

BJ winked at Midnight and said, "Let's leave these two alone, huh?"

Midnight glanced at Joe, noting that the fight had left his mind.

BJ stood in the doorway, holding his hand out to Midnight in invitation. "Come along, love," he said, smiling wickedly.

Midnight shook her head, grinning all the same, and walked to the door. She had to push Jordan gently toward the bed where Joe sat, and then closed the door behind her.

Midnight and BJ went out to the living room. Midnight sat down on the couch, watching BJ as he prowled around the room. He was definitely a compelling figure, with his long dark brown hair, shot through with rich auburn highlights. He was tall, taller than Joe, standing about six foot three or four. He had a build similar to Joe's, but a bit more lean. His eyes were his major selling point; they were a light green, with a hint of blue making them almost aqua in color. He was dressed in black leather pants that looked so soft as they moved with him, black rocker-style boots with a slight heel, a long leather coat that fell to mid-calf, and a jade green shirt that opened at the neck to reveal a gold chain with a gothic-looking cross hanging from it. His face was handsome, with a rakish, thin goatee and smooth, tanned skin. His teeth were movie star perfect, and his smile could melt even the coldest woman's heart. He was definitely an attractive man. On top of his looks, he had a kind of animal magnetism that just emanated from him. As if that weren't enough, he had a voice that could make angels green with envy. His tone was so clear and perfect, even as a rocker, that he'd received critical acclaim.

Midnight's cat-like green eyes tracked him, even as her face remained passive.

"So, where's the husband tonight?" he asked, turning to look at her.

"He's at work."

"And did I hear right—you're the actual Chief of Police?"

"You heard right."

"How does one become a Chief of Police?" BJ asked, sitting down next to her on the couch, stretching his long legs out in front of him.

"You interested in changing careers, Mr. Sparks?" Midnight asked, raising an eyebrow at him.

He grinned engagingly. "Tell you what," he said, his voice lowered an octave. "You can call me Brenden if I can call you."

"Is that what the *B* stands for?" Midnight asked, a smile playing at her lips.

"Brenden James."

"Ahh…" Midnight said, nodding.

205

"So, can I?" he asked smoothly.

"Can you what?" she asked, a grin playing at her lips.

BJ smiled brilliantly, and there was no telling what he was asking her. "Oh, I can think of a number of things I'd like to do with you," he said, staring directly into her eyes.

"Do I even want to ask what?" Midnight asked.

"I do," came another English-accented voice.

Midnight glanced up to see Rick standing in the front doorway.

BJ didn't even bother to glance back. He simply continued to stare at Midnight, his eyes taking on a look of almost pure evil. In them, Midnight could see Christian Collins for a moment. And she knew he was about to bait Rick.

"Oh Lord..." Midnight said under her breath as Rick walked over to her.

She glanced up. His eyes were on BJ, and the look in them didn't resemble anything friendly.

"Rick..." Midnight began.

"You're the husband," BJ said, his stare appraising.

"Yeah, I'm the husband," Rick replied, his eyes narrowing slightly.

BJ nodded, looking back over at Midnight. "You favor Brits, eh?"

Midnight didn't answer. She was too busy trying to think of a way to defuse the fight she could feel brewing in Rick.

"Just this one," Rick replied for her.

"S'okay, man, I'm Irish," BJ said blithely. "Maybe she's ready to change sides."

Midnight saw Rick's eyes narrow dangerously, and she stood up.

"Okay, boys," she said, glancing back at BJ. "Let's drop the testosterone levels a bit here and relax, okay? Brenden, don't overestimate my husband's tolerance for flirtatious rock stars. It's about nil."

BJ grinned. She'd called him Brenden. "S'okay, beautiful. I've taken on bigger and better."

"Jesus…" Midnight said, jumping out of the way as Rick stepped forward to test that out. She grabbed his arm, pulling him back. He hissed in pain.

"What?" she said, concern instantly in her voice.

"Nothin'," Rick said, determined to beat the shit out of BJ Sparks.

"Bullshit, nothing!" Midnight said, getting in front of him and pushing him back, grabbing his hand and shoving his jean jacket off his shoulders.

"Night!" he growled. "Leave it."

"Richard, don't piss me off here," she snapped as she caught sight of the bandage on his arm, which already had his blood soaking through it. "What happened?" she breathed.

"We had a raid. Some kid tried to skip," Rick said offhandedly.

"And you stopped him with your arm on his knife?" Midnight asked, touching the bandage carefully.

He hissed as she pulled the tape away to look at the cut. "It's alright," he said irritably.

"Yeah, I can see that," Midnight said, giving him a vile look. "You need stitches in this, babe."

"I don't need stitches, Night, I'm fine."

"Don't make me put you on report, Lieutenant," Midnight said seriously.

207

"Do it," Rick said, his blue eyes looking down at her.

"You know," she said, reaching up to kiss him softly, "you take all the fun out of being chief."

"I've heard that," Rick said, grinning.

Brenden had watched with interest. He noted how quickly he was forgotten in the face of her man being hurt. He grinned to himself. He'd been told by Jordan about the legendary Debenshire love affair; now he'd witnessed it first-hand. His ego took a hit, but he gained a great deal of respect for Rick Debenshire in that moment. Rick obviously had something that his wife loved, and she obviously had something that Rick was willing to fight anyone to keep for himself. It was a rather interesting combination.

Brenden couldn't take his eyes off the two as they talked. He watched as Rick reached up and re-taped the bandage on his arm, pulling his jacket back on. Midnight turned around, obviously having remembered Brenden in that time. Rick's uninjured arm snaked around her waist, pulling her back against him possessively, his deep blue eyes reflecting supreme confidence in his hold on her. Brenden stood up, his eyes alighting on Midnight again, his look almost regretful. His eyes connected with Rick's then—connected and held for a long moment. Then Brenden inclined his head in deference to Rick's position. Rick nodded slowly, accepting Brenden's unspoken surrender.

"Think they've made up yet?" Midnight asked, nodding toward Joe's bedroom.

"I haven't heard any breaking glass," Brenden said, grinning.

"That's always a good sign," Rick put in.

"Should we check?" Midnight asked.

Brenden glanced back at the closed bedroom door, then shook

208

his head. "Nah, I'm sure they're just fine." He turned back to Rick and Midnight. "So where's a decent place to get a steak around here?"

Midnight laughed. "Well, we could take you to dinner, but that would require at least one autograph for our daughter."

"You don't want one?" Brenden asked, winking at Midnight. "I'm crushed."

"Sorry," Midnight said, shaking her head sadly. "The boys listen to you, but I really don't know all that much other than the fact that you're considered rock's biggest bad boy, and that you win Grammys a lot."

"You know that, eh?" Brenden asked, grinning.

"My daughter goes on and on about you and Jordan, and Billy and the Kid, and so on and so forth."

"Yadda, yadda, yadda," Brenden said. "Okay, take me to dinner and I'll buy. Hell, how old's your daughter?"

"Not old enough," Rick said, but his grin spoiled the attitude he was trying to convey.

"Well, bring her along anyway. It would be nice to have one person who appreciates me at dinner."

Midnight laughed, shaking her head. "Come on then," she said, motioning for Brenden to precede her and Rick.

Jordan stood looking at Joe after Midnight closed the door behind her. She found that she actually ached at seeing him again. He still looked incredible, but the cynical disgust in his eyes burned her to the core.

"You've been drinking," she said. It wasn't a question.

Joe nodded, his light blue eyes narrowing slightly. He could see

209

she'd been indulging too. She wore no makeup and she had dark circles under her eyes. She also looked like she'd lost weight.

"A lot?" she asked.

"Enough."

Jordan nodded, shifting her eyes to the bedspread instead of looking at him.

"So, when did you and Randy start seeing each other again?" she asked, trying to keep the hurt out of her voice.

Her eyes narrowed at the spot on the bed she was staring at in her effort to keep from trembling. She didn't really want to hear the answer, but she knew she needed to hear it so she could get past it and him.

Joe nodded, the look on his face saying, *I knew it*. "We didn't."

Her eyes went to his then. "Bullshit, Joe. She was here. I know it."

"When?"

"What?" she said, surprised by the simple question.

"When was she here that you *know* of?"

"The night the story broke about me and Bren."

"You and Bren, huh?" Joe said sardonically.

"That's not what I meant," Jordan said. "Don't change the damned subject, Joe. Randy was here. You can't deny that—I fucking heard her!"

"Heard her?" Joe asked, looking doubtful.

"I called to explain about being out with Bren, and she answered," Jordan said, her look triumphant at having caught him.

Joe gave a short laugh. "Yeah? And if you'd called about a half hour earlier you could have gotten Night, or Rick, or Dave, or Steve,

210

or Christian, or even Kyle, since they were all here too."

"Why?" Jordan asked, the steam going out of her.

"Oh, I dunno," he said. "Maybe to console me about my girl-friend fucking some rock star on international TV."

Jordan was taken aback by his vicious tone, never having actually seen Joe mad before. She wasn't used to it.

"I wasn't dating him," she said.

"Then why were you out with him?"

"He's one of my best friends, Joe."

"Really?" he asked, not sounding convinced. "Seems to me that you told me you dated him at one point."

"Yeah?" Jordan said, putting her hands on her hips. "Seems to me that you used to fuck Midnight Chevalier too, but you don't see me going off on you when you hang out with her, do you?"

Joe stared at her in silence. He didn't like the way she'd put it, but he couldn't argue with her either. Not many women would understand his relationship with Midnight, the fact that they'd been lovers for years, then best friends with nothing sexual between them. It was a rather odd relationship. Yet Jordan had never questioned it; she'd accepted it, and never once hassled him about it.

He closed his eyes for a long moment, breathing a frustrated sigh. He'd let his emotions take over, and he'd been wrong. He'd believed a story on the news, rather than asking her for the truth. How stupid was he? Then again, she'd obviously believed the story about him reconciling with Randy without asking him about it. So she wasn't blameless here either.

"Why didn't you talk to me about Randy?" he asked, his voice devoid of accusation now. He sounded defeated.

211

Jordan looked at him for a long moment, then shook her head slowly.

"I didn't think I could handle you telling me you were going back to her."

"I'm not going back to her," he said softly.

Jordan dropped her head, shaking it miserably. She was terrified that she'd already made too many mistakes and that they couldn't go back now. That thought had tears forming behind her eyes. She kept her head down, not wanting him to see her tears. Bad enough she'd fucked this relationship up; she didn't need to lose her pride now too.

She didn't hear him get off the bed. Suddenly he was there, standing in front of her, his hands on her shoulders, pulling her to him. She put her arms around his waist, burying her face against his shoulder. His arms went around her, holding her. She felt his lips against her head, his hands stroking her back and her hair.

"I'm sorry, Joe. I'm sorry," she said tearfully.

"I'm sorry too, babe," he said, shaking his head. "I guess I just don't know how to handle anything I can't control."

He moved to sit down on the bed, pulling her down on his lap, still holding her. She shifted back to look at him. She searched his eyes, wondering if he'd heard about her drug use. It was something she knew he wouldn't put up with, and she was sure it would end everything. But if she didn't tell him, and he found out later, it would be worse.

"Joe…" she began, not sure how to tell him. "Look, when I thought… well, when I thought you were going back to her, I couldn't deal with it. I couldn't breathe, and I just… I got weak."

Joe looked down at her, his chin coming up a notch as he sensed she was about to tell him something he didn't want to hear. "What

212

did you do?"

Jordan pressed her lips together in apprehension. She wasn't sure how he was going to react.

"I started using again," she said, her eyes dropping from his.

His finger at her jawline brought her eyes back up. "You what?" he asked, as if hoping he hadn't heard right.

She closed her eyes for a second, then looked at him again. "I started using cocaine again."

"Jesus…" Joe said, his expression letting her know she hadn't been wrong about his reaction.

"I know, I know," she said, trying to think of anything she could say to make it better.

"No, Jordan," Joe said, his look very serious. "You don't know." He shook his head, his eyes going to the ceiling. "Jesus, I'm a cop, Jordan. I'm a goddamned captain of vice, over the narcotics unit…" His voice trailed off as he shook his head again. "We bust people for using." He ran a hand through his hair in agitation.

"I know," Jordan said, biting her lip, her gold eyes staring up at him.

They were silent for a long time, during which Jordan moved off his lap, sitting next to him. She didn't know what to say. She had a feeling neither did he. He looked over at her.

"Were you using when we were together before?"

"No!" she exclaimed. "Joe," she said, calming her voice again, "when I met you, I had been clean for almost a year, but even then I thought about it a lot." She reached out, touching his hand, touching the ring she'd bought him. "When I was with you, I didn't drink. I didn't want to. I didn't think about coke either. I just thought about

213

being with you."

Joe nodded, waiting for her to continue.

She sighed. "I just..." she hesitated, searching for the words to fix this. "I got weak. I saw that story about you and Randy and I just gave up. I started drinking, and one night someone offered me a line of cocaine and I said no. But then I thought about it, and thought, who was I being clean for? So I did it. I wanted to be numb, Joe. I wanted to be mindless." Her eyes pleaded with him to understand.

He did understand needing to be numb; he'd been self-medicating for days. But the cocaine, the need for a drug, he didn't understand. And he couldn't deal with her doing that either. It went against everything he'd been fighting against for years.

He shook his head. "Jordan," he began, his tone so full of resolution she knew what he was going to say before he said it. "This just isn't going to work. It's just going to be a constant series of misunderstandings and being alone for both of us." His eyes met hers. "It's not your fault, really, but I'm pretty used to my lady being around a lot. This is just... I don't know..." He shook his head again, looking miserable.

"Joe, please," she said, her voice trembling. "Please. We can make this work—we just have to come to an understanding." She put her hand to his cheek, turning his face to hers. "I love you. I don't want to lose you. Please." She was abandoning her pride now. This meant too much to her to hide behind it. "I need you, Joe. I need to be with you. I'll do whatever it takes, whatever you want. Please?"

There were tears in her eyes then, and Joe's resolve crumbled, even if temporarily as he took her in his arms again. He held her until her tears subsided. She lifted her face to his, her gold eyes dark with emotion.

"I don't want to lose you," she said, her voice stronger now. "I won't lose you."

Joe's light blue eyes searched hers, but he didn't say anything. Jordan didn't know if he still meant to leave her, but she meant what she'd said. She had no intention of losing him.

\*\*\*

After five days in Seattle, Kevin finally felt like he was getting a handle on things. He'd convinced his mother that his father had indeed had more than "a couple of beers" before driving. He'd spoken to the investigating officer, a former colleague of his. The officer suggested that Kevin have his father prepared to go to counseling and rehab. Kevin also got in contact with a lawyer, who said that John Elmasian would have an easier time of it considering he hadn't injured anyone else or caused very much property damage. He'd hit a tree and damaged some guard rail.

When he talked to Erin that fifth night, he told her he planned to go over and see Emily the following day.

"That's great," Erin said, smiling at how enthusiastic he sounded.

"Yeah," he said. "The only problem is, Stacy's being difficult about letting me take her out alone."

"Is that going to be a big problem?"

"Stacy likes to be center stage."

"Oh," Erin said. "That's why she wants you to stay there with Emily."

215

"Yeah," he said, shrugging. "I'm used to dealing with her attitude though."

"Then you already know how to handle her, right?"

"Yeah. So what's up with you down there?

Erin grinned. "You mean other than freezing my butt off?"

"Why?"

"Oh, the heater in the house quit. The landlord is out of town, so we have to wait to get it fixed."

"Is it still really cold there?"

"It's been chilly. We've all been walking around in socks, sweatpants, and sweatshirt and or sweaters."

"Babe," Kevin said, leaning back against the headboard, blowing out cigar smoke. "Why don't you and Steven just go stay at my place?"

"It's okay," she said, not wanting to impose on him.

"Erin, if Steven gets sick, you'll be next. You know how many kids are coming down with colds at his school. Just go to my place. Hell, I'm heating it and I'm not even there. So go make it worth my money."

She sighed. "Are you sure?" she asked, not wanting him to know how excited she was at the prospect of being warm again. Not to mention the fact that she'd get to sleep in his bed, where she knew she'd feel close to him.

"I'm sure. Pack up some stuff and take Steven over there."

"Okay," she said, smiling. "Thank you."

"No problem."

"I miss you," she said then, voicing what she'd been thinking a minute ago.

"I miss you too, babe," he said, honestly feeling it. "So you gonna go over tonight?"

"Yes, if you're really sure."

"For God's sake, Erin, don't make me come down there and move you myself."

She laughed softly. "Okay, okay, I will. I promise."

Kevin could hear the smile in her voice. He'd found that he thoroughly enjoyed doing things for her. He liked making her happy. It made him feel so good to hear her sigh happily, or laugh. It wasn't something he'd ever cared to do for anyone else. He knew it was because he'd never been with someone who honestly appreciated the things he did. Erin did, and she showed him that, and he reveled in the feeling.

That night, Erin fell asleep happily holding on to his pillow, her face buried in it. His cologne was still on it, and she could imagine he was there holding her. Later, Steven crawled into the big bed with her, putting his face into Kevin's pillow. It was obvious her son missed him too. She smiled wistfully and thanked whatever fates had brought Kevin Elmasian into their lives.

After a day and a half of not hearing from Kevin, Erin was worried. She'd expected him to call after his visit with Emily, but he didn't. Her mind started imagining any number of things that could have happened. What if he'd had an accident? He'd told her about patches of black ice that had sent him skidding a couple of times already. What if he'd gotten sick, or hurt, or something else? What if his father had taken a turn for the worse? She worried all day long and that night when he didn't call. The next day she started trying to call him.

She dialed his cell phone number and got his voice mail. She left message after message. He never called back.

That night she got a call, and was relieved when she saw Kevin's cell number on her screen.

"Hello?" she said.

There was silence for a long few moments, then a hesitant voice. "Is this Erin?" It was a young woman.

"Yes," Erin said, her worry stepping up again. "Who is this?"

"This is Samantha. I'm Kevin's sister."

"Samantha," Erin said, trying to tamp down on her nervousness. "Where's Kevin?"

"He's here," Samantha said, not sounding very confident. "I'm scared for him."

"Why, Samantha? What happened?" Erin asked, closing her eyes for a moment, almost afraid to hear the answer.

"I don't know. He came home yesterday. There was blood on his shirt. He went to his room and hasn't come out. He won't talk to me."

"Oh God…" Erin breathed. "Can you take the phone to him? Tell him I want to talk to him."

"Okay," Samantha said, sounding relieved.

Erin heard Samantha knock on a door. She heard Kevin's muffled voice saying, "Sam, go away."

"Erin's on the phone, Kevin!" Samantha called. "She wants to talk to you."

Erin heard the door snatched open.

"What are you doing with my cell phone, Sam?" Kevin practically snarled.

"Erin wants to talk to you," Samantha said stubbornly.

"How did you get ahold of her?"

"You left your phone on the counter—I used your call list."

Erin heard a thud and a yelp of fear, then silence and a muffled sound of the phone being moved around.

"Hello?" she queried, not sure what had happened.

"I'm here," Kevin said, his voice lifeless.

"What did you do?" Erin asked worriedly.

"I didn't hit her, if that's what you're thinking," he said as he lay back down on the bed.

"What did you hit?"

"The wall."

"Does your hand hurt now?"

Kevin looked down at his hand, flexing his fingers and noting the blood on his knuckles. "A little."

"Kevin, what happened?"

Kevin shook his head and remained silent.

"Kev," Erin said softly. "Please talk to me."

"I just…"

"Okay, just tell me how you're feeling right now."

"Awful, mad as hell…"

"Okay. Are you feeling like you want to drink?" Erin knew she was pushing it, but she wanted to know.

"Yeah," he said, swallowing against the lump in his throat, sounding so dejected it made Erin wince.

In truth, he felt so weak, he was ashamed. It was why he'd avoided her for the last two days.

219

"Okay," Erin said. "Tell me what I can do, Kevin. I don't want you to drink."

Again, he shook his head and was silent.

"Kevin?"

"Yeah?"

"Tell me something," she said, her tone changing. "When you went through rehab, when you were getting sober, it was pretty awful, wasn't it?"

"Yeah…" he said, not sure what she was getting at.

"Did you go through rehab in a hospital or a center?"

"Hospital," he replied, still hesitant.

"Okay, so what was the place like?"

"Cold and sterile."

"Sterile?" Erin echoed. "Like clean? Did they use a lot of cleaning stuff?" she asked as she got up from his bed and walked toward the kitchen.

Kevin took a long few moments to answer. "Yeah, I guess. Why?"

"Well, what did they use? Pine-sol, Lysol… bleach?"

She'd looked under his kitchen sink, where she saw the first two. Then she'd walked into his laundry room. He didn't have bleach.

"Yeah, bleach. Why?" he asked again, sounding irritable now.

"Does your mom have bleach there?" she asked, praying he wouldn't lose patience with her and hang up.

"I have no idea."

"Tell you what," Erin said. "Go to her laundry room and see. If she does, open it and smell it."

220

"Smell it?"

"Trust me."

Kevin sighed loudly, putting down the phone and doing as she asked. Erin waited, holding her breath. She'd just started to worry that he wasn't going to come back when she heard him pick up the phone again.

"Kevin?"

"You win," he said grimly.

"Are you okay?"

"Yeah," he said, shuddering. "Effective deterrent, babe."

"I figured the smell might bug you, if it's one that you associate with that difficult time in your life."

"I never even realized that was why I hate bleach so much," he said, shaking his head in wonder.

"The sense of smell is the fastest and strongest memory trigger."

"I guess…" Kevin said, agreeing with her totally.

"So you ready to tell me what happened yet?" she asked gently.

Kevin sighed. "It's just drama, babe."

"Go ahead and tell me. I missed my soaps this week," she said with a wink in her voice.

Kevin laughed softly, already feeling better.

He went on to tell her about the incident with Stacy. Stacy had lost her temper when he'd commented about the apartment she had Emily living in. He sent her five to seven hundred dollars a month for child support; he wasn't seeing that the money was being used effectively. Stacy had flown into a rage, picking up a crystal ashtray and throwing it at him. A sharp corner, already broken before she'd thrown it, caught him on the neck. She'd gone after him with her

221

nails then, clawing his neck further and drawing blood. It hadn't been a good visit. Fortunately, he hadn't made the mistake of making the comments in front of Emily; she'd been down for her nap at that point. He'd left right after that.

Erin and he ended up spending the next six hours talking. He told her a lot about his childhood, and about being diagnosed with ADD. She was very unhappy to hear about how his mother had treated him. She also began to see why he was so emotionally closed off with many of the people in his life. By the end of the call, Erin felt like she knew him so much better, that she understood him so much better than she had before. Kevin lay in his bed in Seattle wishing like hell he was home in his bed with her.

The following evening Erin was a little bit worried when he didn't call, but figured she'd wait until the next day to phone him again. She didn't want to drive him crazy with her constant need to know he was okay. It was fairly obvious that he wasn't used to so much "mothering," and she didn't want to get him to the point of telling her to back the hell off. All the same, she went to bed that night feeling a knot in her stomach. What if he'd been lying to her about being okay? What if he'd started drinking? She tossed and turned for two hours before falling asleep.

The smell of smoke reached her first. She came awake with a start, but suddenly she realized what she was smelling was cigar smoke. Turning over to look at the clock, she saw him there. Steven's night light was on in the hallway, so she could see him clearly—standing by the window, the fan on, blowing the smoke out of the room. He was leaning against the wall, his face turned in her direction.

"Kevin?" she said hesitantly.

"Yeah?" he answered, as if he'd been home this whole time.

She sat up, unknowingly looking extremely attractive to him, all tousled from sleep with his Quiksilver shirt on. "Is everything okay?"

He nodded. "Everything is fine. I needed to get home."

"What about Sam? Is your mom home from the hospital? Is your dad out?"

Kevin grinned. Erin couldn't help but worry about everything. "Sam's here—I put her in the third bedroom. Speaking of which, be careful—you have a little person beside you," he said, nodding toward the bed.

Erin glanced to her side. Sure enough, Steven had crawled into bed with her again.

"I didn't even feel him get in," she said, shaking her head. She looked back at Kevin. "When did you get home?"

"About two hours ago," he said, taking a long drag on his cigar.

She grimaced. "And here we are hogging your bed."

Kevin canted his head to the side. "I like the way you look in my bed."

Erin smiled, liking the way he said that.

Turning, he stubbed out his cigar, and lit another one as he sat down on the chair next to the window. He started to unlace his boots. Erin watched him, then glanced down at Steven. She got up and picked him up to take him back into the second bedroom.

By the time she got back, Kevin had stood up and was unbuttoning his shirt, his cigar having been put out again. She walked over to stand in front of him, her eyes going to the still bloody scratches and cut on his neck. She touched them gently, then looked at him.

223

He was watching her, and his hand came up to touch her cheek. Leaning down, he kissed her, his lips moving over hers with reined-in hunger. Her hands went to the back of his head as she kissed him back, pressing closer to him.

Within moments the heat caught between them. His shirt was on the floor and his hands were working on taking off hers when there was a knock on the door. Kevin made an irritated growl in the back of his throat as he pulled his head away.

"What?" he snapped.

Samantha opened the door.

"Did I say come in?" Kevin growled.

"I… no," Sam said, looking down for a moment. Then she glanced up at Erin. "Hi. You must be Erin."

"Hi, Samantha," Erin said, smiling warmly to try and take the bite out of Kevin's words.

"What do you need?" Kevin asked, a little less irritated, having seen Erin's smile.

"I was going to take a shower before I went to bed," Samantha said. "I didn't know where to find towels."

"Hall closet," Kevin said simply.

"Okay."

"Goodnight," Kevin said pointedly.

"Goodnight," Sam said, looking at Erin again. "Nice to meet you. Kevin was right about you."

"Right about me?" Erin couldn't resist asking.

Samantha nodded, glancing at Kevin to see him narrow his eyes at her. "He said you were beautiful and that you were very nice."

Erin smiled, glancing up at Kevin. He looked down at her and saw the smile. Then he turned back to Samantha. "We'll see you in the morning, Sam," he said, his tone much nicer this time.

"Okay. Goodnight, Kev," Sam said, smiling as she turned to leave the room.

Once the door was closed, Kevin pulled Erin closer again, reaching up to take the shirt off once and for all, tossing it aside. Erin grinned at the look he gave her. They made love then, and lay together afterward, talking.

"I've been thinking…" Kevin began, glancing down at her and catching the look of worry that came into her eyes. "What?"

"What?" she echoed.

"What was that look about?" he asked, his eyes searching hers.

Erin didn't answer, not sure what to say. Yes, she'd instantly been worried that he was going to say something like, *We shouldn't spend so much time together.*

"Erin," he said seriously. "I'm not Donovan or Tyler, okay? I'm not going to automatically disappoint you at every turn."

Erin nodded. "I'm sorry."

"Anyway," he said, giving her a pointed look. "Like I was saying, I've been thinking." He put his hand to her cheek, leaning forward to kiss her, then pulled back to look at her. "I want you and Steven to move in here with me."

Erin didn't say anything for a moment, her heart was too busy doing cartwheels. "Really?" she finally eked out.

He grinned. "Yeah, really. I want you here when I get home. I want you here in my bed with me when we sleep. I just want you."

Erin bit her lip, her eyes shining brightly in the semi-darkness of the room. "Okay," she said simply, her eyes speaking volumes

225

more.

"Can you move in today?"

"I think I better give my roommates some notice," she said gently, not wanting to disappoint him but wanting to be fair to them too.

"I'll pay your share of the rent for the next two months," he said, having thought about that already.

"Kevin…" she said, appreciating the fact that he wanted her that soon but not wanting to take advantage of him.

"Please, Erin? I want you here."

She smiled. "And I want to be here too."

He grinned. "So quit arguing with me."

"Okay, okay, you win," she said, biting her lip again. "I missed you so much."

"I missed you too," he said, leaning down to kiss her.

They fell asleep, both of them feeling content.

# CHAPTER 8

It had been two weeks since their reconciliation of sorts. Jordan had gone back to her tour the morning after their argument, but Joe still felt like everything was up in the air. They'd talked on the phone a few times, both of them feeling strained.

Jordan's European tour was going to end in two weeks. Joe looked at his calendar that morning, taking that in and wondering if she'd come to the States or just go back to London.

That was the day he saw the first poster. It was flashy with lots of color and metallics. The header read, *The Concert to bring UP the House!* It went on to list the headliners: BJ Sparks, Billy and the Kid, and Jordan Tate. The date was three weeks away, and all proceeds would benefit Sinclair House. Joe stared at the poster for a full five minutes. Then he made his way over to Sinclair House, looking for Randy.

She came up to the front, with a smudge of blue finger paint on her cheek. Joe grinned, reaching up to rub at the spot with his thumb. Randy glanced at his thumb when he pulled it back, and laughed. They walked outside, sitting down on the porch swing.

"So, did you know about this concert?" he asked.

Randy nodded. "Jordan called me last week."

"Any reason she didn't tell me?"

Randy looked at him for a long moment. "She's not sure what's happening between you two, Joe. She's afraid she's losing you. But I'll warn you—she's determined not to."

Joe pursed his lips, not sure how he felt about that. "She was using again, Randy."

Randy nodded; Jordan had told her that part too. "Is it really that big a deal?"

Joe looked at her like she was crazy. "I'm a cop. Have you forgotten that?"

Randy gave him a look that said, *Duh*. "No, Joe, I haven't forgotten that, but have you forgotten that you're only a cop here? And have you forgotten that people make mistakes?"

He narrowed his eyes at her. It was obvious she had been talking to Jordan. "How would that look, Randy? My girlfriend is a coke user? Think that's going to help the department out?"

"First of all," Randy said, "I don't think it's your sole responsibility to support the department's image. Secondly, I'm sure that Jordan is aware that she can't be with you and be doing drugs. In fact, I know she is—I warned her of that myself." She pinned him with a look. "Do you love her?"

He nodded, realizing that Randy was about to nail him.

"Then you have to remember that everyone has weaknesses. You resort to tequila when you're upset; she resorted to cocaine. She realizes now that she can't do that and keep you. But you need to forgive her, with the understanding that it doesn't happen again."

Joe nodded, then gave her a pointed look. "You do know how weird this is, right? You giving me relationship advice."

"Yeah? So?" she said, grinning. "I just want you to be happy, Joe. I don't know if Jordan is the one to make you happy forever, but I

228

don't want to see you throw away someone you love because she made a mistake." She grimaced. "Hell, look how many I made, over and over and over again. You forgave me, right?"

"You were my wife," Joe reminded her gently.

"Yeah," she said, nodding. "And she's your girlfriend, so you need to cut her a little slack." She held up her hands. "I'm not saying cut her so much slack as to compromise your own values. But you have to realize that not everyone is as strong as you are, and not everyone takes legal methods to resolve their hurts. Okay?"

Joe gave her a stubborn look that reminded her of JT when he didn't want to agree to something. Finally he nodded.

"So what's going on with you, anyway?" he asked. "Any relationships on the horizon?"

Randy looked pensive, and Joe knew she was hesitating about telling him something. "Come on… give," he said, grinning.

"Well, I have been asked out by someone, but I'm not sure…" she said, shaking her head.

"Why? Don't like the guy?"

"It's not that."

"What is it?"

"He's kinda at the department," she said, looking worried.

"And you're worried about hurting me?" he asked, easily discerning her angst.

"Well, Joe, I don't want to repeat old mistakes. And the last thing I want to do right now is hurt you, or make you look bad."

Joe nodded, appreciating her concern. "Who is it?"

"John Tearney," she said, grimacing slightly.

"The guy that runs the juvenile division?"

229

"Yeah. I've been working with him a lot over the last few months, since we're starting to get more older kids." She hesitated, not wanting to tell Joe more than he wanted to know. Joe nodded, motioning for her to go on. "Well, apparently he somehow heard some of the details about the divorce, and mentioned to me how 'decent' he thought it was that I didn't ask for half of everything you had..." Her voice trailed off as she looked at him. "How did he hear about details of our divorce, Joe?"

Joe chewed at the inside of his cheek, looking down at the ground guiltily. Again, he looked very much like his son when he got caught at something.

"I just didn't want people thinking you were taking me for everything," he said. "You still have to work with some of these people, like Tearney."

Randy nodded. "Well, I don't care what they think, but thank you for trying to help."

"So, do you like the guy?"

"He seems very nice."

"So go out with him."

Randy stared at him for a long moment, then sighed. "I don't know..."

"What are you worried about?"

"I'm worried that it's too soon. That people will think I was having an affair again or something."

"Randy, it's been months," Joe said. "And you know what? These people are going to think what they want to anyway. Do what makes you happy."

Randy looked at him, her teal eyes searching his. "We're really

230

going to manage this, aren't we?"

"What?"

"This," she said, indicating the two of them. "Being friends."

He grinned. "What, you thought you were getting away that easily?"

"I should have known better," she said, grinning back.

He hugged her then, holding her for a long time, then kissed her on the top of the head. "Do what makes you happy, Randy. Please."

She nodded against his shoulder, feeling very happy that she was still friends with him.

\*\*\*

Stevie and Kevin were on an operation together, working some diversion cases. They were hitting pharmacies and passing forged triplicate prescriptions for pharmaceutical narcotics. The intent was to see which pharmacies weren't following procedure in processing the prescriptions. Pharmaceutical narcotics were becoming a big problem on the street, and they needed to find out where it was coming from.

Stevie glanced over at Kevin as he drove. He was definitely a quiet one, but she was finally getting used to that. She watched as he smoked a cigar, blowing the smoke out in a long stream.

"You inhale those?" she asked, noting the difference between the time that he took a drag and the time he blew the smoke out.

"Yeah," he said, glancing over at her. "Old habit from when I smoked cigarettes."

"Isn't it kind of a moot point to quit smoking if you're only going to smoke something else that's probably just as bad?" Stevie asked, never one to keep her thoughts to herself.

Kevin stared at her for a long moment, then grinned. "I didn't quit smoking," he said. "I quit drinking. Cigarettes were too closely associated with the taste of alcohol for me."

Stevie gazed back at him, then nodded. "Alcoholic, huh?" she said, having seen enough of them in law enforcement during her lifetime.

Kevin glanced at her again. She didn't look affected at all, just matter of fact. He nodded after a long pause.

Stevie nodded. "Does that account for your hands shaking sometimes?"

Kevin grinned. Stevie O'Neil was not shy, was she? "No, that has nothing to do with it."

"Then why do your hands shake?"

Kevin took a long drag on his cigar, squinting at her through the curling smoke. "Do you ever let your curiosity go unsatisfied?"

"Not too often, no," she said, grinning unabashedly.

Kevin nodded, aware that he wasn't getting out of this now. Erin had told him over and over again that he could trust the people he was working with. He was about to find out.

"I have ADD," he said. "When I don't get home to take my Adderall, I get edgy. That makes my hands shake sometimes."

"ADD? Attention Deficit Disorder?"

"Yeah."

"What happens with that?"

"It means that without medication, my mind acts like a ball in a

232

pinball machine."

"All over the place, huh?"

"Yeah."

"Anything we can help with?" she asked sincerely.

Kevin had noted the "we," and he knew that was her way of letting him know she expected him to tell the whole team. He shook his head.

"I pretty much have a handle on it."

"Except when you don't get Adderall," she pointed out. "We do a lot of all-nighters, Mace."

Kevin nodded. "I need to start carrying it on me."

"Yeah," she said. "But if we understand what happens to you, we might be able to run interference."

"Maybe," he said, realizing she was right.

Stevie looked at him for a long moment, assessing. "You know, Mace, you have to trust us."

Kevin nodded, having been told that already.

"I mean, really trust us," Stevie said pointedly. "We're your lifeline out there sometimes."

Kevin took a deep breath, reaching for another cigar. "It's just not something I'm used to."

"Well, we'll get you used to it then," Stevie said, grinning.

He grinned too, liking that she didn't take no or maybe for an answer. He generally liked her a great deal; she was very genuine. There were no games with her. If you wanted to know what she thought, all you had to do was ask. Kevin tended to think that he didn't always want to know what she thought of him.

233

They were silent for a while as they headed for the next pharmacy they were targeting, across town. They needed to space them out, not wanting them to start warning each other that the heat was on.

"So, Erin moved in with you, huh?" Stevie said.

Kevin looked over at her. "Is anything ever not public knowledge with this place?"

"Not on this team, no," Stevie said, grinning unrepentantly. "So, we talking wedding bells here?"

"Wedding bells?" Kevin looked almost disgusted.

"Oh, God, don't tell me you're another one like Collins and you don't believe in love," Stevie said, rolling her eyes.

"There's no way not to believe in love around here, O'Neil."

"How's that?"

"Well, look at you and Collins, and Curtis and Jeanie, and hell, the chief and Debenshire." He shook his head. "It would take a world-class cynic not to believe in love around here."

Stevie grinned. "It does seem to be a department-wide epidemic."

"Uh-huh."

"So you love her, but marriage is out for now," Stevie said, shrugging.

"Who said I love her?" Kevin asked, looking thoughtfully at the cigar in his hand.

Stevie raised an eyebrow at him. "You've known her all of what, two months? Mace, is there another reason you'd have her in your house?"

Kevin shrugged. "Donovan had her in his, right?"

"Donovan was protecting her from that bastard of an ex-husband."

"Okay, but who says it's not just the sex?"

Again Stevie regarded him for a long moment, then shook her head. "If that's all you were into, you would have picked someone more your speed."

"My speed?" Kevin asked, grinning in spite of himself. Stevie O'Neil was sharp as hell.

"Yeah, fast, loose, wild," she said, without a hint of apology.

Kevin stared at her, wondering if she ever even bothered to attempt to be tactful.

"Okay, so… I care about her," he said.

"Care about her," Stevie repeated slowly, then nodded. She knew he was deluding himself, but she didn't figure it was her place to dispel that notion at this point. He'd figure it out eventually. Men like Kevin Elmasian couldn't be pushed.

Midnight drove her classic Corvette, listening to music and thinking about all the things she needed to accomplish that day. She'd already talked to Joe that morning, hearing all about his latest with Jordan and Randy and all that. Her mind was going a mile a minute, and her daughter, who sat in the passenger seat, was watching her. Mikeyla had been getting interested in the circles her mother moved in, especially since the other night when she and Rick had shown up at the house with BJ Sparks in tow. Mikeyla had been sure she was going to die right there on the spot.

They'd all gone to dinner, and BJ had jokingly called Mikeyla his "date" all evening. Mikeyla reveled in the attention he lavished on her. He told her in no uncertain terms that she was every bit as beautiful as her mother, and even more so, he'd said in an aside, "Since you're not already in love." He'd grinned, making at face at Rick. Rick had shaken his head, smiling all the while. Mikeyla had been aware that her "uncle" Joe Sinclair was dating Jordan Tate, but she'd never imagined that would involve anything to do with her parents.

When Midnight had explained that Mr. Sparks had called her at the office to set up a meeting between a fighting Jordan and Joe, Mikeyla had realized that her mother was indeed a celebrity in what she did, if people like BJ Sparks knew who to call and how to get ahold of her. In truth, Midnight was a celebrity in the law enforcement community, but as with normal teenagers, Mikeyla Debenshire equated everything to Hollywood.

Thinking along those lines, Mikeyla had asked her mother if she could accompany her to work. Midnight had hesitated, thinking about all the things she needed to do that day, but finally agreed, seeing that Mikeyla was making an attempt to be closer to her. Midnight also suspected it had everything to do with the visit Mikeyla had had with BJ Sparks. She hadn't stopped talking about it since that night. Midnight found it endlessly amusing.

***

Angelica Muñoz ran into Christian, who was headed into Rick's office. There had been a cooperative effort between FORS and Rogue Squadron to take down some gang members that were heavy into trafficking. Rick had asked for Rogue Squadron's support, and Spider had of course approved the request. Christian was bringing Rick the reports he and Stevie had prepared for the squad's part in the raid.

236

Angel, as usual, paid particular attention to the appallingly handsome Christian Collins.

"Hey, Blue," she said, smiling brightly. "Good work this morning, huh?"

"Uh-huh," Christian said, with a knowing nod. "'Cept you fucked up."

"What?" Angel asked, thrown off guard.

"You fucked up."

"How?"

"Far too many eyes caught that act with Debenshire this morning."

Angel made a dismissive sound. "Oh, that. What about it?"

"It's a good way to get your ass kicked," Christian said conversationally.

Angel rolled her eyes. "I'd be more afraid of your lady than his."

"Oh really?" Christian said, raising an eyebrow.

"Yeah, really."

"And where do you think my lady learned everything she knows?" he asked, his grin sardonic.

"Bullshit," Angel said. "I don't believe it."

"Believe it, Angel."

Angelica still looked cynical.

"She'll nail your ass to the wall, I'm warning you," he said.

"Yeah, yeah," Angel said airily.

Christian shook his head and shrugged, walking away.

Angel watched him go, wondering who he thought he was to warn her.

237

She began hearing later that morning that Midnight Chevalier was out for her blood.


Rick had called in an hour after Mikeyla and Midnight got into the office. He told Midnight on the speaker that they needed to talk about "a certain reoccurring issue." Midnight knew that the fact that he didn't tell her what the issue was meant it was something he didn't want their daughter to hear. His caution was for naught, since Midnight started receiving reports on the incident shortly after that.

She was informed that during the raid that morning, Angelica Muñoz was pointedly touching Rick while "making sure he was okay." Midnight heard it from a number of people, all of whom would be more than happy to watch Midnight take Angelica Muñoz apart. It had become known among the members of the Gang that Angelica had been relentlessly pursuing Rick. Well known, and collectively frowned upon.

After yet another member, Spider, left her office, Mikeyla looked at her mother.

"She's been after Daddy?" she asked, surprised.

"Yes, Keyl, for a while now," Midnight answered carefully.

She was having to tamp down on her desire to walk downstairs and beat the living shit out of Angelica Muñoz. If for nothing else, for being stupid enough to challenge Midnight's hold on Rick's heart, and for being so blatant about it.

"What are you going to do?" Mikeyla asked.

"What do you think I should do?" Midnight said, curious as to what her daughter thought.

"Can't you fire her?"

238

Midnight shook her head. "No, I can't do that."

"Why not?"

"Because there's a difference between business and personal. Her being after my man isn't business—it's personal."

Mikeyla noted the fact that her mother said "my man" rather than "my husband." Midnight was always up to date on the way she talked; it was indicative of someone in touch with current trends.

"Okay," she said, still not understanding the logic. "But if you fired her, who's going to argue with you—you're the chief, right?"

"True, Mikeyla," Midnight said, sitting back in her chair and looking at her daughter. "But the thing here is, as the chief I have to set an example. If I fire the first person that makes me mad, besides the fact that I'll probably end up with half a department"—she grinned lopsidedly—"I'll also in effect be telling my management that I condone such practices."

"So you're saying, if you do it, everyone else will think it's okay for them to, right?"

"Right," Midnight said. "And that's not how I do business."

Mikeyla nodded, starting to grasp the level of balance her mother had to keep in order to do her job. Mikeyla knew that if she was in her mother's position, she'd have fired Angelica instantly, without stopping to think of how it would look. It made her realize how complicated life could get when you were older. She gained a little more respect for her mother in that moment.


Later that morning, Joe sat in Rick's office, in front of his desk, much as he had years before when talking to Midnight when she'd run FORS. Angelica knocked and walked in, noting that Captain Sinclair was there. Rick and Joe looked up at her, and Joe shot Rick a look that was very definitely surprised. In fact, Joe was surprised that she would simply walk in without waiting for Rick to tell her to do so.

Angel looked at both of them. She knew the two men were good friends, so she wasn't surprised to see the captain. Joe Sinclair was a looker too, with a ton of money, from what Angel understood. But he was dating a rock star now, so he was, in her mind, unattainable. However, for both men's benefit, she put on her best pout, moving to sit down next to Joe.

Rick looked back at Joe, spreading his hand in front of him, as if to say, *See what I have to deal with?*

To Angelica he said, short and to the point, "What is it, Angel?"

Angelica was surprised by his tone, and her face reflected that surprise. She glanced at Joe to see if she was getting any sympathy from that arena. Joe was slumped casually in his chair, his leg crossed at the knee, leaning his right elbow on the arm of the chair, his chin on his fist. His face was impassive as his glance skipped from Rick back to Angel. Angel thought she could read amusement in the captain's eyes, and she didn't understand that.

"I keep hearing that the chief is out to get me," Angel said, sounding hurt.

Joe sat up, dropping his leg that had been crossed casually, as if the whole tone of this meeting had just changed. Indeed it had. Joe's eyes connected with Rick's for a moment, pointed. Joe was fully aware of the brewing situation between Midnight and Angel. He and Rick had been discussing options for defusing it before Midnight found it necessary to handle it herself, thus putting her career in jeopardy. Both men knew Midnight well. She didn't take insults lightly, and Angel's pursuit of Rick was the ultimate insult. Neither of them

240

thought Angel fool enough to come crying to Rick for protection from his wife. They'd been wrong.

Rick looked back at Angel for a moment. "That I'm aware of, the chief isn't out to get anyone," he said passively.

"Midnight, on the other hand..." Joe put in mildly.

Angel glanced at him sharply, remembering how Midnight had differentiated between being Chief Chevalier and Midnight Debenshire. Did they all think the same way?

"What's the big deal?" she asked. "I don't see why everyone's making a big deal about all this."

"Angel," Rick said, sitting forward. "I think you know why it's a problem."

"Jesus!" Angel exclaimed, rolling her eyes. "Most guys would be stoked at having another woman wanting him."

"We already had this discussion," Rick said. "I told you what would happen if you didn't back off. You didn't heed that. Now I'm working on trying to find a transfer for you."

"A transfer?" she echoed, shocked.

"Yes, I'm trying to figure out where else in the department we can place you."

"Problem is," Joe said, "nobody else has a need for your, ah, services."

Angel narrowed her eyes at Joe. She knew he was taunting her.

"So," Rick said, giving Joe a pointed look, "chances are you'll end up having to look at another agency. Maybe the Sheriff's Department. I can give you a recommendation, and Joe knows the lieutenant over there."

241

"Why should I lose my job over this?" Angel asked, irrate. "Because your bitch of a wife can't handle competition?"

"Be very careful…" Joe practically growled, his eyes narrowing dangerously.

"Angel," Rick said, trying to defuse the situation that was occurring right in front of him, his own ire raised by Angel's comment. "Your behavior is unacceptable to me as your supervisor—I don't need a lot more than that to terminate you. If that's what you'd like instead, I'm sure I can accommodate you."

"Bullshit!" Angel screamed. "You have to have documentation! You can't just say that I'm not acting right now and fire me," she said, proud of herself for knowing that.

"How do you know it hasn't been documented?" Joe said, his light blue eyes staring into hers.

"I'd know," Angel said, not liking the way Joe was looking at her.

"Personnel issues are kept confidential, Ms. Muñoz," Joe recited. "However, Lieutenant Debenshire spoke to you regarding correcting your inappropriate behavior toward him in a meeting at your home. A meeting that was made at your private residence at your request, I do believe…" Joe's voice trailed off menacingly, letting her know that he was fully aware of what she'd done in front of Rick at her house.

Angel swallowed convulsively, not liking the way this was going at all. "You can't do that," she said, shaking her head.

"Do what?" Joe asked. "Fire you? I assure you, we can. And if you continue to piss me off, I promise you, I will do so personally."

"You can't do that. I'd sue."

"Sue me," Joe said. "Find out how far you'll get."

242

Angel looked at Rick. He sat back in his chair, his elbows on the arms, his expression telling her he had no intention of defending her. She'd pushed it too far. She'd assumed Rick had only turned her down that night at her house because Midnight had been aware of her play to get him. She'd figured if she laid low for a while, she could try again when Midnight wouldn't be watching him so closely. She still assumed that he wanted her.

Standing up, she left the office without another word. She went down to the parking lot. She was furious. She couldn't believe this was turning out this way! How dare that bitch get them to fire her! Who did she really think she was? Angel was forgetting she'd expected Midnight Chevalier to fire her long before now, and never had. Instead she was telling herself that Midnight had told Rick to fire her.

"Well, if I don't have a job here anyway…" Angel said to herself, grinning.


That afternoon, Midnight and Mikeyla were walking out to Midnight's car. Midnight had been told about what had occurred in Rick's office. She'd already flat out told Joe that he was not to start termination procedures on Angelica Muñoz. Joe had argued with her about it, but Midnight was adamant that it wasn't how things were going to be handled by her or anyone in her department.

"Goddamned stubborn female," Joe had muttered as he walked out of her office.

"I love you too!" Midnight had called after him, winking at Mikeyla.

They'd both heard Joe's rumble of laughter as he left her outer office.

243

They'd just reached Midnight's Corvette when Midnight's name was called. She turned and saw Angelica Muñoz striding over to her. Midnight set her briefcase on the ground, tossing Mikeyla the keys to the car so she could open the passenger door for herself. Midnight then proceeded to lean against her car, waiting to see what Angel had to say.

"You think it's that easy, puta?" Angel sneered.

"That easy to what, Angel?" Midnight asked, not rising to the bait.

"You think you can just have your friends fire me and I'll go hide?"

Midnight looked back at the younger woman for a long moment. "Why would you need to hide, Angel?"

"'Cause your friends saw me talking to your man, and now they tell me you're out to get me," Angel said, not liking being on the defensive.

Midnight's look was sardonic as she raised an eyebrow. "Well, you're here now. What is it you think you want?" she asked condescendingly.

Angel stared back at Midnight for a long moment, then said, "You said you think you can take me. I want to see you try."

Midnight's expression didn't change. She crossed her legs at the ankles, looking back at the young woman who'd just challenged her. "What do you hope to gain from that?"

"I knew it, you're all talk," Angel said disparagingly.

By this time a couple of officers had noticed Angel's raised voice and walked over. They noted that the chief was involved, so they didn't say anything.

Angel paced back and forth in front of Midnight. "You're not such a badass puta when it comes down to it, are you?" she said, sounding all gang member now.

Midnight hadn't moved, but she was endeavoring to keep from grinning. This girl was unreal in her stupidity. In truth Midnight didn't want to fight her, simply because she felt as chief she needed set a better example than that. It had nothing to do with fear of the younger woman.

"Mom?" Mikeyla said, having watched the whole conversation with a look of fear.

Midnight didn't take her eyes off Angel, but spoke to her daughter. "It's okay, Keyl."

"Yeah," Angel spat. "Your mom's just a chicken shit."

"Don't talk to my daughter like that," Midnight said mildly, her eyes narrowing slightly.

"What are you going to do, Chief?" Angel asked. "Fire me?"

"That's not what I had in mind, no," Midnight replied, her voice still frustratingly calm.

"So step up, if you think you can take it."

Midnight sighed, shaking her head. "Little girl…" she said, then her eyes went back to Angel. "Do you have any idea what you're talking yourself into?"

"Kicking your ass?"

"Hardly."

"Yeah, yeah, so you say. I don't see you steppin' up though."

Midnight nodded. "As the Chief of Police, I feel it necessary to point out to you that your current action would be considered harassment of a peace officer, which carries a fairly stiff penalty. Now if

245

we get down to it and fight, you're then guilty of assault on a peace officer, whether you actually manage to land a punch or not." Midnight's look was assessing. "You sure you want to take all that on?"

"Figures you'd charge me with something if I touch you."

"I won't," Midnight said. "Like I already told you, I can take you and ten of your friends. However," she said, her hands indicating the officers standing nearby, whose number was growing every moment, "this audience your big mouth has garnered you will be legally responsible for filing such charges."

"Just admit you were going to have me fired for taking your man," Angel said, putting her hands on her hips. She figured that if she aired the dirty laundry, Midnight would look bad in front of her officers.

"You didn't take anything, little girl. Rick is, was, and will always be mine," Midnight replied calmly. She pushed off her car, shrugging out of her jacket. "That being said, are you sure you want to push this?"

"Bring it," Angel said, her look confident.

"Mom!" Mikeyla screamed.

Midnight shook her head, her eyes on Angel. She had no intention of throwing the first punch; if she did, she was guilty of assault. Angel shifted her weight back and forth between her feet. Midnight didn't react, simply waited.

"Come on, Muñoz, you all show and no go?" yelled someone from the crowd.

Angel's head snapped around, trying to find the source of the comment.

"Yeah, Muñoz, either put up or shut up," shouted another voice.

246

Midnight was fairly sure she recognized both of them, but didn't turn to look.

The comments had goaded Angel's anger and she charged at Midnight, catching her mid-section. Midnight went down, but put her boots to Angel's mid-section to throw her off, spinning to her feet. Angel was stunned to have been thwarted so easily. Midnight waited for the next attack, not moving far from where Angel had fallen. Angel climbed to her feet, watching Midnight warily.

Midnight motioned with her fingertips for Angel to bring it on again. Angel went for it, throwing a punch. Midnight moved out of her range at just the right instant; a seasoned fighter, she knew which way Angel was going to throw next, but this time with her weaker arm. Midnight allowed the second punch to hit its target, her jaw. Her head snapped back, but Midnight found that Angel didn't hit very hard with her weak arm, definitely not as hard as Midnight had been hit in the past by other gang members she'd fought.

"That the best you got, Muñoz?" Midnight said, reaching up to finger the spot on her jaw. "I bet my kid hits harder than that—the little one, that is." Her cat-like green eyes were glittering, her tone taunting, and that irritated Angel even more.

"You want to see what I got for you?" she said.

Reaching into her pocket, she pulled out a switchblade, depressing the button. The blade jumped out, and no sooner had it clicked into place than the rustling sound of guns clearing their holsters was heard.

Midnight threw up her right arm, yelling "Hold!" in her most commanding voice.

The look she threw Angel was all gang leader and as threatening as any member of the department had ever seen. The Gang didn't witness that look, since they'd mobilized the minute Midnight had yelled out. Joe, Rick, Spider, Tiny, Kana, Dave, Christian, Donovan, Jeanie, and Stevie moved into the crowd, telling officers to put their weapons down, that Midnight would handle this. All that the officers knew was that they'd just seen someone draw a weapon on their chief.

Kyle stepped into the clearing where Midnight and Angel still stood, holding up his arm for everyone's attention.

"Put your weapons down. Chief Chevalier is in control of this situation." His look at Midnight was pointed. She nodded, confirming what he'd just said, her eyes still on Angel.

"You just fucked up big time, little girl," she said. "You just drew a weapon on a Chief of Police with about forty law enforcement witnesses. You should consider yourself lucky, however, that I have the best trained officers in the city when it comes to lethal force, or you'd be on the ground with about forty holes in you."

Once again, she motioned with her fingertips for Angel to bring it on. "Now, let's finish this, because I'm getting tired of playing with you. You're going down, Muñoz," Midnight said, her tone all gang leader.

Angel hesitated, but then decided she'd gone this far. "If I'm going down, you're going with me," she yelled, taking a run at Midnight, the knife itching to find a purchase.

Midnight waited, counting beats in her head. She stepped aside just as Angel's knife would have hit her. She heard Mikeyla scream, and had the impression of Rick moving to their daughter's side. She turned, throwing a punch at Angel as she stumbled forward, having missed her mark. Midnight's fist didn't miss its mark, and like many before her, Angel was stunned at how hard the petite Chief of Police

248

could hit. The first punch knocked Angel to the ground, but Midnight didn't give her the chance to recover this time. Instead, she grabbed her by two handfuls of her shirt, dragging her up off the ground. Angel struggled and managed to free herself, shoving Midnight back. Midnight dropped back two steps, which Angel mistook as a retreat, and she lunged at her. Midnight used Angel's momentum, grabbing her arm and putting her hip into her side, literally throwing Angel over her shoulder. Angel lay on the ground, stunned, looking up at where Midnight stood over her, barely even breathing heavily from the exertion.

"You want to fuck with me, that's fine. You want to fuck with my husband, that's fine too. But no one fucks with the safety of my officers—no one," Midnight said, once again sounding like the Chief of Police that she was.

She glanced at Tiny and Dave, who stood nearest to Angel. "Get her out of here," she said, then turned and walked away.

She headed toward her car, seeing Rick standing there with Mikeyla at his side. She walked right up to him, her eyes on his. He reached out, touching the bruise starting at her jaw.

"You okay?" he asked.

Midnight nodded, grinning. "I'm sure the press'll hear about this one."

Rick laughed. "Likely."

Midnight took a deep breath, blowing it out slowly as she moved her neck around. Rick watched, knowing she was working at regaining her composure. She turned to Mikeyla then, and saw that her daughter was still watching her with nothing short of awe on her face.

"You okay?" she asked Mikeyla, smiling.

"Yeah, Mom, but... wow..."

Mikeyla was stunned to have seen her mother fight like that. She'd heard over the years that Midnight was a good fighter, but she'd never seen her in action.

Midnight shrugged. "Guess you never saw that before, huh?"

"Um, no, I haven't," Mikeyla said, still looking shocked.

Joe walked up then, looking Midnight over. "You okay?"

Midnight grinned, feeling like everyone was repeating themselves. "I'm fine," she said brightly.

"Uh-huh," Joe said, nodding with a knowing grin on his lips. "You'll be feeling it tonight—how much you want to bet?"

Midnight rolled her eyes. "God! Don't remind me!"

"Way to go, Debenshire," Spider said as he walked by, grinning. "Got the prettiest girl in school to fight your battles."

"Fuck you, Spider," Rick said, laughing.

"He does have a point," Christian said, coming up with Stevie.

"He doesn't have a point, he's being an asshole," Rick said, grinning at Christian.

"Maybe, but she is awfully pretty," Donovan said as he joined them, winking at Midnight.

One by one the members of the Gang came up to check on Midnight. None of them were surprised by the way the fight had turned out; they'd all seen Midnight in action at some point.

"I can't believe Muñoz was stupid enough to try you," Joe said, shaking his head.

"I tried to warn her," Christian put in.

"So did we," Rick said, nodding at Joe.

"She had plenty of warning," Midnight assured them.

"She just wasn't smart enough to heed any of it," Stevie said, leaning back against Christian.

"Gang members don't always learn quickly," Rick said, shaking his head.

"Yeah, but to be dumb enough to pull a weapon on a cop in front of other cops?" Donovan said. "How stupid can one person get."

"Midnight was right," Joe said. "She's lucky she didn't end up dead on the spot for that move."

It was well known that to pull a weapon on a cop was a quick way to suicide. Midnight had been adamant about the use of lethal force being taught well in the academy, with instruction on when an officer should and should not fire their weapon. Joe had been further adamant that the officers be well trained on hitting what they shot at when they drew their weapon. So there was no doubt Angelica would have been hit had they fired.

"So, why didn't they fire?" Mikeyla asked, glancing around at what was basically her extended family.

"She wasn't within easy reach of Midnight," Dave said, having just come up in time to hear the conversation.

"If she had made any move to use that knife on your mother…" Rick said.

"They would have dropped her," Joe finished for him.

Mikeyla glanced at her mother, and Midnight nodded. "She wouldn't have had much of a chance to use that knife."

"But you told them not to, right?" Mikeyla said, remembering how Midnight had yelled "Hold."

"Right, because it would be my officers at risk. I wasn't going to have that for this bullshit," she said, gesturing to her bleeding knuckles.

251

"That's what you meant by the safety of your officers?"

"Yes. They would be liable if they fired on her, and there was always the chance of a misfire or a bad shot. I wouldn't want one of my officers hurt over this."

Mikeyla nodded, still shocked by what she'd seen. "Hey, Mom?"

"Yeah?" Midnight said, taking the gauze Tiny handed her.

"Think you could teach me to fight like that?" Mikeyla asked, garnering a number of grins and chuckles from the Gang.

Midnight glanced around at her friends, and grinned. "Yeah, I can, Keyl, but," she said, giving Mikeyla a pointed look, "I only intend to teach you how to finish fights, not start them."

"Finish them?"

"Yeah," Rick said, putting his arm around Midnight. "Your mom and the rest of us didn't change who we were so we could watch you become who we were."

Mikeyla stared around her, once again seeing the faces of the people who'd been in her life since she'd been born. Remembering that most of them had been gang members at one point, she nodded.

That night the news reported the incident. Mikeyla ran into her parents' room, turning on their TV and telling them there was going to be a report. Rick and Midnight had been lying on their bed, Midnight in his arms. They both moved to sit up, and Midnight winced as her back complained about the movement. Rick's hands moved to massage the spot, even as the news story started.

"Today, Chief Midnight Chevalier was reportedly in an altercation with a disgruntled employee," the reporter said. "The street-tough chief was reportedly headed to her car when the employee confronted her. Witnesses stated that Chief Chevalier attempted to calm

252

the woman, but to no avail. Things escalated when the employee pulled a knife on the chief. The officers at the scene reportedly drew their weapons, but the chief told them not to fire. It was later reported that the disgruntled employee was booked for assault on a peace officer. It is not known at this time what complaint she had, but I believe it's safe to say that whatever it was, she handled it the wrong way." The reporter grinned. "This certainly won't hurt Chief Chevalier's influence over her department. One of the officers witnessing the incident was quoted as saying, 'Chief Chevalier doesn't take anyone's shit, and she can give it back tenfold, but today, she was more worried about us than she was herself.' That's a cop's cop," the reporter finished, smiling again.

Midnight glanced at Rick, and he grinned at her. "Who said that?" she asked, sure it had to be one of the Gang.

"None of us that I know of."

"Sure, right," Midnight said, unconvinced. She never believed she was as popular as she was in her own department.

# CHAPTER 9

Jordan finished up her tour in Europe on a Thursday night. She was on BJ's plane an hour later, headed for California. She had every intention of spending the entire week with Joe, even if she had to kidnap him to manage it. She'd missed him so much, not having spent near enough time with him after the fight.

BJ's plane got her into California at 4 a.m. BJ had a car waiting for them; he'd come with her, since he needed to be there for the show too.

"What the hell are you going to do in San Diego?" Jordan had asked him.

BJ had shrugged. "Score a couple of blondes?" he replied, grinning rakishly.

Jordan shook her head at him. He wasn't quite the tramp everyone thought him to be. In truth he was a very sweet man with a lot of anger built up over things that had happened in his life. It came out in his music, even if his incredible voice made even anger sound good. He was a cynic about love, but he didn't sleep with just anyone either.

He'd been known to date groupies, other rockers, cocktail waitresses, black jack dealers, whoever caught his fancy. But any woman that dated him found out quickly that he could either be sweet or he could be indifferent. Most strived to see the sweet side of him more often; many failed. BJ was careful about who he opened up to, and

254

once he had, he expected total loyalty and confidentiality. Anyone caught carrying tales about "the real BJ Sparks" was summarily dismissed from his life forever. He liked his bad-boy image, and was capable of being the worst bad boy of them all, given the opportunity or need.

Jordan had often experienced the sweetest he could be, and she enjoyed it. He was one of her very best friends. They'd dated and slept together often in the six years they'd known each other. BJ said they were kindred spirits. He also knew that she deserved the best, and to be loved totally—that was why he had let her go. He didn't think he was capable of loving anyone, and he wanted her to have a chance at real love. She'd never loved him—and he knew that—but she cared very deeply for him. It was for that reason that BJ was very glad she'd found Joe. She'd now experienced real love, and he wanted her to keep it.

Jordan knocked on Joe's door at 5 a.m., praying that she wouldn't find him in bed with someone else, or that he wouldn't be mad that she'd just shown up. To her utter shock he answered the door fully dressed, in jeans, a black polo shirt, and black boots. He looked good, as usual, and Jordan stood staring up at him for a full minute.

"Well, what do we have here?" Joe said, grinning at her.

"You're dressed?"

"No, I just slept in this," he said, opening the door wider so she could step inside.

"Uh-huh," she said, smiling up at him. "More likely you never went to sleep."

"Wrong again," he said, reaching out to pull her into his arms, his lips finding hers quickly.

"Mmm…" she murmured. "I've missed you," she said as their lips parted.

"I've missed you too," he said, looking at his watch. "Didn't you have a concert last night?"

"Yeah," she said, happy that he remembered her schedule so well. "And then I came here."

Joe nodded. "And you're gonna drop any minute," he said, looking down into her eyes.

"Nah. I'm on my second or third wind now."

Joe laughed, walking toward his kitchen. "You want coffee?"

"Sure," she said, leaning against his counter. "So what's going on today that has you up so early?"

He handed her a cup of coffee and pushed the sugar toward her. "I'm doing some training at the range today."

"Can I come watch?" she asked, sipping at her coffee.

"Sure," he said, shrugging. "It'll probably bore you to tears."

"That's what you said last time."

"Yeah, you just hid it well then."

A little while later she changed her clothes, putting on jeans and a T-shirt with her tennis shoes, grabbing her jean jacket as they left. She got to spend the day watching Joe drill everyone, and even got to watch Joe shoot, since all the recruits insisted he show off for his girlfriend. Jordan was suitably impressed, seeing the way he moved and hearing how incredible it was that he hit a perfect score every time.

In the end it was a nice week spent together. Jordan took care of details for the concert on her cell phone while watching Joe do any number of "cop things." She'd gotten to watch him on a raid as well.

There had been no end to how much Joe amazed her and excited her senses. Watching him doing his job with his gun in hand had been exciting, and she'd even gotten the opportunity to see him chase a suspect down and tackle him. She'd been standing by the car, as he'd told her to, when the team had gone in, waiting for someone to give her the all clear sign so she could go inside, when she'd heard a yell that sounded like Joe.

"Freeze!"

The next thing she'd seen was a man running out of the house and right by her. Joe hit the door moments later, and she saw that he was holstering his gun. His long legs carried him past her in seconds. Jordan straightened up and felt a hand on her shoulder.

"Stay here," Rick said when she glanced back at him.

"Does he do this a lot?" she asked, wincing when she saw Joe launch himself at the man and tackle him to the ground.

"Pretty much," Rick replied, grinning.

Joe had sustained a few minor cuts, scrapes, and bruises from the tackle, but Jordan had also learned how physical his job really could be. She understood why he kept fit; it was dangerous not to.

She also witnessed the abuse, both verbal and physical, that officers took when arresting suspects. The man Joe had chased down spewed any number of expletives about what Joe could do with his "rights," and what he was going to do when he got out, on and on.

Jordan shook her head, surprised that anyone could hold their temper when suspects got so insulting. Joe and Rick had just looked at each other and made jokes about whether or not the man could even follow directions, and should they supply him with a map so he could come kill them when he got out. Jordan was amazed.

"How do you put up with that?" she'd asked Joe that night.

They were lying in his bed after he'd taken a shower. He glanced over at her, then shrugged. "You don't have a choice."

"Why not?"

"Well, if you get pissed and rack the guy upside the head, he turns around and sues you for assault under the color of authority. No one cares what he said to you to piss you off—all they care about is that you struck a cuffed suspect."

"Yeah, but it's a normal human reaction to get mad when someone starts cussing at you like that," Jordan pointed out.

"Yeah," Joe agreed. "But getting mad is one of the things we're not allowed to do."

"But you do, don't you?" Jordan asked, seeing how complicated his work was.

"Yeah. But that's when you take it out on the punching bag at the gym, or the pedal of your sports car, or the hammer of your gun."

"Or a bottle," Jordan said, seeing easily how officers became alcoholics.

"Sometimes."

"And I thought my job was difficult in terms of temptations," she said, shaking her head.

"Just a different kind of difficult, love."

Jordan agreed with him wholeheartedly. They talked for a long time that night. She told him that she hadn't had a drink since they'd made up, and definitely hadn't done any cocaine. Joe was relieved to hear that, knowing that things would get very difficult very fast for them if she started using again. It was something he didn't really want to think about.

258

The day of the concert for Sinclair House dawned. Joe woke first thing in the morning. He'd scheduled a range day long before the concert date had been set. He'd set it up for both the current academy class as well as for requalification for any officer that needed it.

He and Jordan had spent the entire week together. He'd enjoyed the time with her. She was a constant flurry of activity, always happy to go anywhere with him.

Leaning over, he kissed her lips softly. She stirred and woke up.

"Mmm," she murmured, kissing him back.

"Good morning to you too," he said, smiling down at her.

She wrapped her arms around his neck, kissing him again.

"Where are you sneaking off to this early in the morning?" she asked, noting that he was already mentally getting ready.

She'd been with him long enough now to see when he was preparing for his day. Mornings when he had nothing to do, he'd lie with her for hours, his manner totally relaxed.

"I have the range today, babe," he said.

Jordan narrowed her eyes in thought. "And you told me that already, didn't you?" she said, annoyed at herself for not remembering.

Joe smiled indulgently. "Yeah, but you have a lot going on in your head right now, with the show tonight and the tour coming up."

"Yeah, but you keep all that in your head and your own stuff," Jordan said, curling her lips in self-derision.

"Jordan, I've been doing this for years."

She shook her head. "Still, I'm in love with you. The things you do are important to me—why can't I remember them?"

"Honey, it's just the range," Joe said, grinning.

"And I'm making a big deal out of nothing, right?" Jordan said,

259

catching the amused sparkle in his eyes.

"Basically."

Jordan sighed and nodded. She knew she was always going to compete with the ghost of the woman he had loved for so long, and she never felt like she measured up. She knew in the very depths of her heart that Randy Sinclair had kept everything in her head. She'd been on top of everything, always. She'd known Joe so well, she'd been able to predict him.

"What is it, babe?" Joe asked, seeing the unhappy look on her face.

"I'm just never going to be Randy," she said softly.

"Jordan," Joe said, sitting up and pulling her with him. "If I wanted Randy, I'd still be with her. What is it you think you're letting me down on?"

Jordan shrugged, her eyes not meeting his. "I just can't remember everything like she could, like with the penicillin in the hospital. She kept track of everything for you, and I can't do that."

Joe reached out, tipping her face up to his. "If I want someone that keeps track of everything for me, I'll hire another secretary. I want someone that loves me, someone I enjoy being with, who enjoys me."

Jordan sighed again, nodding.

"Randy wasn't always on top of everything, you know."

"Right, sure, like what? Maybe forgot to do your socks once, right?"

"Actually," Joe said, "a bit bigger than that."

"What?" Jordan asked, aware that she shouldn't be so interested in hearing how his ex-wife had goofed up.

"Couple of years ago, I'd been coughing a lot, which was a sure sign I was headed for pneumonia. I'd noticed it, but really didn't take the time to do anything like get it checked. I figured if it was bad enough, Randy would tell me to go to the doctor—she usually did." His expression indicated the chagrin he felt at being so reliant on his ex-wife to the point of his health hinging on it. "Well, she was so busy with the center that she wasn't home or around me enough to notice how long I'd been coughing. Eventually, I went to the department doctor for my annual physical. That's when the doctor saw the spot on my lung."

"Oh my God," Jordan said, her voice a whisper.

"Yeah," Joe said, nodding. "It turned out okay, just an infection that caused the spot, but the fact was, Randy thoroughly castigated herself for not noticing my coughing before that. It wasn't her fault— it was mine. I'm an adult, I know what my coughing means. But see, babe? She knew me better than anyone, and she didn't catch it. She wasn't perfect, and I never expected her to be. I'm far from perfect— I don't expect the woman I love to be either. Okay?"

Jordan smiled softly. She knew she'd been silly about Randy, but she had a feeling she always would be. Randy was the woman he'd been married to for thirteen years; it was a big pair of shoes to try and fill. She did, however, like the fact that she honestly felt like Joe was the one man she couldn't just expect to drop at her feet. She had to keep up with him, and she enjoyed the challenge of that.

"Can I go to the range with you?" she asked.

"It's gonna be boring," Joe warned her. "You sure you don't have anything better you'd like to do today?"

"Better than watching my extremely handsome man shoot a gun?" she asked, sounding like she thought he was crazy. She shook

261

her head. "I don't think so."

Joe grinned, loving that she always made him sound so irresist-ible. He didn't believe for a minute that he was, but he loved that a woman as beautiful as she was loved him like that. It was a major ego boost.

They took a shower and got dressed, and were at the range an hour and a half later. Jordan got to watch as he ran the academy class through their paces. She was particularly intrigued with the hypo-thetical situation work they were doing. Joe would have the recruits hold a pad and a pencil as if they were interviewing a suspect. He'd call out, asking if everyone was ready on the left side of the firing line, and then the right.

He'd hold up his hand, then tell them to "go." A few moments later, he'd blow a whistle. The recruits would drop the pads and pen-cils and draw their weapons, firing once then standing at the ready position, their arms rigidly extended in front of them, their weapons up. Joe would blow the whistle again, and the recruits would holster their weapons. Jordan stood behind the recruits, watching Joe's eyes as he scanned each of them.

Jordan was surprised when the student in front of her raised his hand right after Joe had blown the first whistle. Joe blew the whistle again and then walked over to the recruit. Jordan edged closer and to the side so she could see what was going on.

The recruit was yanking at the top part of his gun. The slide had jammed halfway back. He was pulling at it, trying to put it back into place. Joe stood watching him passively, raising his eyebrow when the kid started cussing at the weapon.

"When you wear yourself out, let me know," Joe said calmly.

262

The young recruit glanced at Joe, seeing the look on his instructor's face. He worked harder, trying to fix the jam. Joe's eyes narrowed as he noted that the muzzle of the weapon was slowly but surely making its way toward him.

"I'll tell you right now, recruit," Joe said, his voice harsher than Jordan had ever heard it. "That muzzle gets any closer to pointing at me, and I'll put your ass down right here. And once you pick yourself up off the ground, you'll be out of a job."

The recruit glanced at the muzzle of his weapon, realizing that it was indeed dangerously close to pointing at Joe. He dropped his hands then, the gun in his right hand, nearest to Joe. Joe gave the younger man a pointed look, then reached out to take the weapon. He held it up to all the other recruits on the firing line.

"This is what we call a stovepipe, a jam," Joe said, his tone instructional. His eyes fell on the recruit as he continued, loudly enough for everyone to hear. "The way you clear a stovepipe is to tap and rack. Tap the butt of the gun to settle the round back into place, and rack the slide back."

Joe held the gun in his right hand and held his left hand palm up. He struck the bottom of the gun against his palm, then reached up with his left hand, gripped the slide, and pulled it back into place. The slide moved back easily, clicking into place. He handed the gun back to the recruit, leaning in to talk to him.

"Don't you ever even come close to pointing a weapon at an officer on my line again, or you'll be off my line for good. Understood?"

The recruit nodded, his eyes not meeting Joe's. "I'm sorry, Captain."

Joe grinned. "Just be careful, Simms, okay?"

"Yes, sir," the recruit replied, looking relieved.

263

"Problems?" Midnight asked as she, Rick, and Spider walked up.

"Nothing I can't handle," Joe said, glancing up at her and smiling.

All the recruits craned their necks around to see the Chief of Police. Midnight was still a matter of legend with the department. It was one thing to be instructed by a living legend such as Joe, but to actually get to see these two together...

"Mind your weapons!" Joe said, noting that a few guns had strayed.

The recruits snapped to attention again.

Midnight grinned at Joe, seeing that he had them well trained.

"The Gang gonna requal today?" Joe asked Midnight, having spotted Dave's Charger pulling into the lot with Kana's Navigator right behind.

"Yep," Midnight said. "Figured I better do it while I had the best range master available."

Joe grinned. "You figured I'd pass you no matter how shitty you shoot."

"Fuck you, Sinclair," Midnight replied, smiling all the while.

"Didn't we cover that a while back?" Joe asked, grunting as Midnight poked him in the ribs.

"Yeah, and I've yet to deck you for it," Rick said, his look pointed, but with a grin twitching at his lips.

Dave, Donovan, Jeanie, and Kevin walked up, followed by Tiny, Kana, and Jessica.

Kana glanced at Jordan then gave Joe a pointed look. "If I'd known girlfriends were welcome..."

"You could have invited Palani," Joe said.

"You're usually a stickler about that stuff, Joe," Kana said.

Palani had asked Kana if she could come to the range that day. Palani was ever fascinated with Kana's work and wanted to see her "in action." Kana had told her no, because Joe was usually really strict about no civilians being on the range. Now, she pulled her cell phone off her belt, calling Palani at the house. Palani excitedly agreed to be there as soon as she could.

"She's right," Spider said, referring to Kana's comment about Joe being a stickler.

Rick laughed. "Yeah, you losing your edge, man?"

"Drop dead, Debenshire," Joe said, grinning back at his best friend. "I'm just in a good mood."

"I hear a lot of sex will do that to men," Midnight said, winking at Jordan.

"Only a lot of good sex," Dave put in wryly.

"There's bad sex?" Donovan asked.

"Just not with me, babe," Jeanie said, laughing.

Donovan nodded. "Oh, yeah, that's it."

Stevie and Christian joined them.

"What's it, when?" Christian asked, always wanting to be in the thick of things.

"Good sex," Tiny informed him.

"At the range?"

"Only at night shoots," Joe said.

"Oh-ho!" Rick said, laughing. "I think that's more than I want to know."

"Well, I wasn't tellin' ya nothin'," Joe said. "Shall we shoot?"

Everyone nodded, having gotten their usual ribbing out for the

265

moment.

The academy class was fairly excited at getting to see the Gang in action. As usual, they were well known to most of the recruits, and those that didn't know about them did shortly thereafter.

Joe cleared the firing line, instructing the recruits to take a break. Naturally, their idea of a break was sitting down to watch seasoned officers shoot. Just as Joe was getting ready to run Tiny, Jess, Rick, Midnight, Spider, and Dave through the first paces, with himself included in the shoot, Palani drove up in her white Mercedes. She got out of the car and walked up to the range. Kana glanced over her shoulder. Palani was wearing jeans, a sweatshirt, and tennis shoes, and her hair was up in a ponytail. Kana thought she was incredibly beautiful. She stood near Kana, but didn't touch her or anything. Kana had been very definitive about her concern that Midnight should never be embarrassed in any way with how her officers behaved. Palani knew this, so she was very careful as well. Kana looked back at her, smiling and giving her a wink. Palani smiled warmly.

Joe began the shoot then, having nodded to Palani in welcome. The recruits quickly found that Joe rode his friends just as hard as he rode any recruit. Sometimes more so, because he was constantly aware that these were people he loved, and he wanted to make sure they were as prepared to be on the street as anyone.

"Tiny, pick that range up. I want you hitting center mass," he called to Tiny, who was at the end of the firing line. "Jess, if that gun's still jamming, use your backup, and I want to see it after this." Jess nodded, holstering her weapon and leaning down to pull her backup from her ankle holster.

"Night, I know you can hit better than that," Joe said chidingly.

266

"Tighten your grip—your muzzle is bouncing a bit." Midnight nodded, her hands tightening.

No one ever questioned Joe on the firing line. He was the best shot in the department and knew how to make everyone else a good shot too.

"Dave, you're dropping to the right a bit—pull it back up," Joe called. Dave nodded and corrected his range.

"Spider, pull back a bit, man. You're bouncing too,"

"Sorry, Joe," Spider said, moving his neck a bit to get centered better, then fired again.

"Better," Joe said.

"Not going to start on me today?" Rick asked with a grin, even as he squeezed off another shot.

"I know you'll do something I can yell at ya for. I just have to give you time," Joe assured him, grinning too.

Joe called the cease-fire then, and beckoned the rest of the group to the firing line.

Kana, Christian, Stevie, Donovan, Jeanie, and Kevin were next up.

"Oh good, I get to shoot with the kids," Kana said, grinning.

"Don't worry, we won't out-shoot you," Christian said, then paused. "Much."

"You know where you can stick that, right, Collins?" Kana said, smiling broadly.

"Nowhere near you, right?" Christian said, grinning.

Kana winked. "For you, I might make an exception."

"Ohhhh…"

"Watch it, Collins," Stevie said, narrowing her eyes at him.

267

"What?" Christian said, his light blue eyes dancing with amusement. "You can't be jealous."

"Maybe I can," Stevie said, giving him an amused look. "Maybe I'd like to be Kana's exception."

There was a round of "Ohhhhs" from the Gang, in varying tones of chagrin and laughter.

Christian stared openmouthed at his wife as Kana said, "Honey, for you, I don't need to make an exception. You just tell me when and where and I'll be there." She winked at Stevie to let her know she was joking.

Stevie laughed. "I'll let you know," she said, still chuckling at the look on Christian's face.

"Excuse me," Palani said, giving Kana a narrowed look of her own.

"Uh-oh," Rick said.

"Kana's had it now," Dave said, shaking his head.

"Yep," Tiny said. "The little woman looks none too pleased, K."

Kana glanced at Palani. "Now, honey…" she said placatingly, which had the rest of the Gang breaking into laughter. "Don't we need to shoot or something?" Kana asked once she'd gotten a smile from Palani.

"Yes," Joe said, giving everyone a serious look, then grinned. "Firing line ready?"

They all nodded. Joe blew his whistle. Palani watched as Kana drew her gun and fired. She hit center mass for all but two shots, and even those were respectably close.

Joe blew the whistle again, calling out, "Reload!"

The six released their ammunition magazines, pulled out new

268

ones, and slid them into their weapons, clicking them into place. They pulled back the slides, chambering a round.

Joe blew the whistle again. "Fire!"

Again they brought their weapons up.

Just after Joe called a cease-fire, Christian squeezed off an extra shot.

"Blue, you know better than that," Joe said.

Christian nodded. "Got a little over-zealous," he said, grinning.

"Happens a lot," Stevie said.

"Bite me."

"Where?"

"Easy, kids," Rick said from behind them.

"Okay, next up," Joe said, shaking his head and rolling his eyes.

He ran Midnight's group through kneeling and shooting, and a reload like he had the others. Jordan was surprised as she watched how good these people were with their weapons. She couldn't help but admire how well they got along, and the fact that they did indeed know what they were doing on a range. Joe most of all. His score was perfect, dead-on every time. He never missed a shot. She glanced to her side and saw that Kana was watching the shooting closely.

"Kana?" Jordan queried.

Kana's dark eyes turned to her. "Yeah?"

"You did pretty good against 'the kids,'" Jordan joked.

Kana laughed softly. "Thanks. I hate shooting with these hot shots—always makes me feel like a recruit."

When it was time for the second group to go up again, Palani moved to Jordan's side.

"She can't be much older than those other people," Jordan said

269

in an aside to her.

"She's older than she looks," Palani said. "Not that you can tell from her appearance though."

"How old is she?"

"Thirty-eight."

"Really?" Jordan said, surprised. "Never would have guessed that."

Palani smiled. She knew what Jordan meant.

Joe now had them do an exercise where they had to move from one side of a five-foot section of range to the other and shoot. It was an evasive tactical maneuver.

Christian was first up and completed it with an admirable hit pattern.

Stevie was next; she did rather well, hitting an almost perfect score.

"Been workin' on that, huh?" Joe commented.

"Oh yeah, can't have the range master disappointed in me," she replied with a wink.

Jordan caught Christian's eyes as they narrowed slightly, but that was the only indication that the conversation bothered him. She suspected there was a lot of residual anger there, but that Christian wasn't willing to cause a scene about it. Jordan glanced at Joe, and noticed that he had seen exactly what she had. He pressed his lips together, looking unhappy for a moment.

"Okay, Donovan, let's see what you got," Joe said then, his voice sounding normal.

Donovan did well, only making one bad shot.

"You're dropping that shoulder again," Joe said.

270

Donovan grimaced. "Rammed it into a door the other day."

"That'll do it," Joe said. "Okay, Jeanie, you're up."

Jeanie did well, receiving the best score up until that point.

Kevin shot next, receiving the same score as Jeanie. Everyone started joking about Jeanie and Kevin spending way too much time together. Kevin just shook his head, grinning, but said nothing. He still wasn't at the point of being so comfortable with these people that he could joke with them easily.

Then it was Kana's turn. Palani watched as she took a long, deep breath, blowing it out slowly and moving her neck and shoulders around. She was centering herself, Palani knew, as did everyone else.

Kana drew her gun and proceeded with the exercise, making a perfect score.

Everyone clapped. Kana inclined her head to the younger people in the group.

"Now, that's the way I want you all shooting," Joe said, smiling broadly at Kana.

"When I've been with the department for twenty years, I will," Donovan said, grinning.

"Not likely," Christian put in.

"Up yours, Collins," Donovan said, grinning still.

"Boys..." Jeanie said.

"Yeah, knock it off, or we'll send you to clean all the guns," Stevie said.

Everyone laughed.

The next group was back up. Joe called for a prone firing position.

"Sinclair," Midnight said, narrowing her eyes at him. "I'm so not

271

in the mood for this today."

"You're saying that like I care," Joe replied sweetly.

"You will, next time you get your prob report," Midnight replied with equal sweetness.

"Oh, that's intimidating," Joe said, rolling his eyes.

"You know…" Midnight said, giving him a sour look.

"Yes, love, I know," Joe replied, winking at her.

Midnight shook her head, glancing at Rick, who sighed.

"Never tell him you don't want to do something, babe. You know he'll insist then."

"Yeah, could you not like something a little less dirty next time, Chief?" Spider asked.

"Yeah, and could you make sure it pertains to higher pay, lighter caseloads…" Dave put in.

"If you'd take the lieutenant's test…" Midnight said, moving to kneel on the ground, as the others were doing.

"Oh, no, no, no," Dave said, shaking his head and drawing his weapon as he lay down.

"See?" Spider said. "You just like working too hard."

"I do it to make you look good, man."

"And Spider's got the best case record in the department to show for it," Rick put in.

"Fuck you," Dave said.

"Are we there again?" Rick asked.

"God, I hope not," Tiny said from down the line.

"Honey, stay out of it," Jess said.

"Yes, dear."

"Can we just shoot? I have a concert to get to sometime tonight," Joe said, having listened to the preceding with an indulgent grin. He winked at Jordan, who smiled warmly at him.

"So do we," Midnight said.

They got back to work.

That night at the concert, the Gang had front-row seats. Jordan had insisted on that much, wanting to do something for Joe's "family." They also went backstage before the show for a party. Joe was there ahead of time, having arrived with Jordan for her sound check. He wore all black, his gun in a holster at the small of his back, his badge in his pocket. Midnight, Rick, and Mikeyla arrived an hour later. Midnight wore black jeans, high-heeled boots, and a jade green silk camisole under a long black jacket that fell to her calves. Joe told her she looked like she could be a rock star. She laughed and reminded him how old she was. Rick raised an eyebrow at her, reminding her quietly that she'd better not start that again. He wore blue jeans, a black shirt, black boots, and a black leather jacket. With his long hair, he looked like he could be a member of the band too. Mikeyla was dressed in black and was actually wearing darker makeup than normal, and it was obvious she was becoming as much a beauty as her mother. Joe commented on the makeup to Rick and was told to "shut the hell up."

Kyle, Rhiannon, Stevie, Christian, and Nick arrived next, all dressed casually. Nick made his way over to Mikeyla, and the two were inseparable the rest of the night. Christian, of course, commented on how good Midnight looked. He was elbowed by his wife, and given a fairly threatening look by Rick, to which he grinned wickedly.

273

The rest of the Gang arrived for the most part at the same time, creating a chaotic scene of joking, comments, and laughter. BJ Sparks wandered into the midst of it all, catching sight of Stevie O'Neil and making a beeline for her. Meanwhile, Billy Montague, of Billy and the Kid, was busy working her charm on Christian. Jerith "Kid" Michaels, the band's guitarist, was talking to Joe and Jordan, and ended up in a very interesting discussion about law enforcement with Midnight.

Before long there came comments about who was losing who to one of the rockers, and Joe had to call everyone to order before things got out of hand.

"Hey, hey," he said, getting up on the nearest table. Jordan watched him with a smile. "Settle down here, people, settle down," he said, grinning at the comments he got about Toastmasters needing their mouthpiece back. "Look, I just want to take this opportunity, before we're all too drunk to think straight, to thank Jordan, BJ, Jerith, Billy, and the rest of their crews for doing this. It's for a good cause and—"

"It gets Joe out of paying for it anymore," Rick interrupted, grinning.

"Hey!" Randy said, swatting him on the arm.

"Yeah, tone it down, Debenshire," Tiny said from across the room.

"Can't anyone keep a leash on him anymore?" asked Spider.

"Midnight keeps him leashed pretty good," Dave put in.

"Rabid as he is," Kana said, grinning widely.

"Alright now, let's not start," Joe said, laughing even as he did.

"Speaking of which, where's the tequila?" Christian yelled.

274

"Hell yeah!" Rick agreed.

"Oh Lord," Midnight said, shaking her head.

"Can I finish?" Joe asked, even as the bottles of tequila were passed around along with shot glasses.

"We're not sure, but go ahead and try," Rick said.

"Anyway, thanks to the rockers for this night," Joe said, smiling as he was handed a shot of tequila. "I guess this would be the music world's equivalent of a toast," he added, holding up his glass.

"Don't do it to FORS this time," Spider said, grinning.

"And why the hell not?" Rick asked, raising an eyebrow.

"Boys!" Midnight yelled, giving them both a narrowed look.

Joe turned to Randy, smiling at her. "This is Randy's night, so the toast will be to her, and to the center she built," he said, inclining his head.

"With Joe's money," Randy put in, grinning at him.

Joe laughed. "And your hard work, love," he said, winking at her.

"Hear, hear," Midnight said, raising her glass, as did everyone else.

Joe hopped down off the table and walked over to Randy. He hugged her. She smiled up at him as Jordan walked over to them.

"Jordan," Randy said, turning to the other woman. "Thank you again for doing this. I can't ever thank you enough."

Jordan smiled. "It's a good cause, Randy. It's my hope that people will get the idea that this is something every city needs. Kids can't be sheltered enough from the bad things in life, or the bad choices of their parents. What you're doing here is important."

Randy smiled, tears coming to her eyes. It felt good to know that the work she'd been doing was viewed as important by someone other than her close friends and family. It was something she needed to hear.

The concert was a resounding success, bringing in over three million in revenue for Sinclair House. On top of which, BJ Sparks donated half a million, and refused to allow any paper to print that information. Randy called him and thanked him personally; BJ told her that he'd raised a daughter himself and knew that what she was doing was important.

Randy sat back and looked at her life then, seeing the changes that had occurred in the last year. It amazed her, the direction life's path could take you. How you could start going one way, thinking your life was going to be a certain way, and end up somewhere totally different. She'd always pictured herself being a wife and a mother. She'd always pictured being married to Joe. Never had it occurred to her that she'd start something that could be the beginning of something very important. Sometimes, she guessed, you just need to go all in on an idea to make it a reality.

You can find more information about the author and series here:

www.sherrylhancock.com

www.facebook.com/SherrylDHancock

www.vulpine-press.com/midknight-blue-series

Also by Sherryl D. Hancock:

**The *WeHo* series** follows a group of women from Los Angeles as they navigate the ups and downs of love, life, work, and everything in between.

www.vulpine-press.com/we-ho

**The *Wild Irish Silence* series**. Escape into the world of BJ Sparks and discover how he went from the small-town boy to the world-famous rock star.

www.vulpine-press.com/wild-irish-silence-series

www.ingramcontent.com/pod-product-compliance
Lightning Source LLC
Chambersburg PA
CBHW020308200626
46814CB00006BA/2139